C000039749

THE STRONGHOLD
©2023 JAKE BIBLE

ALSO IN SERIES

ONE
THERE WAS AN OLD WOMAN...

The body hangs like a limp bundle of sticks and rags, unaffected by the intense cold and wind that comes whipping down off the Rockies. The four people carrying the limp body, a man and three women, move cautiously through the debris, their feet expertly avoiding the stray hunks of metal and junk that litter what was once an airstrip of the former Peterson Air Force Base.

Now the tarmac is nothing but dead weeds and stunted trees that are almost finished dropping their autumn leaves. The dry vegetation pushes up through the asphalt, cracking the blacktop into hundreds of ankle-breaking pieces.

The four move on, picking their way around hunks of old and rusted aircraft close to being decommissioned before Z-Day hit.

Z-Day—when the dead decided they no longer wanted to be dead and that walking the Earth would be a much better option. No explanation, no warning. Corpses began to dig themselves out of graves, sit up in morgues, fight their way out of body bags and caskets. And they were hungry. Attacking the living and feasting off their flesh, the undead—the zombies, the Zs—multiplied quickly as the victims themselves turned into monsters and became part of the undead ranks.

That was on a Sunday.

By Monday evening, everything was lost and those still alive began their never-ending fight to survive.

Four people, descendants of some of those survivors, carry the human bundle of sticks around a large piece of a jet engine and then stop, their heads turning this way and that, back and forth as if they are scanning the area with some unknown sense. Two of them turn and look over their shoulders, back at the broken tarmac and the long shadows coming off the towering pines and firs that ring the old base, their roots able to find plenty of purchase and nutrients. The tall trees almost mock the scraggly ones that struggle against the inhospitable remains of an asphalt world.

But the two people aren't looking at the scraggly trees, the broken tarmac, the tall trees outside the fence line, or anything at all. Looking, seeing, watching with their eyes is not an option. Only empty sockets stare out at the landscape, the holes rimmed with long scars, both old and fresh.

The two others turn their heads, eyeless as well, and join their comrades in an impossible study of the area. It has been said that when one sense is lost, the others compensate. For these four people, the compensations have increased exponentially.

Scents from a thousand sources waft on the cold wind and the four take deep breaths, their brains processing the data instantly. Sounds from just as many sources reach their ears, separating and compressing into different aural streams, each with its own influx of information. One of the women opens her mouth and tastes the slight mist the wind brings, a portent of a late autumn storm to come. A second woman rolls her head on her neck, letting the air currents drift across her skin.

"What do we have?" the man asks. "Sheila?"

"Unsure," Sheila, the tasting woman, replies. "Vicky?"

"Possible snow," Vicky, the air currents woman, responds. "Missy?"

The third woman, Missy, takes another deep breath through

her nose. She hesitates and takes a third breath, then shakes her head.

"I don't smell snow, but I trust Vicky," Missy replies. "Confusing scents. A lot of elk urine. Must have been a herd come by recently. That's all I have. Jack?"

"I don't remember hearing or feeling a herd anywhere in the area," Jack says. "But they don't tend to stay put, do they? Too many undead around."

Jack tilts his head as if looking down at the body the four carry. It is a woman, head shorn, face crisscrossed with scars and age lines, dressed in a tattered long coat made of deer hide with matching pants. Her shirt is a crude weave of hemp and wool. The boots on her feet are new, however, or new as can be when boots haven't been mass-produced in a hundred years. Black with thick soles and obviously reinforced toes, the boots are worth almost as much as the woman.

But considering how much of a fight the woman put up when found, despite her emaciated appearance, Jack believes the information the woman can provide is the true treasure. He knows Skye will be pleased to have such a survivor in her presence. With the increase in Z activity and their undead numbers seeming to grow day after day, a little intel from an outside source is almost better than food.

Especially with their plan almost ready to launch.

"Something funny?" Vicky asks.

"What? Yes, I made a mental pun," Jack answers. "Just thinking about how the plan is almost ready to launch."

The other three chuckle with him.

"The day of the Code Monkeys is almost at hand," Missy says. "We will bring justice to this horrid place. Wipe the unworthy from the landscape."

"Wipe all from the landscape," Vicky says.

"An honor to die for such a cause," Sheila sighs. "Such an honor."

The woman in their hands moans and Jack frowns. "She shouldn't wake up for hours. This one heals fast."

"Explains how she has survived alone out in the wasteland," Missy says. "I do smell a strong life force about her. She will not leave this plane without some violent help."

"That will be up to Skye to decide," Jack says. "For now, we deliver this woman and let Skye sort out her worth and fate."

The four nod as one and turn back to their task of carrying the unconscious woman across the base. They reach a small hut, barely half the size of a normal-sized Quonset building, and set the woman down on the ground while three of them lift a metal hatch hidden beneath a pile of refuse. Once the hatch is open, Vicky and Missy descend partway, then reach up for the woman as Jack and Sheila ease her down to them.

The woman lowered below and the task done, Jack climbs down and grips the hatch with a gloved hand. His eyeless head turns back and forth over and over before he grunts then drops inside, the hatch clanging loudly behind him, followed by the sound of heavy locks *thunking* into place.

The pile of refuse shifts back over the hatch, a series of pulleys and platforms expertly placed on and around the hatch so that the illusion of a trash heap is all a casual observer will see.

The cold wind blows and the late autumn sun begins to set behind the Rocky Mountains, casting the world in an orange glow that resembles fire.

Or Hell.

Depending on one's perspective.

———

Beneath the tall firs and pines, covered by various branches, leaves, twigs, and dried weeds, two figures slowly crawl backward on their elbows and tips of their boots, their bellies barely an inch off the ground. The branches, leaves, twigs, and dried weeds move with them, glued to their backs in arrangements of perfect camouflage.

Blending into the surroundings is a key to survival in a wasteland populated by Zs, crazies, cults, cannibals, and various other factions fighting for just one more day of life.

Never wavering from their slow, low crawl backward, the two figures leave the protection of the tree line and keep going through the tall yellow grasses of a wide meadow dotted with oaks. Once fully obscured by the three-foot-high grass, the two stop and wait. After a minute, they both hear a short whistle. It sounds like a lone bird, but to their ears it is the signal that the coast is clear.

"Go," one says to the other.

The other nods and crouch runs through the meadow to a stand of pines at the far edge. The one left waits until another whistle is heard, then gets up and follows quickly.

Once in the shadowed safety of the pines, the two figures strip off the branch/leaf/twig-covered ghillie suits to reveal beige military fatigues underneath. They are each handed gear-laden vests and packs, and they quickly put them on as three others clad in military fatigues wait patiently.

"Damn, you two stink," Dead Team Alpha Team Leader Cole Wright whispers. Except for the pink scars that crisscross his cheeks and neck, his dark skin blends in with the deepening shadows. He shifts away from the two new arrivals, his wiry muscles moving him silently in the thick underbrush. "Mandatory showers when we return to barracks."

"If they let them in through the gates," DTA Team Mate Dorothy "Tiny D" Peters laughs quietly.

Tiny D's hair is in tight black cornrows, stretching into braids that go all the way down her back, fanned out across her pack. Normally the tips would shine from the small, barbed blades that hold the ends of the braids together. But Tiny D has made sure each barb is dulled by mud so as not to give off their position in the pines. But it's a wash considering the bright white of her teeth as her nearly pitch-black face splits into a wide grin.

"Yeah, some of the elk piss soaked through the ghillie suits," DTA Team Mate Alastair Swancutt replies. "We may stink, but the piss works."

"It was close," DTA Team Mate Valencia "Val" Baptiste says, taking a cautious whiff of herself. She frowns and looks at the ghillie suit she had just taken off. "I thought they'd sensed us for a second there, but they kept going and disappeared into that hatch of theirs."

"Still using just the one entrance?" DTA Team Mate Lyle Diaz asks over his shoulder. He is down on one knee with an M-4 carbine to his shoulder, his full attention on the meadow between DTA and the firs and fence that rims Peterson AFB. "That's a big risk. Any number of hostiles could see that and try to get in there."

"I don't think they're too worried," Val responds.

She picks up her own M-4 and stands, stretching out tight muscles that were close to cramping from hours of being in one position as she and Alastair surveilled the Code Monkeys' hide-out. Twenty-three, tall, blonde, dark brown eyes, and built like a dancer who's all muscles and grace, Val starts to roll her head on her neck, then stops when Cole gives a slight cough.

"The way your vertebrae crack, you'll bring that whole nest of Monkeys down on us," Cole says, standing as well. In his thirties and only an inch taller than Val, Cole surveys the rest of DTA. "Ready to move?"

"You know it, TL," Diaz says as the rest of DTA get to their feet. "But I'm not carrying those."

"We got them," Alastair says. A couple years younger than Cole, Alastair is average height but holds himself like a prize fighter who's ready to spring from toe to toe at a moment's notice. His pale skin is windburnt, making his usually rosy cheeks stand out even more. "But next time you guys get to wear the piss suits."

"We'll Rock, paper, scissors for it," Tiny D says. At her full height, Tiny D is almost the tallest of the Team. She looks down at Alastair and pats his shoulder. "Or we could wrestle."

"Cut the chatter," Cole orders. "We have a long haul ahead of us."

"Where we headed?" Diaz asks. "All the way back to Denver?"

"We'll see," Cole says. "I'd prefer to get as far as possible. But, with the weather looking like it is, we may want to find shelter."

"Let's not risk it, TL," Tiny D says. "Getting stuck in a storm would suck."

"True," Cole says. "We'll assess the weather when we hit the stadium. If we think we can move on to the next safe spot, then that's what we do."

"Remember when Silo Teams used to be the ones who went out into the wasteland and DTA only handled Denver?" Alastair sighs. "Good times."

"That was before the Code Monkeys came and fucked the Stronghold up," Val says. "Or tried to. Didn't quite work out."

"I hear that," Tiny D says and high fives Val.

"That's chatter," Cole says. "Which I said to cut. Silence from here on out until we are well away from Colorado Springs."

"What's with the springs?" Alastair asks as he hurriedly stuffs a ghillie suit into a duffel and tosses it to Val. He grabs up the second one and stuffs that into a different duffel, then throws it over his shoulder. "Are there actually springs around here? Because I've never seen any."

"They don't exactly have signs pointing to them," Diaz replies. "I'm sure some of the old-timers up at the Stronghold know where they're at."

"For fuck's sake," Cole snaps. "Chatter. Stop." He locks eyes with each and every Mate in DTA and then nods to Val. "You have point, Val."

"On it," Val says. She secures the duffel to her pack then leads the way, her M-4 up and pointing the way out of the stand of trees.

———

No light. Not even a hint of a candle or a rare glow stick.

The woman with the shorn head rests against the wall, her eyes wide open despite the pitch blackness. Her back is sticky and damp from the slow trickle of water that leaks down the concrete. She is not happy that her captors have removed her long coat. She'd spent years conditioning that coat, applying sheep gland oil across its surface to protect it, and her, from the dangerously chaotic weather of the wasteland.

She takes a deep breath and her lungs fill with the powerful smells of mildew, mold, and rotting things. Another deep breath and she is thankful that the rotting things are neither Zs nor human remains, just normal smells coming off of a pile of trash in the far corner.

"Rat bait?" the woman asks. "You leave your garbage out and wait for the critters to show up, that it?"

No one responds, but the woman knows she's not alone. Even with the room being completely without light, there are ways to tell when someone is close. Light breathing, the almost imperceptible rustle of clothing, a heartbeat.

Two heartbeats?

The woman shifts against the wall, the sound of her wet shirt scratching against the old concrete like a wail in the night. She adjusts her position, tucking her legs up underneath. In a normal world, she would have looked like a woman poised on a couch, a nice cup of tea by her side and a book in hand. Which is the feeling she wants to portray. She wants the person (or persons) in the room with her to sense that she is completely at ease.

Even if she is only waiting to grab a neck and snap it.

"The rats are big now," the woman says. "I remember when they didn't used to be so huge. Skinny things trying to fight for scraps with the rest of us. Now they don't have to fight. We are the scraps. How many are you?"

An intake of breath, then a shuffle. One of the persons was about to answer. The woman smiles in the dark.

"You gave me a hard whack," the woman continues. "Must be enough folks down here to give some protection if you're willing to bring a stranger underground with you. These days you have to be careful. Unless you're in the Stronghold or one of those random survivor pockets out there, you're on your own."

No response.

"I should know," the woman says, pushing on. "I've been on my own for a long, long time. Used to have others. Used to be part of something bigger. That time has gone."

A scrape of feet, quiet shoes on rough concrete, and a presence just out of arm's reach.

"Go on," the woman says. "Ask your questions. You didn't bring me down here to eat, so you gotta have questions."

"Your name," a woman's voice asks from across the room.

A third person the shaved woman didn't pick up on. That is troubling, since she rarely gets something as easy as a head count wrong.

"You first," the shorn woman responds, turning to face the woman's voice. "You're the host."

"Skye," the hidden woman replies. "Your name?"

"Sister," the shaved woman replies.

"Sister?" Sky asks.

"Sister," Sister confirms.

"That is not your real name," Skye responds. "What is your real name?"

Sister laughs. "Been a very long time since I've used it. Can't really remember."

"That is a lie," Skye says.

A fist comes out of the darkness and hits Sister across the cheek. It stings but doesn't do too much damage since she was waiting for the first strike to happen.

"You are fast," Skye says. "Why are you so fast?"

"Have to be," Sister says and shrugs. Something deep in her gut tells her that the three persons in the room can tell that she shrugged. "Two kinds of people in this world now: the quick and the dead. Same with the Zs. Two kinds of them: the quick and the slow. They're all dead though. Dead as doornails and other dead stuffs."

"You ramble," Skye says.

"Do I?" Sister asks. "Hmmmm. Been a few months since I've talked to the living. I guess I have some words built up and they're spilling over."

"What's your real name?" Skye asks. Her voice is steel and razor wire, set hard and losing patience.

"I don't remember," Sister replies.

The fist comes from the dark again, but Sister blocks it easily, causing the owner to grunt and stumble back. The heartbeats, all three, increase, and Sister hears a sharp intake of breath from Skye.

"I'll let you have your lie," Skye says. "*Sister.*"

"Thanks," Sister replies. "You're swell as swell can be. Super swell. The swellingest."

"Where do you come from?" Skye asks. "You know about the Stronghold. You know about other places. What else do you know?"

"Two questions," Sister says.

"What?" Skye asks.

"You asked me two questions," Sister says. "Which one do you want me to answer first? Where do I come from or what else do I know? One's a short story, one's a long story. You want short or long?"

"Where do you come from?" Skye repeats.

"Short story? Okey doke," Sister says. "I come from the Stronghold."

"No, you don't," Skye responds. "Another lie."

"Is it?" Sister counters. "Pretty sure it's not. Now, I ain't been there for a long while. Not living permanently, at least. But it's what I call home."

Skye grumbles, the sound like gravel grating in her throat.

"What you really want to ask is where *did* I come from," Sister says. "Where did I come from when your people found me and took me down. Hard to do. I give them proper respect for ambushing me. Most don't live through that."

"I believe you," Skye says. "You seem well trained."

"I am," Sister says. "So are you folks. At least I guess you are, since you're moving around in the dark like a bunch of bats. You have NVGs? Night vision goggles you found on this base and repaired?"

"Base? What base?" Skye asks.

"Oh, right, sorry, I was supposed to be unconscious when your people brought me down here," Sister says. "Sorry. I woke up before we were halfway across that tarmac. Decided that since I wasn't dead I should maybe ride it out and see where the day takes me. And it takes me into a smelly garbage room."

The sound of a hand smacking flesh echoes in the room and Sister grins.

"Uh oh, someone is in trouble," Sister says. "Who is it? The guy who ambushed me, or one of the three women he was with?"

Sister waits, but Skye doesn't respond.

"I smell testosterone," Sister says, taking a guess in the dark. "So it's the guy. Jack, right?"

Still no response.

"Okay, okay, I can't smell testosterone," Sister admits. "I was playin'."

"Where *did* you come from?" Skye finally asks.

"The East," Sister answers.

"The Consortium holds the East," Skye says. "Do you work for them?"

"I already said I come from the Stronghold, so why would I be working with the Consortium?" Sister asks. "Keep up, Skye. I don't have time to hold your hand through this little interrogation."

"You are lying about the Stronghold," Skye says. "You are not from there."

"Really? Is there a quiver in my voice? Is my heartbeat elevated? Do you smell me sweating?" Sister asks. "Because all of that would be happening if I am lying. Which I'm not."

"Do you work for the Consortium?" Skye asks.

"No," Sister answers.

"Then why were you east?" Skye asks.

"Scouting," Sister answers.

"Scouting what?" Skye asks.

Sister laughs, then clears her throat. "The end of the world, Skye. The motherfucking end of the world."

———

Code Monkeys.

Sister laughs out loud at the name. Skye left her alone in the stinky concrete room an hour ago after Sister dropped the "motherfucking end of the world" news.

News that included, but is not limited to:

There are approximately a total of twenty million Zs still active within most of the major cities of the Eastern United States.

The Zs are getting faster, stronger, and seem to be able to live off sunlight for brief stretches if fresh flesh is not available. Which increasingly it is not, since the survivor levels decrease daily.

About eight million Zs are marching across the Plains and headed west for no apparent reason other than to go for a stroll. Surprisingly, crossing rivers does not seem to be an issue. They just create bridges of corpses as thousands get mired in the mud and the rest stumble over their backs to the other side. Z corps of engineering.

Sister knows the Code Monkeys have almost all the launch

codes to light up all of North America with nuclear mushroom clouds.

Skye seemed quite proud about the last part. Sister knew she would be. She also knew that was enough intel to fry most anyone's brain and wasn't surprised that Skye left without using more drastic interrogation techniques to delve deeper into what Sister knows.

Sister has no illusions that the more drastic interrogation techniques will not be withheld for much longer. Once Skye wraps her head around the news that there are so many Zs still left, with more joining everyday as survivor pocket after survivor pocket fall, then Sister knows Skye will come knocking, and there will be nothing but pain that answers the door.

With her seeds of intel planted, Sister knows it is time to get the hell out of the stinky room and be back on her way. The Peterson AFB is only a detour. A minor detour she didn't plan to have happen so soon but turns out to be a blessing in disguise. Except for the lump on the back of her head. That isn't such a blessing.

It hurts like hell.

Sister is actually a little pissed that the damn Code Monkey had been able to sneak up on her. She is getting old, that is the only reason she can think of.

Fucking Code Monkey…

Sister doesn't laugh out loud this time at the thought of the stupid name. Instead, she stands up and begins to make her way to the door on the far side of the room. She barely has to trace her fingers along the wet, concrete walls. While she talked to Skye, she had gauged the dimensions of the room by listening to the echoes of her own voice. It was a trick she'd picked up years ago out on the wasteland that is America.

One giant, Z-infested wasteland. Go big or go home. USA!

Not that Sister remembers much about the country before Z-Day. Things were confusing back then. Mixed up. Warped. She likes to think that her real life started when she woke up to a zombie boy trying to eat her face. Been nothing but roses since.

Speaking of roses…

"I'm done with the stink," Sister says to herself. "Done, done, done. Done as shit. Shit stinks. This shit stinks. Done with the shit stinking shit."

She reaches the door and tries the knob. Locked. No surprise.

So she knocks.

"Hello?" she calls out. "I'd like to leave now, please."

A woman she'd known many years before, a surrogate mother who meant more to her than her own mother, had always said that politeness was the best way to get what you wanted.

She also said to break a bitch if you need to.

Sister needs to.

"I'm going to count to three," Sister says. "When I get to three, it'll be too late."

She presses her ear to the door. She can faintly hear a person shuffle outside in the hallway.

"One," she calls out.

She snaps the doorknob off, reaches in, and manually turns the catch with her fingers. A sharp piece of metal slices her middle finger, and she winces but doesn't slow down as she yanks the door open.

"Two," she says as the person standing outside the door comes at her.

A fist flies at her face and Sister dodges it easily despite there being zero light in the hallway. The whiff of the attempted blow caresses her cheek. Sister slams an open hand into the throat of the attacker, causing the man to bark out a strangled cry of pain. Another open hand shot to the bridge of the man's nose drops him fast.

Sister places her foot on his neck and stomps hard. The snap is like a grenade going off in the silence of the complex.

"Three," Sister says.

She waits in the hallway, listening to the stirrings of those close enough to hear the commotion. Four people coming from the left, five people coming from the right. Almost even numbers, but Sister is pretty sure she needs to go right. Right feels good.

She takes off running, careful not to trip or stumble on the junk placed in the hallway as a deterrent for those who try to escape. The ones who have taken her captive, the Code Monkeys, are all blind, but in a way that gives them better sight than most people with fully functioning eyes. Sister knows the debris won't slow them down at all. She also knows it won't slow her down. Not much does these days except the occasional flare up of arthritis and the random migraine now and again.

And the cancer. But that's a nuisance she can deal with. An occasional irritant.

The first of the five reaches her and Sister ducks low, avoiding the large knife that slashes through the air where her head had been. She strikes hard and punches the man in the nuts. The clatter of the knife on the ground and the groan of the man tell Sister he won't be a problem anymore.

The second of the five kicks out, trying to nail Sister in the face, but she rolls backward, dodging the blow. She grabs up a handful of trash, sticky and sweet smelling, and throws it at the second attacker. The woman grunts at the impact but keeps coming, her legs kicking out again and again while Sister rolls farther and farther backward until she is almost to the four Code Monkeys coming from the other way.

"Shit fuck," Sister says, finding herself in a position she tried to avoid.

She jumps to her feet and throws a hard right, her fist crashing into the kicking woman's jaw. Then she brings the arm back and slams her elbow into the nose of one of the four behind her. A man moans and falls.

Sister whips about with a powerful roundhouse kick, her left leg snapping another man's head to the right and back. His neck cracks, and there is a tearing sound as his entire head twists about three hundred and sixty degrees. Sister kicks with her right leg, sending the head spinning in reverse until the pliant flesh rips apart and the head tumbles from the body.

Hands grab Sister's shoulders and she thrusts her head forward, headbutting the attacker. The man stumbles back, and Sister begins to press the attack but gasps as a sharp pain explodes in her side.

"Fucking shit fuck!" she yells, her right hand going to the wound, feeling the warm, sticky blood. Her blood. "Lucky fucker!"

She reaches out and grabs the man with the knife around the wrist. She pulls down then twists hard, splintering the bones, sending the knife falling toward the ground. Before the blade hits the junk-strewn concrete, Sister catches it on top of her left foot, then flicks her ankle, sending the knife flying through the darkness.

A woman grunts and a body falls. Sister smiles.

A quick straight-legged kick backward slows another attacker while she reaches forward, stretching until she has a woman by the throat. A hard squeeze and the woman's trachea is old news. Sister kicks backward once more and a body falls. She lets go of the woman with the crushed trachea and that body falls as well, added to the piles of corpses quickly filling the already cluttered hallway.

Her side is on fire with each kick and punch, but Sister ignores the pain and the blood flowing, instead concentrating her attention on the few attackers still coming for her. Sister's ears pick up the sounds of quite a few more feet heading to the hallway. Time to get out, fast.

A jab with her left hand, then a hard strike with her right, and another attacker is down. Sister stomps his face twice before ducking a swipe from a machete as a woman comes at her. Coming up with a brutal left uppercut, Sister sends the machete bitch flying backward. But not before she snags the machete out of the stunned woman's hand.

Slashing with quick, powerful strokes, Sister cuts her way

through the last couple of attackers, dropping them to the floor in pools of their own blood and severed limbs. She reaches the end of the hallway and knows she has maybe five seconds before her exit is cut off by the blind reinforcements heading her direction.

Machete in hand, Sister starts running again, her perfectly tuned senses directing her through the pitch blackness.

———

Eight of them wait for her at the ladder to the hatch that leads outside. Eight very large, very angry Code Monkeys, each at least six feet tall and nearly as wide.

"Skye?" Sister asks.

A seventh figure steps forward, although Sister can't see her since the total lack of light is just as complete near the exit as it was deep inside the bunker.

"I know who you are," Skye states.

"I doubt that," Sister replies.

"No, I do," Skye insists. "Hard to believe, but I am sure it is you."

"You're wrong," Sister says. "But whatever."

"I'm not wrong," Skye says. "We've been wondering if you'd come back."

Sister can feel her shirt sticking to her side, wet with blood and sweat. She places a hand to the wound and winces at the slight pressure. It's deeper than she feared.

"You are getting old," Skye says. "In your youth, not even my people would have been able to wound you."

"I'm tired," Sister admits. "Really fucking tired."

"Then let go," Skye says. "Stop your fighting. Stop your running. Let go and give in. You tried. That is worth some honor."

"Fuck honor," Sister laughs. "Honor means nothing to crazies like you. You talk a talk, but your walk is shit. Fuck your honor and fuck you."

Sister rushes the six huge Code Monkeys.

Her machete does short work of the first one she reaches, slashing open his belly and throat in one continuous, back and forth swipe. Sister uses the falling body as a shield, blocking the swing of a heavy pipe from one of the others. The pipe crunches into the dead Monkey's skull and Sister shoves the body back, sending both the corpse and the pipe Monkey crashing into the wall.

A fist grabs for her throat, but she hacks off the hand, her face instantly coated by the spray of blood that shoots out from the Code Monkey's stump. Sister flips the machete about in her hand, spins her body, and jams the blade into the belly of a fourth Code Monkey.

Where it gets stuck in the man's spine.

Knowing she'll lose precious time trying to free the weapon, Sister dives and rolls across the ground, coming up right in front of the ladder. She hears the fifth and sixth Code Monkeys right behind her. Grabbing the ladder's rungs, Sister pulls herself up, spins her body around, and wraps her legs around the fifth Code Monkey's neck. She uses her momentum to whip her body down and to the side, sending the man crashing upside down and backward into the ladder. His neck snaps before his body crumples to the ground.

The sixth Code Monkey lifts her off the ground by her neck and slams a fist into her face once, twice, three times. Sister's head rocks back and the pitch blackness explodes into stars and motes of bright lights. Dazed, Sister almost forgets what she's doing, but muscle memory and instinct kick in.

Her thumbs find the man's empty eye sockets and she shoves them in as deep as they can go. Despite having no eyes, the empty holes are still sensitive enough to feel pain as Sister's thumbs tear into the flesh at the back of the sockets. The man screams and lets Sister go. He stumbles back and falls hard, tripping over the dead and wounded bodies of his comrades.

Two hard jabs to her wound makes Sister scream as well, but she still refuses to give in.

Sister whirls about, sending a hard kick with her left leg at where she thinks Skye is. Her leg meets empty air. She doesn't have time for this shit. Sister kicks out with her right leg as soon as she has her balance again and clears a path to the ladder. She takes five steps and jumps, launching herself halfway up the rungs.

She grabs on with all her strength and hauls ass up to the hatch. A brief moment of panic hits her when she reaches the hatch.

Will it be locked?

She finds the handle and twists hard, nearly crying with relief when the hatch shifts and cracks open, letting in what is almost a blazing light compared to the total absence she's been trapped in.

"I know who you are," Skye calls from below as Sister shoves the hatch open and pulls herself up into the cold, night air.

"Good for you," Sister says, looking down at the upturned face of the leader of the Code Monkeys. "Won't matter though."

Then she sees what Skye is wearing.

"That's my coat, bitch," Sister says. "I'll be coming back for that."

She slams the hatch closed and stumbles away as fast as she can. Despite it being night, the world around her is bright and clear. It will take her senses a long while to revert back from her blind fight state. Her hand at her side, Sister hopes she has that kind of time, but for now, as she sees a few Zs shuffling around the base, she's just glad for the heightened awareness.

———

Third watch.

Val prefers first watch so she can get a solid sleep for the rest of the night, but second watch is close enough. Unfortunately, she gets third watch. With third watch, you are lucky to get back to sleep just as fourth watch ends and it's time to get your ass up and hoof it down the road.

She stares out at the cold Colorado night, watching huge cloud banks drift quickly past the half-moon that glows in the sky, the intense winds getting even more intense as the oncoming storm draws nearer.

The air does smell like snow, and Val wonders if it will be a heavy snow, one of those thick, wet surprises that happens every now and again. Autumn isn't usually the time for that kind of storm, but then there is nothing usual about the world anymore.

Or not since the Code Monkeys showed up.

A legend amongst the old-timers, and a secret tightly held by the command of the Stronghold, the Code Monkeys hit Boulder hard. They nearly destroyed everything, throwing the survivor enclave into total chaos and fear. It has been months, and people are still struggling to get back to their usual routines.

Dead Team Alpha sure as hell never expects a normal routine ever again. They have always been tasked with the most difficult missions down in the perpetually Z-infested Denver wasteland, but now their missions take them venturing into areas well outside the Mile High City.

North to Fort Collins. South to Colorado Springs. Even east into the high Plains. Dead Team Alpha is now the Point Team for the Stronghold; their job is to get ahead of threats so they can't be surprised again like they were with the Code Monkeys.

Hence their recon mission to Peterson AFB. It had once been the home of the Code Monkeys, years before when Val's mother was TL of DTA, but that Team had cleared it of the freaks.

Not the case anymore. The blind crazies are back in full force.

Val wonders what Commander Lee will think when DTA returns and reports that the Code Monkeys are not only back at Peterson AFB, but they are taking people captive for some reason.

The wind picks up, and Val shivers as she huddles on a ledge of what had once been the football stadium for the United States Air Force Academy Falcons. Whatever an Air Force was. She knows what football is. The Teams play a lot back at the Stronghold. As for an "Air Force," Val only knows what she does from old textbooks she read back in school. But having never seen any working aircraft, let alone a working jet fighter or military plane, it is hard to conceive of the need for an "Air Force."

There is a long, low whistle from the shadows far below the stadium and Val brings up her carbine, her NVGs picking out a small shape working its way through the husks of cars left in the stadium's parking lot on Z-Day, abandoned by the fleeing and doomed sports fans.

The whistle sounds again and Val is puzzled. It's a Team code whistle, letting her know that a friendly is approaching. But the small shape she sees is no friendly she knows. In fact, it looks like…

"Shit," she says and drops off the ledge to the walkway a few feet below her.

Val sprints down the sloping and curving walkway to what used to be a concession stand for those long-dead spectators who had needed hot dogs and beer in between plays by the Air Force football team. Now, instead of hot dogs, stadium cheese-covered nachos, and cheap beer sold at expensive prices, the stand hosts the rest of DTA, all sleeping soundly, grabbing some rest while they can.

"Company," Val whispers as she hurries past the concession stand.

Every member of DTA is awake, alert, and hopping over the concession stand's counter in the time it takes them to open their eyes. Carbines up to their shoulders, they follow Val down the continuously spiraling walkway until they reach a set of wide stairs.

"What we got?" Cole asks, catching up to Val.

"I don't know," Val says. "I think… I think it's that woman the Monkeys took inside their bunker."

"Are you shitting me?" Cole asks. "That old woman? Can't be. No way some old survy like that is escaping the Code Monkeys."

"I said I think," Val says. "Maybe I'm wrong."

When they get to the bottom of the stairs and see the woman

standing at a chain link barricade blocking the entrance to the stadium, Val knows she is not wrong.

"Holy fuck," Diaz says. "She's a mess."

"Hello," the woman says. "I'm Sister."

Then she collapses to her knees, one hand on the chain link, the other gripping her side, blood leaking from between her fingers.

"Shit fuck," Sister whispers before she falls onto her side and her eyes roll up into her head.

"She can say that twice," Alastair says.

TWO
A BITTER PILL TO SWALLOW

"Damn," Alastair says as the Team stares at the unconscious woman they carried up to the top-level concession stand. "How the hell did she get away?"

"She took a beating doing it," Cole says, squatting a few feet from the motionless Sister. "She probably would have bled out eventually if she hadn't found us."

"What are those sores on her skin?" Tiny D asks. "Look at them. They look like burns."

"Not burns," Val says. "Cancer. My mom had some like that before she…"

Everyone nods, no one wanting to think too much about the death of Val's mother. Suicide is not something anyone in the Teams talks about. It is considered a disgrace, despite more than a few of the Team Mates going down that path when they reach the end of their lives.

"Cancer," Cole says. "This chick has cancer and she still got away from the Code Monkeys?"

"Maybe they just didn't see her leave," Alastair says, then shrugs when everyone frowns at him. "What? It's not like they have eyes."

"They obviously know she left," Val says. "How else did she get the shit beat out of her and stabbed?"

"I don't get it," Cole says. "I don't get any of it. This woman escapes the Code Monkeys, which is pretty much impossible, and then she finds us? How did she know to look for us here?"

"Yeah. Why us?" Alastair asks.

"We're DTA," Tiny D responds.

"So fucking what?" Alastair counters. "How the hell does she know that? We've never seen this woman before."

"Maybe she found our trail and figured we could help," Val says.

"Looks like she left a trail of her own," Diaz says from the broken and cracked cement wall across from the concession stand. He nods at the parking lot far below. "Zs incoming. Lots."

Cole sighs and hops the concessions stand's counter, then hurries over to Diaz. They look through the break in the cement wall, which originally had only been a waist-high barrier topped with a row of metal pipe railings so spectators didn't fall several stories to their deaths. Now it is a cracked and jagged example of the old world finally succumbing to the Colorado weather extremes.

"Fifty?" Cole asks.

"More," Diaz says. "I count seventy-five, at least."

"Gates should hold," Cole says. "For now. But we need to move soon."

"This chick ain't going anywhere, Cole," Tiny D says.

"We could use one of the stretchers down in the equipment rooms," Val suggests. "There were two down there when we last took inventory. Unless some wasteland trash has broken in and snagged them."

"Why the hell would wasteland trash want one of those stretchers?" Alastair asks.

"Why does wasteland trash want anything?" Val replies. "Don't try to figure those people out. They live out with the Zs instead of safe with us up at the Stronghold."

"She'll slow us down too much," Diaz says. "I'm looking at a hundred Zs now. We gotta go, Mates. Out the backdoor and we can lose them in that old golf course thing before we cut back to 87."

"Diaz is right. She'll slow us down. I say we leave her," Tiny D says and holds up a large hand before any objections are voiced. "We leave some water and rations and hoof it back to Denver. We can let the DTB that is on outpost duty know she's here and they can send back a rescue Team. Let those assholes carry the stretcher."

"She won't last that long," Val says. "It'll take a day to get to the first outpost and then take them a day to get back. Another day, at least, for her to be carried back just to the outpost and another day to get her up to the Stronghold. We don't have enough water or rations to give her."

"So, what, we stay here?" Tiny D asks. "With her? Diaz said there are a hundred Zs down there. This chick probably left a trail of blood from Peterson to here. That means more Zs are on the way. And Code Monkeys. They can follow a blood trail too." Tiny D looks from Alastair to Diaz and then finally to Cole. "Am I wrong here, TL?"

"No," Cole replies.

"Cole, come on, you can't just leave—" Val starts.

"Hold on," Cole says. "I said Tiny D wasn't wrong, but I didn't say she was right."

"What the hell does that mean?" Tiny D asks. "I'm either right or I'm wrong."

"I'm Team Leader," Cole says. "I'm the only one here who gets to be right."

He rubs at his face, leans over the edge of the level, and looks down at the approaching Zs, then glances sideways at the concession stand.

"Wish we had a Runner," Cole says. "That would make things way easier."

"We can thank the Mayor and the Stronghold council for that," Val grumbles.

"No shit," Diaz agrees.

"Why the hell would they refuse to let a Runner be assigned to DTA?" Alastair asks.

"Not enough of them left," Cole says. "You all know that. They want them close to home in case we come under siege again. Too many huge Z herds about now. And the Code Monkeys could come back at any second and try to finish the job."

"Their job is finished," Sister mutters, then coughs. "They don't care about the Stronghold. Just about the nukes."

Val, Tiny D, and Alastair stare down at the woman. Cole rubs his face once more, then moves to the concessions stand counter and peers over it.

"How long have you been awake?" Cole asks.

"The second you put your hands on me to get me up here," Sister replies, her eyes still closed. "Just been saving my energy. Good job on cleaning and stitching my side. Thanks for that, TL Wright."

"You know my name?" Cole asks. "How the hell do you know my name?"

"I know all of your names," Sister replies. "I know your parents' names and I know your grandparents' names. I know pretty much everyone who lives in the Stronghold."

"We don't know you," Tiny D says.

"That's just the way I like it," Sister replies and smiles. "Makes things a shit ton more fun." She chuckles softly. "Shit ton fun. Rhymes. I like me some rhymes."

"What do you mean they don't care about the Stronghold?" Val asks. "What do you know about the Code Monkeys?"

"Wasn't talking about the Code Monkeys," Sister says. She opens her eyes and stares right at Val. "I was talking about your Mayor and the council. And Commander Lee."

"Commander Lee?" Cole asks. "Who the hell are you, lady?"

Sister responds with a dismissive wave of her hand.

"I'm Sister," Sister replies. "I'm the woman who's going to save the Stronghold. Now help me up."

"You probably shouldn't move," Alastair says. "Not with that—"

"I heal fast," Sister interrupts. "Or used to. Doesn't matter now. Time for it all to be over."

DTA stare at her and she stares back.

"I said to help me up," Sister says. "Hello? You got two hundred and thirteen…" she cocks her head and listens. "Nope, two hundred and fourteen Zs down there. Get me up and we do what Diaz said and go out the back, then cut across the golf course. Any of you play golf?"

"Wait? How many? What?" Cole asks.

"Any of you play golf?" Sister repeats.

"No. No one plays golf."

"I did when I was little," Sister sighs. "I think." She rubs her face and shakes her head. "I don't really know anymore."

"Help me get her up," Val says and glances at Cole. He nods, then snaps his fingers and Alastair moves to help Val.

"Thanks," Sister says as she stands on wobbly feet. "I'll be fine in a few hours. Just have to catch my breath now and then. Old bones and shit like that."

She looks at DTA and smiles as they all stand there, waiting.

"You want me to lead the way?" she chuckles.

"DTA, saddle up," Cole orders. "Val, you have point. Alastair and Tiny D can help our guest while Diaz and I take our six."

"I can manage on my own," Sister says.

"Maybe," Cole says, double-checking his M-4. "Maybe not. Not a risk we can take. Let's move."

———

Getting down and out of the stadium is easy enough. But once outside they slow down considerably.

"What the hell?" Cole whispers as they see a second Z horde

heading toward them. "No way those followed the blood trail. They're coming from the wrong direction."

"They must have heard the other Zs and came to have a look," Alastair says.

"They know we're here," Sister says. "Things are getting smarter as they get older. Faster too." She nods at the second horde. "Thirty-eight slow, six fast in that group."

"Lady, you are freaking me out," Tiny D says.

"Leave her alone," Cole orders. "We keep the stadium between us and the Zs. It'll take us longer to loop around and back to 87, but better than the Zs seeing us. They won't ever quit if they catch sight of Diaz's sexy ass."

"Damn right," Diaz says and smiles.

"We get over this hill, then cut right," Val says as they head for a line of firs and pines that cling to a small red-dirt ridge. "It'll take longer but should keep us from being spotted."

No one argues as Val moves off, heading into the line of conifers. DTA hikes up the small ridge and disappears over the other side. Cole gives a last look back at the far-off Zs and raises a middle finger before hurrying to catch up with the others.

They hike through the trees then cut across an old road, the asphalt completely crumbled and broken. Scraggly weeds poke up through the cracked surface here and there, but mostly the road is marked by the stalks of dead wildflowers, their lives over for the season, their dried petals withered and fallen to the ground.

Val absentmindedly brushes the stalks aside with her boots while she keeps an eye on the way ahead, the barrel of her M-4 leading. The Team makes it across the road and back into the trees without a sign of more Zs.

It's not until they reach the edge of what used to be the Air Force Academy's Eisenhower Golf Course that they run into trouble.

"This ain't nothing," Sister says and grins as the Team looks down at the waist-high grasses and weeds of the old golf course that now play host to dozens and dozens of wandering Zs. "You should see what's coming from the East right now. Oceans of undead."

The Team tears their attention from the Zs and all look at Sister. She shrugs and keeps her eyes on the golf course in front of them.

"Oceans of Zs," she repeats, but more to herself.

"We'll have to go completely around," Cole says. "We fight our way through there and the noise will bring the other hordes down on us."

"Not so hard," Sister says and steps from the trees and into the grasses. "Follow my lead."

"Your wound," Val snaps. "You aren't up for point."

Sister puts her hand to her side and looks down. She scrunches up her face and then punches herself right in the wound. Sister gasps, grits her teeth, then shakes her head.

"I'm good," she says. "I told you I heal fast."

"No one heals that fast," Diaz says.

"You're fucking crazy," Tiny D adds.

"Never said I wasn't," Sister says. "I need a blade."

Alastair pulls a knife from a strap on his thigh and flips it handle first, then holds it out.

"I need a real blade," Sister says. Her eyes turn to Val.

The rest of the Team look at Val as well, their eyes falling to the long, curved blade sheathed on her hip. Val follows their looks and glances at the long blade that has been in her family for generations. Legend has it that the blade was given to Granny G by the Great El herself right before the woman left the Stronghold for the last time.

"No way," Val exclaims. "I'm not handing this over to some stranger."

"Trust me," Sister says, her hand outstretched. "Let me borrow it, and I promise to give it back."

Val starts to protest, but Cole clears his throat and raises his eyebrows.

"Cole? Come on!" Val nearly barks. A few of the Zs slowly turn their undead bodies towards the noise.

"Stop dicking around," Cole says. "Let her have the blade."

"Not like it's really from the Great El," Tiny D says, instantly getting a look of death from Val. "What? Come on, Val. Makes for a nice family story, but the Great El is more a legend than a reality."

"Like a ghost," Alastair says. "People think she hangs around the Stronghold, her spirit haunting the idiots who wander too far from the wall."

"Idiots shouldn't wander," Sister says. "You gonna give me that blade or not?"

Val frowns and pulls the curved blade from its sheath. The blade in her hand is just over twenty inches long, curved with the end wider than the part closest to the hilt. The grip is soft, well-worn leather with steel knuckle guards, making it not only an excellent slashing and stabbing weapon, but one that makes a hell of a skull-crushing punch.

"My mom gave this to me," Val says, reluctantly handing the blade over. "Even if it didn't come from the Great El, it came from my mom. Lose it and I'll fucking kick your ass."

"You can try," Sister says. "But I won't lose it. Just stay close, Mates. Maybe you'll learn something."

Sister hefts the blade and smiles, then walks down into the golf course and straight at a large group of Zs huddled close to an abandoned and almost-rusted-to-dust golf cart. DTA follows close behind, none of them knowing whether to watch the Zs or watch Sister. They err on the side of caution, and their training, and settle on watching the Zs, even though the way Sister swings the blade back and forth draws their attention with its hypnotic rhythm.

The first Zs turn their undead bodies toward Sister just as she reaches them. They moan low and take a couple steps. That's all the steps they get as Sister casually removes their heads with two swipes, sending five bodies falling to the ground at the same time, black sludge leaking from their necks and staining the grasses.

Sister does a hop step to the right and cuts down two more Zs while three on her left reach for her. She hacks off their outstretched hands, which are mostly weathered bone with some strips of dried gristle holding the joints together. The Zs hiss and groan at her, but she ignores their protestations and proceeds to pierce their skulls through their foreheads one at a time.

She looks back over her shoulder and winks.

"Fucking A," Alastair says.

DTA sling their carbines, pulling the straps tight to their chests, the M-4s secure at their backs, resting against their packs, then each pull out collapsible batons and snap them out, showing the sharpened metal points.

"Here we go," Cole says and goes in for the kill as two Zs come for him.

He takes the legs out from under one and spins the baton about to stab the other. It lunges at him faster than anticipated and he misses the kill shot, instead sticking the thing through the throat. The Z on the ground reaches for his ankles and he lifts a boot, then brings it down hard, crushing the Z's skull.

Cole lowers his shoulder and lets the other Z fall across his back, then he stands straight, sending the thing tumbling over him and onto the ground. A hard *thunk* sounds and Cole turns his neck to see Diaz ending the Z's undead life with a hard stab through the back of the head. The thing stops wiggling and truly becomes dead.

"Two more," Diaz says, nodding past Cole.

"Right back at ya," Cole says, nodding himself.

It's Diaz's turn to turn around, and he sighs as four Zs shamble toward him. Or three shamble toward him. One begins to move quicker than the others until it is lumbering at an alarmingly fast gait. Then the gait turns to a brisk walk. From there it starts to become a slow sprint.

"What the fuck?" Diaz mutters as he braces for the attack.

The faster Z reaches for him and Diaz steps to the side, holding out a boot so the thing trips and falls right on its face. Before it can push up, Diaz silences it with a piercing shot to the base of the skull. With the first threat managed, Diaz whips about and takes the fight to the other Zs. He makes short work of them, breaking a few bones before ending the Zs' undead lives.

"Second group coming," Alastair announces as he cracks open one, then a second skull with his baton. Putrid brains spill out of the broken heads, filling the air with a stench that makes him nearly gag. "Jesus. You'd think they'd stop smelling after a while."

"Zs stink," Sister says. She kills three more Zs and glances at Alastair. "Duh."

"Yeah. Duh," Tiny D says as she lifts up a struggling Z and throws it into the second group of undead that wade through the grasses to get to the living. "Zs stink."

Val has moved off away from the Team, her eyes drawn to a shadow in the morning light at the edge of the golf course.

"Val? What the fuck?" Cole asks. "Head in the game, Mate!"

"Company," Val says, pointing with her baton at the shadow.

"Can you identify?" Cole asks.

He slams his fist into a Z's face, crushing half the thing's cheek, shakes off the goo that coats his glove, then grabs it by the back of the head and brings up his knee, slamming both together in a spray of bone and gray matter. Not that the brains are gray anymore. More a brownish black.

"Human," Val says. "Just watching us."

"Code Monkey," Alastair says. He moves at the second group with Tiny D and gets to work on those Zs. "They found us."

"Not a Code Monkey," Sister says as she stabs two Zs through the skulls with one blow. She yanks the blade free and whips it down, cleaning the hunks of gunk off with a flick of her wrist. "Canny."

"A what?" Cole and Val ask at the same time.

"No way," Cole says. "We haven't seen cannies around here for years. They gave up a long time ago."

"Cannies never give up," Sister says. "You're an idiot if you think they do."

"Then where the hell have they been?" Val asks.

She kicks a Z back, giving her space to shove the baton through its temple. The thing dangles from the end of her baton for a second until she pulls it free and lets the corpse fall on top of the others that surround her feet.

"Not much out there for them to eat," Cole says.

"Plenty to eat if you know where to look," Sister says. She wipes the blade on her sleeve and smiles at DTA. "Cannies always know where to look."

Cole and Val exchange a glance, then kill the last Zs in front of them.

"You guys about done?" Cole asks, looking at Tiny D, Diaz, and Alastair as they finish off the second group.

"Gone," Val says. "Whoever it was took off."

"That'll be a problem," Sister says. "Going to go find other cannies and try to ambush us before we get to Denver."

"Or it saw how badass we are and decided to fuck off," Diaz says. He wipes the baton on his pants leg and collapses it, tucking the weapon into a pouch on his belt before grabbing up his M-4. "We're one scary set of motherfuckers, ya know. I'd run off too."

"Didn't run off," Sister says. She takes a deep breath and winces, looking down at her side. There's a wet stain there, but it's small. Nowhere near as bad as it should be, considering the exertion she just put on it. "Cannies don't run. Cannies hunt. Their food runs."

"Then I guess we aren't their food," Alastair says, bringing his own M-4 around and ready. "Because DTA doesn't run."

"DTA doesn't shut up either," Cole says. "Keep moving, same formation. We have a lot of hiking to do before we hit the first outpost."

"You're feeling a lot better," Val says to Sister. "I don't know how, but you are."

"Not really," Sister replies. She rubs at her side. "I just know how to fake it and keep going."

"Then get ready to fake it hard, because we are burning daylight," Cole says. "Move the fuck out!"

Everyone nods, even Sister, and they double time their march across the old golf course, ignoring the groups of Zs that are just now giving chase but far enough off not to be a threat.

———

The golf course ends at a crumbling old building. The remains of rusted golf clubs litter the area around the building as if someone had come along one day and decided to just toss them around for no reason. The husks of broken-down white vans line a cracked parking lot with the husks of various cars and trucks in a lot next to it. DTA doesn't even glance at the remnants of the old world, their focus on the road ahead that is nearly choked out of existence by scraggly pines.

They get to the end of the road where it intersects with one that is almost just as clogged with pines. Alastair kicks a stray pine cone out of the way and it bounces off a tree trunk, ricocheting into Tiny D's shoulder.

"Two points," Alastair says.

"Oh, we playing that game?" Tiny D asks as they make their way across the new road. "Because I'll win. You know I have mad skills when it comes to—"

"Quiet," Cole orders. His voice has a finality to it that shuts Tiny D up instantly.

"What's up, TL?" Diaz asks.

"Show respect," Cole says and nods to a clearing a few yards away.

They follow his gaze and all nod along with him.

"Everyone counts," Cole says.

"We always remember," the rest of the Team answers.

"Why say that?" Sister asks as they skirt the edge of a cemetery that is nothing more than a memorial to giant weeds and broken headstones, the occasional glimpse of a rotted wooden cross peeking out here and there. "Not everyone counts. Trust me. Sometimes you have to purge this world of those who don't need to be here anymore."

"Everyone in the Stronghold counts," Cole says, his voice tight and cold, "and we always remember that."

"If you say so," Sister says, shrugging. "Just always remember to cover your ass if shit goes south."

"What does that mean?" Alastair asks. "What shit is going south?"

Sister stops and gives him a puzzled look. "Everything. That's why I'm here."

"Okay, I'm done," Cole says. He gets right in Sister's face. "Listen, I don't know who you think you are, but you need to step in line and stop being so fucking creepy. You looked half dead when we found you, but now you're ready for a fight."

"I found you, not you found me," Sister says and waves a hand. "Sorry. Go on."

Cole growls and shakes his head.

"You say you know us, but we don't know you," Cole continues. "I need one good reason why we shouldn't cut you loose and leave you to the wasteland."

"I kick ass better than you do," Sister says.

"Not good enough," Cole replies. "And not fucking true."

"Really?" Sister smirks.

"Do better or we cut you loose," Cole says.

"Because I have all the secrets," Sister says. "Commander Lee is going to want to hear those secrets."

"What fucking secrets?" Cole asks.

"Uh, they're secrets," Sister responds. "For Commander Lee, not for TL Wright."

Val gasps and points a finger at Sister.

"You're the spy," she says. "You're the one Aunt Maura hinted at."

"Am I?" Sister replies. "Not like her to be hinting."

Sister looks up into the crisp blue of what is turning into a nice late autumn morning with the late autumn storm far off on the horizon, looking like it will skirt the area and not become a problem.

"I guess it doesn't really matter anymore," Sister says.

"What doesn't matter?" Cole asks.

"The secrets," Sister says. "No use for secrets soon. Not all secrets."

"You were spying on the Consortium," Val states.

"Maybe," Sister says. "Probably."

"Are they coming this way?" Val asks. "Is the Consortium going to finally attack us? They have nukes, don't they?"

"Nukes? The Consortium?" Sister laughs. "No, they don't have nukes. Code Monkeys have nukes, but the Consortium doesn't have shit. Not anymore."

"Okay, crazy lady, game over," Cole snaps. "Talk or you get cut loose. Last warning."

"I don't think that's a good idea," Val says. "Aunt Maura, I mean Commander Lee, will want to speak to her if she's who I think she is."

"And if she isn't?" Cole asks. "We started off helping a wounded and bleeding woman. Now we're just marching back to the Stronghold with a freaky Z killer who knows a fuck lot about cannies."

"Takes one to know one," Sister says.

"What?" DTA asks in unison. M-4s are raised and pointed at Sister.

"What was that?" Cole asks. "What did you say?"

"I said it takes one to know one," Sister answers. "Some of you are related to cannies."

"Fuck you we are," Tiny D says.

"Nope, it's true," Sister insists, her features becoming years younger as she takes on a look of complete sincerity. "Swear to everyone who counts. It was a long, long time ago, but it's true. You think the convoy who founded the Stronghold were all just suburban survivors from that Whispering Pines place?"

"Whispering what?" Val asks.

"Never mind," Sister says. "Doesn't matter. Forget I said anything."

"I vote we leave her here," Tiny D says.

"I second that," Diaz adds. "Lady is freaking me out."

"Jesus," Sister sighs. She pulls the sheathed blade from her belt and holds it out to Val. "Take it."

"Yeah, I think I will," Val says and snatches the offered blade.

Sister puts her hands out and offers her wrists.

"Tie me up, if it will make you feel better," Sister says. "Doesn't make a difference to me."

"TL, we don't have time to deal with this crap," Diaz says. "I say we ditch her and be done."

"We can't ditch her," Val protests. "She has information for Commander Lee."

"Says you," Diaz counters.

"Tell us something that'll keep us from leaving you here," Cole says. "Give me one thing that will make me believe you aren't completely full of shit."

"Really?" Sister responds. "Fine. One thing."

DTA waits as Sister narrows her eyes and thinks it over.

"Well?" Cole snaps.

"Calm down, TL Wright," Sister warns. "I have a lot of info in my brainpan. A lot. Just figuring out what I can say and what I can't."

"The Consortium. Tell us about that," Val says.

"No way we can verify what she says," Alastair states.

"The Consortium? Yeah, I can tell you all about them," Sister says and nods. "They're dead. Gone. No more. Adios, Hotlanta!"

"What?" Cole asks. "The Consortium is gone? Bullshit."

"Not bullshit at all," Sister says. She points at the sores on her face and head. "How do you think I got this shit? Cancer doesn't grow on trees."

"That doesn't make any sense," Tiny D says.

"Shit," Val says. "The Consortium was nuked. That's the cancer you have. Same as the kind my mom had. Severe radiation sickness."

"Bingo was his name-o," Sister says, pointing at Val. "No more Consortium. I found that out the hard way."

"No way," Alastair says. "If you have radiation sickness, you'd be dead."

"Hard to kill," Sister shrugs. "I'm getting tired of mentioning that. And this isn't all from that. I've been to all the hot spots in the old USA."

"What the hell happened to the Consortium?" Cole asks. "If it's true."

"Can't tell you that," Sister says. "I'll let Commander Lee decide what the Teams, and the Stronghold, need to know. But believe the shit out of me, Mates, the Consortium did us a favor by checking out."

"Whoa, whoa, whoa," Cole says. "The Consortium checked out? Are you saying they nuked themselves?"

"Everyone counts," Sister says. "We always remember."

"Why the hell would they do that to themselves?" Cole asks.

"No choice," Sister says. "They were dead anyway. You think there are a lot of Zs here now? Just wait until what's coming this way gets here. Zs as far as the eyes can see."

Cole rubs at his face then looks to DTA.

"On me," he says and walks a few yards away. The Team follows right behind. "Opinions. Now."

"She stays right here," Diaz says.

"That," Tiny D nods.

"I don't know," Alastair says.

"We have to bring her with us," Val says.

"Fuck," Cole grumbles. He looks over at Sister. "Fuck."

THREE
LOOK HOMEWARD, ANGEL OF DEATH

The outpost is built into the remains of what had once been an overpass at the intersection of highways 87 and 470 on the outskirts of the former metro area of Denver, Colorado. The overpass is long gone, but most of the concrete columns and support struts remain, the space between them built up with suspended platforms, connected by long rope and wood bridges. A pyre burns at the top of one of the columns, its black smoke drifting into the twilight sky.

Denver Team Beta One's Team Leader, Stanford Lee, sits a few feet below the pyre that burns, his feet dangling over the ledge of broken concrete, his eyes watching the approaching figures with great interest.

Twenty-three, tall, muscular, with blond hair like his cousin Val, but instead of brown eyes he has ice-blue ones, Stanford swings his legs out and brings them back, out and back, out and back, then stops and gets to his feet as one of the other Mates of DTB1, Shep Wilcox, walks across a short bridge toward him.

"I don't recognize the woman," Shep says when he reaches Stanford. He hands the TL a pair of horribly scuffed binoculars. "See if you do."

Stanford takes the binoculars and puts them to his eyes. He

focuses on the stranger, a woman dressed in some nasty leathers with a nearly shaved head. To Stanford's eyes she looks sickly, but she carries herself with a familiar confidence.

"You don't know her at all?" Stanford asks, moving his view so he can take in DTA as they hike toward the outpost. "Rest of the Team looks okay. They have Z guts on their uniforms, so they certainly got in the shit, but I don't see any wounds."

"The woman is wounded," Shep says. "Check her side."

Stanford moves the binoculars back to the stranger. He studies her for a few seconds more, then grunts.

"Can't be bad the way she's keeping up with DTA," Stanford says. "Her wrists are tied. Maybe she got the nick from one of the DTA Mates."

"Maybe," Shep replies, then looks up at the pyre. "What color do you want me to make it?"

"Red, then green," Stanford responds. "Let the rest know we have some danger incoming but everything is cool right now."

"Will do," Shep says and steps to a rope ladder against the concrete column. He climbs the ladder while Stanford keeps studying the strange woman through the binoculars.

The pyre casts a bright red glow for a few seconds as Shep tosses a signal powder into it. Then he tosses in a new powder and the flames turn a bright green before slowly burning back to their normal yellow and orange.

Stanford waits until Shep has climbed back down before he pulls the binoculars away from his eyes.

"We have any decent food to eat?" Stanford asks. "DTA is going to be hungry as shit after being out in the waste so long."

"Crumble mix and some elk jerky," Shep says. "Breena may have some apples. She always fucking hordes those in her kit."

"See if she does," Stanford says. He slaps Shep on the shoulder. "Ain't outpost life just great?"

"You must have really pissed your mom off if she stuck us with this assignment," Shep says. "What the hell did you do?"

"Who knows?" Stanford laughs. "The mind of Commander

Lee has always been, and always will be, a complete fucking mystery to me."

"You're her son, man," Shep says. "What the fuck?"

Stanford shrugs. "Fuck if I know, Mate. Fuck if I know."

———

"Hey, cuz," Val says as she sees Stanford.

"Val," Stanford says and smiles. "Cole."

"Ford," Cole says, clasping the man's hand as he climbs up the rope ladder and into the outpost. "Good to see you holding things down."

"What'd you do to piss your mom off, dude?" Alastair asks as he follows Cole and Val up, then stands aside as Sister comes up after him.

Stanford only shrugs as he focuses on the new woman.

"What do we have here?" he asks. "Tiny D finally find a cuddle buddy?"

"Suck my dick, Ford," Tiny D replies, following behind Alastair. Diaz is right behind her and turns to pull up the long rope ladder, keeping everyone in the outpost safe from curious crazies or acrobatic Zs.

"Hey now, I'm a TL," Stanford says. "Show some respect."

"Suck my dick, sir," Tiny D replies.

"That's more like it," Stanford laughs. "But seriously, who is this motherfucker?"

"She calls herself Sister," Cole says. "She needs to talk to Commander Lee."

"So she's a masochist?" Stanford laughs. "She'd have to be to want to talk to the old battle axe."

"Not a very nice way to speak of your mother," Sister responds. "You should show more respect."

"Should I?" Stanford asks. "Why? Who the fuck are you to tell me how to talk about my own mother?"

"She is your commanding officer," Sister says. "Team code

dictates you not disparage her name even if she isn't around to hear." Sister looks at the rest of the Mates standing on the outpost platform. "Bad for morale. Makes you a weak leader."

"Who the fuck is this piece of wasteland trash?" Stanford asks, turning to Val. "Is there a reason you didn't put a bullet in her brain when you first saw her?"

"She fought her way free of the Code Monkeys," Val says. "Then found us in the stadium."

Stanford's mouth hangs open briefly, then snaps shut as he blinks, his eyes assessing Sister a second time.

"You? You fought your way out of the Code Monkeys' bunker?" Stanford asks. "How? They must not have been guarding you worth a shit."

"They were guarding me," Sister says. "I killed the guards. Then I killed the others who came to help the guards. I killed everyone in my way, found a ladder, and climbed out. That's how."

"Bullshit," Stanford hisses. "Bullshit, bullshit, bullshit."

"If you say so," Sister says, then smiles. "You'd know."

"What?" Stanford snaps, moving at Sister. "What did she just say to me? Lady, you better watch yourself, or you'll end up learning to fucking fly right off this platform!"

"Ford, stop," Val says and grabs her cousin by the upper arm. He tries to jerk away but she tightens her grip, making it painful enough to force him to look at her. "Let's chat."

"You're not TL, Val," Stanford says. "Cole should brief me."

"I'll let Val do it," Cole says as he moves to a suspension bridge that is just rope and a couple of wooden planks. "I'm going to go take a shit in safety, then find something to eat."

"I'm with TL," Alastair says. "Just in the opposite order. Food first, shit later."

Diaz and Tiny D fall in line with Shep right behind them. The Mates of DTA call out as they see other members of DTB1 perched at their posts along the many platforms and bridges around the outpost. Val watches them go, then looks at Sister.

"Tell him what you told us," Val says.

"Everything?" Sister asks.

"Everything," Val says.

Sister repeats what she had said to DTA about the Consortium while Stanford stands there, looking bored and pissed at the same time. When she's finished, he glances at Val and shrugs.

"None of that means shit," Stanford grumbles. "Wasteland gossip from some crazy woman."

"What's wrong with you?" Val snaps. "You're acting like a Z crawled up your ass."

"That would suck," Sister says and shakes her head. "Really suck. Nobody likes a Z up the ass."

Stanford stares at the woman for a couple seconds, then focuses back on Val.

"Get this whacko nutjob off my outpost," he says.

"Yeah, that's not happening," Val replies.

"Really?" Stanford snarls. "Because Team code dictates that the TL of the Team in charge of the outpost calls all shots when it comes to who is and who is not allowed up into the outpost."

"Cole is TL of DTA," Val counters. "Technically, he outranks you and could override any order—"

"Nope," Stanford says and smiles. "TL of the Team managing the outpost makes all calls. This is my outpost, whether I want it to be or not, so I make the call. If I want this bitch gone, then she is gone, and there's nothing that Cole or any of DTA can do about it."

Sister clears her throat and raises her hand.

"Is she kidding me with this?" Stanford barks.

"May I speak, sir?" Sister asks.

"Fucking A. Yeah, go ahead and speak," Stanford says.

"I'm the only person who has been inside the Code Monkeys' bunker," Sister says. "As far as you know, I'm the only person who has ever escaped them. I'm pretty sure that makes me an A-1 important person. Also pretty sure your mother, Commander Lee, will want to talk with this A-1 important person face to face."

"A-1 important person?" Stanford asks. "What the hell is she saying? Who talks like that?"

"You should have known me when I was younger," Sister says and grins. It's a wide, honest grin. "I used to drive everyone crazy back then. Man oh man, those were the days."

"Your mom told me a while ago, a few months after the Code Monkey attack on the Stronghold, that she had a spy in place," Val says. "Sister is the spy. She's the one who has been feeding your mom intel on what's happening with the other survivor enclaves. You heard what she said about the Consortium, right? We need to get her through Denver and up to the Stronghold. We'll let Aunt Maura take it from there."

"No," Stanford says. "This is my call. I'll send a Runner, but that's it. If the Runner comes back with an order from her majesty, then you and DTA can take her up there. I'm not going with. DTB1 has a job to do. This is my outpost, this is my sector to protect. I'm going to stay right the fuck here."

"You're an idiot," Val says.

"Fuck you too," Stanford replies.

"I used to know siblings who acted like you two do," Sister says. "A brother and a sister who would bicker. It's because of the love. So much love you hold inside that fear makes you say stupid things because you're afraid to feel pain if one of you gets hurt."

"She keeps talking and I toss her to the ground," Stanford warns.

"Love?" Val muses, then looks at Stanford. "Too much love—? Jesus fuck, Aunt Maura didn't assign you to this outpost, you volunteered. Benji dumped you, didn't he?"

Stanford points a finger at Val and starts to respond, but all that comes out is a choking noise. He jabs the finger at her a couple of times, then shakes his head and walks away.

"She's your responsibility," Stanford says as he climbs a ladder up to one of the topmost points of the outpost. "You watch her ass. Anything happens and I blame you, cuz."

"Ford," Val calls after him. "Ford! Oh, for fuck's sake! Come on! Talk to me!"

"No," Stanford says as he reaches the top and is lost from sight.

"Was he in love?" Sister asks.

"Drop it," Val says quietly. "Come on. We'll get some chow and then bunk down. Ford will send a Runner out and all we can do is wait."

"That's not all we can do," Sister replies. She shrugs when she gets a look from Val. "Just saying. I kinda need to see your aunt. We're wasting time sitting here playing with our dicks."

"Neither of us have dicks," Val says.

"Tiny D does, she said so," Sister replies.

"It was a joke," Val says. "She doesn't really have a dick."

"I know," Sister responds and sighs. "I was just playing."

Val stares up the ladder Stanford had just ascended.

"Family is hard," Sister says, clapping Val on the shoulder, making the woman jump and spin around. Sister holds up her bound hands. "Sorry. Sorry. Jumpy soldiers. I always forget. All I was saying is family is hard. So much love."

"Whatever," Val says and nods to the rope bridge. "You need help getting across with your hands tied?"

"Nope. I got it," Sister says.

She steps onto the bridge and nearly sprints across. The ropes and boards barely even move, she's so fast. Val stares for a second and shakes her head.

"You can get out of those ropes at any time, can't you?" she asks as she walks across the bridge and joins Sister. "I mean, if you want your hands free they'd be free, right?"

"I don't want to make any of you nervous," Sister answers, holding up her bound hands. "It makes things easier."

"If you say so," Val says. "Come on."

———

The noise is subtle, quiet, not the sound of a shambling Z moving through the debris at the bottom of the outpost. No, it's a deliberate noise, the noise of someone not wanting to be heard but not quite getting the job done.

Denver Team Beta One Team Mate Carlotta Schuemaker cocks her head as she listens to the sound. Perched on a small hunk of concrete jutting out from the outpost, Carlotta leans over, peering down into the gloom of the shadowed ground below. The night is clear, but the moon has already fallen, leaving the world draped in darkness.

The sound comes again, but from a different direction. Over toward the main access point of the outpost. She swivels about, her eyes trying to pierce the darkness. Then a third noise, off to her right, the complete opposite direction of the main access point.

Carlotta frowns and growls low in her throat, not happy with what she's hearing. She puts her fingers to her lips and lets out a long, slow whistle. It's not very high pitched, sounding more like someone blowing over the neck of an empty bottle. She waits a couple of beats and repeats the noise.

A scuff from behind and above makes her turn slowly. She looks up to see Tommy Bombs' face, his eyes shining in the dark, wide and questioning.

She points at her ears then off to the left, off to the right, and directly below. Tommy Bombs holds up three fingers and Carlotta shrugs, then nods. Tommy Bombs nods back and is lost from sight as he moves away from the edge of his perch.

Carlotta brings her M-4 to her shoulder and looks through the scope. The narrow view of the world is lit in greens and grays, the night vision tech changing the unseen into a visible spectrum. Usually only DTA is allowed to use the advanced tech left over from a civilization long gone, but after the devastation the Code Monkeys brought to the Stronghold, Commander Lee decided the other Teams should have their fair share of tech available to them as well.

Unfortunately, that tech is very limited and spread very thin amongst the Mates.

Knowing she has an advantage the others don't, Carlotta takes her duty very seriously and slowly scans the area below the outpost, her enhanced vision hunting for the sources of the quiet sounds. She does a thorough sweep to the left then a sweep back to the right, but she doesn't see anything out of the ordinary.

Except…

Straight down, tucked into the debris the Teams intentionally litter the ground with to act as a barrier and early warning system in situations just like this, Carlotta sees a boot. It's a nasty, hole-ridden boot, easy to mistake as something lost long ago. But her eye picks up the very subtle movement of something inside the boot. A toe. A toe twitching.

There's a scrape of concrete above and behind her again, but she doesn't turn around. Instead, she holds up a fist, then her index finger, and points down at the ground. A low whistle sounds, and in seconds there's more scraping on concrete.

"What do we have?" Stanford whispers as he crawls on his belly to Carlotta, patting her on the ankle. "Zs? Code Monkeys?"

"Not sure," Carlotta whispers back. "Not Zs though. Gotta be a target directly un—"

Before she can finish, the edge of the perch close to her face explodes into shards of concrete. She scrambles back and turns her head toward Stanford, eyes wide with surprise and fear.

"Looks like they have fucking guns!" Carlotta shouts.

"Do you think?" Stanford says, grabbing her uniform and pulling her back to better cover as the perch continues to be ripped apart by gunfire. He looks up over his shoulder and sees Breena Lang and Shep standing there, M-4s at the ready. "You fuckers ready to light some crazies up?"

"Sir, fucking yes, sir!" they shout and dash off in different directions.

Gunfire erupts from the left of the platform, then from the right.

"Oh, it is so fucking on!" Stanford yells, and the first genuine smile in a long time spreads across his face.

———

Cole sighs at the sound of gunfire and sets the plate of food aside as he reaches for his carbine.

"Not our outpost," Val says, a sneaky smile on her face. "Ford was very clear about that."

"Funny," Cole says and stands up, his M-4 at the ready.

Tiny D joins him, followed by Diaz. In less than a second, Alastair shows up, buckling his belt and looking for his kit and weapon.

"Thought that shit would never end," Alastair says as Tiny D tosses him his gear. "But as soon as the shots started my asshole clenched shut and probably won't open back up until Christmas."

"That's a good one," Sister says, still sitting, still eating, not showing any sign she is affected by the shouts and the gunfire that echo around her. "Asshole clenched shut."

"Watch her," Cole says to Val.

"Me? You may need me," Val responds. "We can tie her to a post. She's not going anywhere."

"I'm not going anywhere," Sister says. "I'm not done eating. And you guys are going the same way I am, back to the Stronghold, so I might as well hang for a while."

"You watch her," Cole says to Val again, his tone very clear that there is no arguing the point.

"Fine, I'll watch her," Val says, holding up her hands. "But you owe me, dickhead. I haven't fought non-Zs in forever."

"Yeah, yeah, you can fight the next batch of crazies we run into," Cole says as he hurries off with the rest of DTA. "I promise."

Val watches Sister take a few bites, then shakes her head.

"Who the fuck are you?" she mutters and holds up her hand before Sister can answer. "Sister. I know. You don't have to say it."

The second there's a break in the gunfire, Stanford leans over the concrete and returns fire. His M-4 barks in the night, the suppressor on his muzzle keeping the barrel flashes from blinding him. His shots are spaced out, each hitting the ground four feet apart as he fishes for the locations of the attackers.

A voice cries out after his last shot. Stanford grins and takes aim, sending three more bullets to the same location. The voice screams, then is cut short.

"That's right, fucker," Stanford says as he sprints to the closest ladder and hurries down, his hands barely touching the ropes, his feet only nudging at the steps.

Stanford drops the last couple of feet and whips around, his M-4 leading the way. He steps through the piles of trash and debris, hunting for the attacker he just took out. It only takes him a few steps before he sees the blood pooling from around a pile of rags.

He nudges the rags with his boot and it rolls to the side, lifeless eyes staring up at him. Stanford studies the attacker, taking note of the pale skin, the sunken eyes, the mottled flesh. If it wasn't for the blood, he'd think it was a Z. He jams the barrel of his carbine into the person's mouth and pulls down, revealing a row of sharp teeth filed to points.

"Cannies," Stanford mutters. "Fuck."

A grunt and scuffle from his right makes him spin about, and he finds himself face to face with a very large man. A very large man with very large teeth that are as sharp and filed as the corpse at Stanford's feet.

He squeezes the trigger, but the canny grabs the M-4 by the scorching hot barrel and shoves it aside, sending the shot far to the left. Stanford lets go of his M-4, knowing the carbine is useless while in the grip of the canny behemoth, and pulls his 9mm pistol from the quick release holster on his hip. He fires two shots into the man's thigh, but the huge canny doesn't go down.

"Oh, shit!" Stanford cries as he finds himself lifted into the air by his neck, a massive hand about to crush his windpipe. His next few curses are nothing but choked, garbled coughs.

Then Stanford is flying through the air, his back slamming against a concrete support, his body sliding down into the trash pile underneath.

"Fuck," he croaks as the huge canny stomps toward him.

"Cover up!" a voice shouts from above, and Stanford instinctively wraps his arms around his head and tucks his legs up into his chest.

The air explodes with gunfire, and it's only Stanford's training that keeps him from crying out. That, and his throat feels like he's eaten ten pounds of ground glass after the fist hug it got from the huge canny. He hears the clicking of an empty magazine and risks a peek from between his arms.

The huge canny stands there, still towering over Stanford, but the man's chest is nothing but gaping holes and pouring rivers of blood. Yet the son of a bitch doesn't fall. The man sways back and forth, his crazed eyes locked onto Stanford. Impossibly, the man snarls and starts to reach down, ready to finish what he's started. But before he can bend a foot, the front of his face explodes in a mass of blood and skull.

Stanford shuts his eyes as he is sprayed with gray matter and bone. It keeps the gore from getting into his eyes, but it also keeps him from seeing what's coming right at him. The corpse of the huge canny. Stanford shouts as the big body collapses on top of him, blood soaking into his uniform instantly.

"Hold on," Cole says as he struggles to pull the giant corpse off Stanford. "Don't move."

"Wasn't going to," Stanford replies.

"Nice voice," Cole says as he finally gets the huge dead canny off Stanford. "You sound like the old guy who lived down the street from me when I was a kid. My dad says he rolled his own cigarettes and smoked like a chimney."

"Smoked? What? Tobacco was gone decades ago," Stanford

said as he's helped to his feet by Cole. "What the hell was he smoking?"

"I think my dad said it was newspaper and old insulation," Cole answers. He looks Stanford up and down. "Any of that blood yours?"

"Not that I know of," Stanford says and pats his body. "Nope. All good."

Gunfire from the far right of the outpost draws their attention. Before they can move that way, a screaming woman rushes them both. Cole drops her with a shot between the eyes as Stanford scrambles to pick his M-4 up off the ground.

Flesh from the dead giant's hands is stuck to the barrel, and Stanford frowns at the crispy skin.

"Oh, that is gross," Cole says. More gunfire. "Shit. Come on."

Then gunfire from the far left stops them before they can go more than a couple of steps. They look at each other and sigh.

"Right," Cole stays and takes off running.

"I'll take left then!" Stanford shouts after him. "Thanks for the choice, asshole!"

Stanford runs off in the opposite direction as Cole, muttering about how the outpost is his and he should be the one to choose which direction to go.

————

"I bet they could use our help," Sister says to Val as the woman sits with her back up against a post, watching Val pace back and forth. "I'm done eating now. We don't have to stay up here."

"I have my orders," Val says. "I'm watching you while DTA and DTB1 take care of business. They can handle it."

Sister cocks her head as gunshot after gunshot after gunshot echoes through the night. She frowns and winces as someone screams.

"That was one of yours," Sister says. "Breena? No, maybe Carlotta. Hold on." She keeps her head cocked and waits. When there's another scream she nods. "Breena Lang. Yep, That's her. Took a bullet to the leg. Maybe even had her knee blown out."

"How the fuck could you know that?" Val snaps. "There is no way you can know that."

"I've been around," Sister replies. "That woman needs our help. The closest Mate is a hundred yards away and is very busy fighting off three cannies. Diaz? No, Tiny D. Yep. Tiny D. Damn, she can fight."

A third scream and Val winces.

"We have to stay here," Val says.

"If you're trying to convince yourself, you're doing a shitty job," Sister says, grinning. "You already have one foot toward the ladder."

Val stops pacing and looks Sister square in the face.

"You're staying here," Val says. "And I'm tying you to that post."

"I can help," Sister responds, shrugging. "You need me."

"You're sick with radiation poisoning and you're still wounded," Val says. "Best to leave you up here. You die down there and Commander Lee will rip me a new one."

"Nah, you're her favorite," Sister says. "And family. She has a soft spot for family."

"Tell that to Ford," Val says as she moves to tie Sister's hands behind the post.

"Really?" Sister asks. "What if one of the cannies gets up here? I won't be able to defend myself."

"I highly fucking doubt that," Val says. She stands and points at Sister. "Do not go anywhere. Stay right here. I'm only doing this to help Breena. I'll already be in deep shit with Cole for leaving you. Do not make my life harder by getting yourself free."

"Life is hard enough without me making it worse," Sister says. "I promise not to go anywhere or get myself free."

More screaming.

"Someone is hurting her," Sister says and frowns. "Bad. Hurry."

Val gives Sister one last look, then scrambles to the closest ladder and drops from sight. Sister looks up at the night sky and sneers.

"What the fuck are you looking at, stars?" she says. "People are dying. Stop looking so smug." A shooting star rockets by. "Ooh, pretty."

———

Tiny D slams two heads together and the air is filled with the sound of skulls shattering.

She tosses the bodies away, one to either side of her, and grabs her 9mm from her hip, firing point blank into the face of a woman coming at her. The woman's screaming face is obliterated into a thousand shards of teeth and bone, blood spraying everywhere.

Tiny D scowls as she wipes gore from her eyes. She doesn't wipe fast enough to see the man coming at her. He tackles her from the side, knocking her to the ground and into one of the dead bodies. A small geyser of blood shoots into the air from the body, caused by Tiny D's weight and the heavy man who has her pinned down, his hands trying to wrap around her thick neck.

"You picked the wrong fight, fucker!" Tiny D bellows as she boxes the man's ears.

He growls and bares his sharpened teeth. Tiny D laughs and boxes him again and again until his hands on her neck loosen and he wobbles, wobbles, then falls over. She sends a hard elbow into the bridge of his nose, and he screams as half his face caves in.

"Shut the fuck up, bitch," she says as she gets up, retrieves her 9, and puts two bullets in his forehead and then one in his chest.

She spits on him for good measure.

There's a noise above her and she looks up. Her eyes go wide as a woman leaps from one of the rope bridges, knives in both hands, teeth glinting in the night. Tiny D can't get out of the way fast enough, and she goes down hard as the woman slams into her. Pain radiates up from her belly, and she barely gets a second to look down and see one knife sticking from her gut before the woman tries to slash at her face with the other.

The woman tries but does not succeed as Tiny D blocks the attack and spins her arm around the woman's, gaining enough leverage to snap the arm at the elbow. The woman shrieks in pain and Tiny D shuts her up fast with several hard punches to the jaw. The woman's sharpened teeth tumble from her mouth and clatter on the old and broken pavement. Then Tiny D grabs the woman's lower jaw and pulls hard, tearing it off in one yank.

"Jesus Christ, Tiny D," Alastair says as he pulls the dying canny off the Mate and tosses her aside. He puts two rounds in the canny's chest and one in her head with his M-4 before turning back to Tiny D. "Did you have to rip her jaw off? Oh… shit…"

He stares at the knife Tiny D has clutched in her hands. The knife bobbing to Tiny D's heartbeat as blood pulses around it, pouring from the wound in her gut.

"Fuck," Alastair says and sets his M-4 aside. He pulls off his pack and digs inside for the med kit, his eyes darting from the pack to Tiny D's belly. "Hold on, D. Just hold on."

"What the fuck else you think I'm going to do?" Tiny D asks. "Go for a fucking morning jog?"

"Right. Yeah. Sorry," Alastair says as he sets the med kit next to the large woman. He pulls out a small cylinder and a pad of bandages. "This is going to hurt. Bad."

"Just do it, asshole," Tiny D snaps and closes her eyes as Alastair looks at the knife.

He grabs the handle, says a quick prayer, then pulls it free. Instantly, dark red blood begins to flow everywhere. He pops open the cylinder, pours the black powder inside it onto the wound, then presses down with one of the bandages. He counts to ten, says another prayer, reaches into the med kit, pulls out a match, lights it, and places the flame to Tiny D's wound.

Alastair cringes at the scream Tiny D lets out. It is loud enough to break glass if there was any glass left intact nearby. There is not.

"Oh, you fucker," Tiny D gasps, looking at her gut as Alastair packs it with bandages and then holds both hands on it. "I'm gonna make you pay for that."

"Make me pay?" Alastair says. "What the hell? I'm saving your life."

"Oh, you better hope so," Tiny D says, her voice weakening. "You better fucking hope so."

Her eyes roll up into her head as it falls back on the pavement. Alastair watches her chest rise and fall, rise and fall, showing she only passed out and didn't die. He turns his head this way and that, looking for the attack he expects to happen at any second since he's now completely helpless. He can defend himself or keep Tiny D alive. He can't do both.

"Shit," he whispers. "Shit, shit, shit."

———

The shadow reaches the concrete column and scurries up it. Val slides to a stop, seeing the person's feet just as they are lost from sight. Instead of heading to the rope ladder a yard away, she turns around and sprints back across the bridge to the platform the column juts out of. M-4 to her shoulder, she looks up toward the top of the column.

And the flames that start growing higher from the pyre on top.

"Dammit," Val says. "What the hell did the canny do that for?"

She watches as the flames continue to rise higher and higher, hoping for a clear shot of the canny. She really does not want to have to climb up after the son of a bitch. Then she stares in horror as burning logs are flung from the column, landing onto bridges and platforms. Bridges and platforms that are made of hemp rope and wood.

The flames spread quickly and Val opens fire, spraying the top of the column with bullets. She doubts she hit the person, and it's too late anyway since the damage is already done, but she knows the gunfire will draw attention to her position and the flames that are already engulfing a quarter of the outpost.

"I got it," Sister says from behind Val, making the Mate jump and almost turn her M-4 on the woman. "Sorry. Didn't mean to startle you."

"What the hell?" Val snaps. "I told you to stay put!"

Sister shrugs and scrambles up the column and is lost from Val's sight. She hears a man shout, then a heavy *thunk* and thud. Shadows dance against the flames of the pyre, but they are warped and twisted, making it impossible for Val to tell who they belong to. There's another shout, another set of *thunks* and thuds, and then a man goes flying out over the edge of the column, arms and legs pinwheeling as he falls into the flaming wreckage of the platform next to Val's.

Sister climbs back down and stretches her side.

"Ow," Sister says. "That canny had some skill. Probably would have hurt you bad if you'd gone up there. Good thing you didn't."

"You weren't supposed to get free," Val snarls. "And I can't find Breena. That wasn't her screaming, was it? Was that all just bullshit to get me to leave?"

"Maybe," Sister laughs and walks away. "Come on, Little Baptiste, time to fetch the other Mates and get the hell out of here. This outpost is lost."

"Hold up!" Val yells after her. "If DTA sees you without your restraints, they'll open fire!"

"Don't think so!" Sister calls back. "They're all a little busy!"

———

The members of DTA and DTB1 stare as the outpost crumbles into ashes, the ropes and wooden structures lost in only a matter of minutes.

"Glad to see you aren't dead," Val says, turning from the outpost to face Lang.

"Huh? What do you mean?" Lang asks.

"Nothing," Val says and glares over at Sister, who is giving her a wide, shit-eating grin. "I just thought I heard you scream is all."

"I did scream," Lang replies. "Fucking canny nailed me in the knee with a baseball bat. Hurts like hell, but I'll live."

"And the canny?" Val asks.

"Two in the chest, one in the head," Lang says. "He won't be coming back."

Everyone stares at the conflagration for a few moments, then Cole steps forward.

"We sure we got them all?" Cole asks Stanford. "Did you see any get away?"

"I'm sure some did," Stanford replies, shrugging. "But not my biggest problem right now."

"Oh? What the hell is your biggest problem right now?" Cole asks.

"How the fuck to tell my mom I let the outpost burn down," Stanford replies.

"Not your fault, Ford," Val says. "No way to know the cannies would use the pyre against us."

"At least the others know we're in deep shit," Tommy Bombs says, hooking a finger over his shoulder. "Red pyres for as far as the eyes can see."

The Teams turn and look at the far-off flames that burn from the pyre stations set up throughout Denver. One by one they turn from orange to bright red, signaling to each consecutive pyre that trouble is going down.

"Fucking great," Stanford says. "We'll have at least one DTB coming to check things out. That means I have to tell either Holly Moore or Gary Hoffman that I couldn't hack it as a TL."

"Don't worry about that, buddy," Cole says, clapping Stanford on the shoulder. "Everyone already knew you couldn't hack it. If it wasn't for all of us, you'd have been Z food years ago."

"I could shoot you now and blame the cannies," Stanford grumbles.

"Too many witnesses," Cole laughs.

"Damn witnesses," Stanford mutters.

"We've got her secure," Alastair says, grabbing onto the end of a makeshift stretcher. Diaz is on the other end, and the two men lift Tiny D up slowly, careful not to jar her too much. "We going or what?"

"Yeah," Cole says. "Val, you and Shep take—"

"I'll take point," Sister says, raising her hand. "Val and Shep can follow behind me. I'm better at point than them. They can't see in the dark like I can."

"You can see in the dark?" Stanford scoffs.

"No," Sister replies. "It's a figure of speech."

"A figure of speech? By who?" Stanford asks.

"By people who can see in the dark," Sister replies and winks. Then she is off, moving quickly ahead of the two Teams, her legs taking long, confident strides.

"I'm not cool with her leading us and definitely not cool with her not being restrained," Stanford says.

"Not much we can do about it," Cole says. "You heard what Val said."

They watch Val and Shep fall in line behind Sister and the two TLs glance at each other.

"Who's in charge around here?" Stanford asks.

Stanford gives one last glance over his shoulder at the burning outpost, then shakes his head and starts marching with the other members of the Teams.

FOUR

THE FREAKS COME OUT AT NIGHT

The line of flaming pyres can be seen for miles. The red flames reaching high into the sky, alerting all of the Stronghold crews, whether Teams or reclamations, that danger is knocking on Denver's door. There is no way to tell what the exact danger is, not without a Runner going from station to station with specific intel, but Denver Team Beta Two's Team Leader, Holly Moore, doesn't need specifics.

She only knows that shit is going to get fucked up if she doesn't get Reclamation Crew Twelve out of their sector and back to the trolleys on the Turnpike.

Light brown skin with almond-shaped eyes and blazing red hair, TL Moore shows her heritage of a mix between Scottish, Thai, and Cherokee. Bordering on a little person, she is barely five feet tall, at least officially. Unofficially, she is a couple inches south of five feet.

Not that it makes much difference. Known throughout the Stronghold as a wicked hand-to-hand and melee fighter, Moore's reputation as a TL leaves not just Mates, but many civilians shaking when she starts barking orders.

"I want this camp broken down and packed in five minutes!" Moore yells at the scared faces of the reclamation crew her Team is assigned to protect as they strip a long-forgotten storage warehouse on the northeastern edge of Denver's downtown. Mainly looking for copper and other precious metals they can use to keep their pedal-powered electrical system going, the warehouse turned out to be a bonanza when first discovered by a scout team.

Row after row, crate after crate, box after box of electronic equipment fills the warehouse, stacked nearly from floor to ceiling. Old Blu-ray players, stereos, TVs, audio speakers, video game systems, everything Americana needed to fight the threat of boredom pre-Z sits in the warehouse, waiting for years for someone to claim it.

Moore grumbles as she knows that the good luck of the reclamation crew is now for nothing due to their evacuation. Any rations bonuses, or possible leave time she and her Team would have received, could easily go to a new Team depending on who gets reassigned to protect the reclamation crew once the latest crisis is over.

To top it off, it's bitter-ass cold out and Moore hates the cold. She dreams of a day when someone says, "Hey, screw this Colorado winter shit, let's move to Florida!" But she knows it'll never happen.

For one thing, no one even knows if Florida exists anymore. Not like anyone who has ever been there is alive. She's only seen it in books from the library, and even she has serious doubts it was a real place. Too many smiling, leathery faces and bright colors.

For another thing, it's hard enough just getting up and down the Turnpike from the Stronghold to Denver and back using the interlinked trolley system, let alone trying to travel all the way across the continent to visit some dreamland that may or may not even be viable.

"TL?" Team Mate Billy Chase asks as he jogs up to the thoughtful woman who is busy staring out the warehouse bay doors at the pyres. "We have a problem with one of the foremen of the crew."

"Why?" Moore asks, pulling her attention from the primitive, yet effective, warning system. "It's your job to make sure we don't have problems with foremen, Chase. Are you unable to do your job?"

"No, sir, I mean, yes, sir, I can do my job," Billy replies. "But you'll need to talk to this guy. He's getting others on his side fast."

"What side is that?" Moore asks.

"He wants to stay and lock down the warehouse until we get the all clear," Billy says. "He thinks running in the night is foolish and will get us all killed."

"You see that?" Moore asks, pointing out the bay door at the pyres. "That tells us that if we don't run, then we will get killed. Danger, Chase. Red means danger. And it's red all the way up."

"I know, sir," Billy sighs. "That is what I have been trying to tell—"

"Who is it?" Moore interrupts.

"Cain Goss," Billy says.

"Goss? Fuck that guy," Moore says and pushes past Billy. "Where is he?"

"In the back," Billy says. "He has almost the whole crew back there buying into his shit."

Moore stops and looks around, realizing for the first time that her order to pack up has been completely ignored, except by her people. She's been so wrapped up in watching the pyres, and hating the cold, that the thought that she'd be ignored never entered her mind.

She intends to fix that.

"Go get Santiago and Spence," Moore orders.

"Spence is outside, sir," Billy says. "She's scouting the streets to make sure we have a clear run for the Turnpike."

"Fine, send me Price instead," Moore says. "Once you do that then you're on the doors. First hint of trouble and you let me know. We are still leaving in five minutes."

"Yes, sir," Billy says and nods. "Good luck."

Moore shakes her head and frowns as she walks away. A harsh

blast of wind whips through the bay doors, following her like a frigid taunt. She curses under her breath, breath she can now see, as she marches toward the back of the warehouse. Small barrel fires light her way and she pauses briefly to press her hands against one, getting the muscles and tendons warm in case she needs to give Mr. Cain Goss a lesson on how things work when down in the wasteland of Denver.

"There she is," a deep voice laughs. "Right on time. Was it Chase who went and tattled to Mommy?"

"Cut the shit, Goss," Moore barks as she shoves through the crowd of reclaim crew members to get to the foreman holding court. "This ends now."

"Does it?" Cain Goss laughs again. He holds out his hands and looks around. "We barely got started, TL Moore. And we don't intend to leave until we're finished."

Six feet even and almost two hundred pounds, Cain Goss is a well-muscled, fit-looking man in his mid-thirties. Close-cropped hair, weathered brown skin, and hazel eyes, Goss has been one of the Strongholds' more successful reclamation crew members, having a knack for sniffing out caches of hidden resources. He has a reputation for earning high rations bonuses, which means the crew members who face him all have a vested interest in hearing what he has to say.

They don't have much interest in what TL Moore has to say, considering her view is to abandon the treasure trove around them and risk it being assigned to another reclaim crew.

"The pyres are red," Moore states. "Protocol is to fall back to the trolleys and assess from there. Staying here is no longer an option. So I need everyone to stop listening to this jackhole and return to gathering their things." She looks about but no one moves. "Or leave your things, I don't care. Either way, this salvage op is over and we are moving out in two minutes."

"You are welcome to leave, TL Moore," Goss says. "But we are staying. We'll lock down the bay doors and ride out whatever is going on out there. This isn't my first time in danger."

"It isn't?" Moore chuckles. "Oh, okay then. You've been in danger before. Good for you." She scratches her head for a second and glances around at the crew members. Most of them are giving her hard looks, but she can see fear on some of the faces and knows all she has to do is push a couple of buttons and Goss's hold will be broken. "What happened when you were in that danger?"

"I survived," Goss says, grinning from ear to ear.

"I can see that," Moore sighs. "But how did you survive? By fighting off a horde of Zs on your own? Or did you take out a gang of crazies who had come to rape your ass? Did you use firearms?" She pats her M-4. "Put a couple rounds between some crazy eyes? Is that how it went down?"

Goss doesn't say a word in response, but the murder in his eyes is all the answer Moore needs.

"Exactly," Moore says. She turns to the crowd. "You know how he survived his dangerous situations? By having his ass saved by a Team. I should know, since I was there one of those times." She smiles over at Goss. "Remember that time in Sector Twenty-three? The hotel incident? Why don't you tell them about that?"

"I would have been fine," Goss growls. "There was a fire escape right outside the window."

"A fire escape that was made of rust and spit," Moore laughs. "My Team had already scouted it and declared it useless. If you had stepped onto it, you would have fallen five stories to that Z-choked alley below. Even if the fire escape didn't break, there was the Z-choked alley! Where the fuck were you going to go?"

"I've survived worse," Goss says.

"Jesus, Goss, let it go," Moore says. "This situation sucks for me and my Team too. We stood to benefit from the rations bonuses as well, so I know exactly what losses we're taking here. But none of that matters. Red pyres. We are leaving now."

Two Team Mates come jogging up behind Moore, both of them

large and well-scarred, looking like they have zero intention of letting their TL's orders go ignored again.

"Mates Santiago and Price? I want this reclaim crew ready to march out in thirty seconds," Moore says. "Anyone who refuses will have their name reported to the Stronghold council's office. Their rations will be forfeit. That includes any due to their family members."

There is some loud grumbling and Moore turns on the crowd, her face red with anger, matching the pyres that light up the Denver sky.

"I am not fucking around!" she shouts. "You leave now or suffer the consequences!"

There's a high-pitched whistle from the bay doors, and Moore turns to look down the long row of boxed TVs toward Chase.

"Go see what he's got," Moore orders Santiago. The man turns and sprints back to the bay doors. "Price? Help these fine citizens of the Stronghold gather their belongings as we leave this damn place."

"Yes, sir," Price nods and turns to the crowd. "Come on, people! Meeting is over! Let's move!"

"I'll be talking directly to the council about this," Goss snarls as he stomps up to Moore. He towers over her, but the small woman doesn't even flinch as she stands in his shadow.

"Oh, no, not the council," Moore says. "What ever shall I do?"

"We have rights, you know," Goss spits. "The Teams may be the backbone of the Stronghold, but that doesn't mean they always will be. Cultures change, and when they do, sometimes there are casualties left behind."

Moore is about to haul off and slug the man in the gut when a cry from the bay doors gets her attention. It's a panicked cry, one filled with immense amounts of fear. And fear is contagious. In less than a second, more cries ring out and the warehouse is filled with scared voices and those shouting for answers. But answers to what?

"Not over," Moore says, pointing a finger at Goss. "We'll both discuss this again in front of the council. Then we'll see about your culture change, you fucking opportunistic cowardly piece of shit."

She takes off running, leaving Goss to stand there and fume.

———

Her uniform covered in blood, Team Mate Kerry Spence sits just outside the warehouse's bay doors, her legs dangling over the loading dock, one arm hanging limp while the other is pressed against her neck, a once white rag now dark red.

Billy stands behind her, his M-4 up and pointed at the crowd of reclaim crew members, his eyes narrowed and steady.

"She's been bit!" a woman shrieks, pointing at the sagging form of Mate Spence. "You have to put her down before she turns!"

"She isn't going to turn right away," Billy snaps. "And nothing happens to her until TL Moore gets here."

Mate Spence looks over her shoulder and several people gasp. Even more back away, some crossing themselves at the sight of her face.

Long strips of skin hang from her cheeks. Half of her nose is gone, as is a huge chunk of flesh from just below her right eye. Blood has soaked her uniform and she looks like she is three seconds from passing out. But her eyes are clear and determined, and she glares back at the panicked crowd.

"Listen the fuck up," she snaps in a voice thick with pain. "I'm not coming inside, okay? All of you back the fuck off and get ready for lockdown."

"What?" Billy asks. "Lockdown? What the hell is coming, Spence?"

"Everything," Spence says. She sways a little but holds on as she glances up at Billy. "A whole fuck lot of everything."

"What's going on?" Moore shouts as she shoves her way

through the crowd. "Chase? Why the hell do you have your weapon pointed at these...? Holy shit, Spence."

"Yeah," Spence says. "I'd get up and salute, but that's not happening."

"Report," Moore says.

"Zs," Spence replies. "I barely got away. A couple hundred are only a half mile away, blocking our run to the trolleys."

"I'm sorry to hear that," Moore says. "Then we'll have to go around."

Spence shakes her head. "No, you won't," she says. "I had a feeling the horde was just a symptom, so I climbed the steel tower over on 47th Street. There's nowhere to go, TL. There's a herd coming that has to be over a hundred thousand strong, easy."

"A hundred thousand?" Moore asks. "You're mistaken, Spence. You've been attacked and you aren't thinking straight."

"Oh, I'm thinking straight," Spence says. "I'm thinking you're all going straight to hell if you don't get this warehouse locked down now. You have maybe five minutes. Ten tops until they are on you."

"On us?" Billy asks. "What do you mean by us, Spence? What about you?"

Mate Spence smiles up at Billy. It's a gruesome sight, and the man can't help but shudder.

"Me?" Spence laughs. She pulls her 9mm pistol from her hip. "I'm taking point. See you all in Hell soon."

She puts the pistol to her temple and pulls the trigger. Blood and brain splatter across the loading dock as her body tumbles forward, landing on the old concrete below. People start screaming and scurrying about, retreating back into the warehouse as they try to put as much space between them and the horror outside as they can.

"Motherfucker!" Moore yells and then points at Billy. "Strip her gear and pull that body inside! I don't want it to attract Zs, do you hear me?"

"Yes, sir," Billy says, his voice choked with emotion.

"These doors are yours to close and secure," Moore shouts. "I'm going up onto the roof to see if what she said is true. I'm praying she was losing her mind because of the trauma."

"Me too," Billy says as he slings his M-4 and leans down to pick up Spence's 9mm from the loading dock. He straightens and tucks it into his belt. "I got this, TL. You go see what's coming."

———

Goss sneers at the panicked people that stream past him, all racing to get to the center of the warehouse and the carefully stacked boxes Reclaim Crew Twelve had set up when they'd first arrived just in case they needed a semi-secure fallback point. Now it looks like they do.

"What's happening?" Goss asks, grabbing a young woman by the upper arm as she hurries past. She struggles for a second, but Goss just grips her harder. "Hey! What is happening?"

"Herd of Zs," the young woman replies. "One of the Mates blew her brains out because she got bit. She said there are like a hundred thousand of the monsters coming this way."

"A hundred thousand?" Goss chuckles. "Okay. Sure."

He lets the young woman go, then searches the crowd for a familiar face. There, off against the far wall, TL Moore is dashing through a doorway, a pair of weird-looking goggles in her hands. Goss shoves people out of the way, determined to follow the woman and see what bullshit she's up to now.

He makes it to the doorway, ignoring the shouts from desperate people trying to get his attention, and shoves through, finding himself facing a dark stairwell. He hurries up the stairs, cursing as the door below him swings shut and he is plunged into darkness. One hand grasps the railing, bits of old, flaking paint scraping against his calluses as the other hand feels along the wall.

He slows down and carefully takes the steps one at a time, not wanting to be the idiot who dies because he trips in a stairwell. It takes him a lot longer than he'd like, but Goss finally makes it to the door at the top of the stairs. He shoves it open and sees TL Moore standing by the edge of the ware-house's roof. She turns to face him and takes off the weird goggles.

"Here," she says, offering the goggles to him. "Best you just see for yourself."

Goss is puzzled. He expected her to yell at him for not being downstairs. Or at least yell at him for following her and trying to interfere. He didn't expect her to offer him the use of what he can now see are one of the rare pairs of night vision goggles the Teams are assigned.

"What is it?" Goss asks, crossing to TL Moore and taking the NVGs. "What am I looking at?"

"You'll see," Moore replies, a soft chuckle mixed with a half sob.

"Where?" Goss asks, putting on the goggles.

"Everywhere," Moore replies, switching the goggles on for him.

The Denver night erupts into greens and grays, a world of light and shadows like nothing Goss has ever seen. At first he finds it hard to focus past a few feet, then he lets his eyes relax and do what they naturally do. That's when he sees the tsunami of Zs overtaking the warehouse district they are all now trapped in.

"Oh, my God," Goss whispers. "How many are there?"

"Thousands," Moore replies. "Tens of thousands. Maybe more."

"Maybe more?" Goss asks as he stares through the goggles at the impossible number of Zs that fill almost every roadway for as far as he can see. "How many more?"

"You do the math, Goss," Moore says. "Once you get past tens of thousands, what's next?"

"Hundreds of thousands," Goss replies, his earlier bravado completely gone. Now he sounds like a man who just wants to hide and curl up into a ball. "How do we survive this? How do we get away?"

"We don't," Moore says, gently pulling the NVGs from Goss's face. "Looks like you get your wish. We're locking down and staying here."

"I... I don't want this," Goss says.

"Well, want it or not, we got it," Moore says. She grabs him by the elbow and spins him around to look directly at her. "Can I count on you to help, or will you continue to undermine my authority tonight?"

"I'll help," Goss says. "Just get us out of this shit."

Moore gives him a weak smile.

"Sorry, Goss," she says as she walks back to the roof access door. "I don't think any of us are getting out of this shit."

Goss watches her go, his mind struggling to make sense of her last statement.

"What? Wait! What do you mean we aren't getting out of this shit?" he cries once his brain catches up. "Moore? It's your job to keep us secure! Moore!"

———

Team Mate Billy Chase's efforts to get Spence's body inside, and her blood scrubbed from the loading dock, make no difference. The woman left a trail of her scent all the way back to the warehouse, leading the massive herd right to the bay doors.

"Stack the boxes deeper!" Moore yells at the people struggling to shove dollies filled with the largest, heaviest boxes they can find against the bay doors. "We need more weight!"

Unfortunately, the electronic equipment that existed when Z-Day hit was made of light plastic and barely weighed more than a few pounds. Gone were the days of heavy TVs and massive Hi-Fi stereo cabinets. Even twenty boxes high and just as many deep, the barricade is more volume than mass.

Goss's voice echoes through the warehouse, coming from the

opposite end as he orders crew members to work harder and faster.

Two sets of loading docks. Two sets of bay doors. The warehouse was set up so that trucks could access it from both sides. One side for deliveries, one side for pick-up. American commercial efficiency at its finest.

"How's Goss doing?" Moore asks as Santiago runs up to her.

"He's doing his best," Santiago reports. "But we're going to need a backup plan. Maybe start tearing down the shelving? Or try to move the structures intact? If we can get just a few of them in front of these bays, then we might have a chance—"

The rest of his sentence is drowned out as the bay doors in front of them shudder and clang. Voices quiet and people stop moving, all eyes and ears focusing on the noise. For a few seconds nothing happens and some people begin to relax, ready to start moving boxes again. But the silence doesn't last and the doors shudder once more.

Then they don't stop shuddering.

People begin to cry out and scream as the sounds of thousands of Zs just outside the warehouse reach their ears. The task of stacking boxes is quickly forgotten and loaded dollies are shoved aside as people scramble to get as far away from the bay doors as possible.

"Shut up!" Moore calls. "Be quiet, you idiots!"

But the people do not get quiet, they do the complete opposite as the bay doors begin to bend inward from the outside force. Men and women scream and run, heading toward the opposite side of the warehouse.

Moore shouts at them, telling them to get themselves under control, to stop acting like wasteland rookies and start acting like citizens of the Stronghold. Reclamation Crew Twelve was not made up of newbies. They were an experienced crew that had been down in the heart of Denver many times. Back when Moore had been TL of DTB1, before Stanford Lee took it over when she was injured in the last DTA trials, she'd accompanied Reclaim Crew Twelve on dozens of missions.

It was one reason she and Goss didn't get along so well. They had plenty of history, not much of it very good.

But, as Moore stares at the panicked people, she doesn't recognize any of the fearlessness and grit that has historically made up Reclaim Crew Twelve. All she sees are scared sheep bleating and shaking where they stand. And that shaking and bleating is making things worse.

"I'm going to start putting people down," Moore snarls.

Santiago looks at her quickly, his eyes wide. "You don't mean that, TL," he says. "You can't shoot people for being scared."

"I can if they don't shut the fuck up," Moore replies. "The crybabies are going to get us all killed unless they calm down and SHUT THE FUCK UP!"

Her voice cuts through some of the panic and the din decreases to half. Which is still too much noise, proven by the bay doors bending even further under the weight of the crush of Zs outside.

"We'll have to get to the roof," Moore says to Santiago. "Tell the other Mates. We're going to get the weakest up top first. The slow ones who'll just get in the way."

"And the rest?" Santiago asks.

"We stay down here and see if we can ride this out," Moore says. "Double our efforts to get the barricades secure. Maybe we can buy some time."

Santiago starts to reply, then shakes his head and takes off running. Moore watches him go before she turns her attention back to the bay doors. For now they hold, staying in their tracks, only bending instead of breaking. But Moore has no illusions as to the doors holding forever.

———

His attention drawn to Mate Price as the man begins tapping people on the shoulders and leaning in to whisper, Goss walks away from the stack of boxes he's helping to erect in front of his bay doors and stomps up to the Team Mate.

"What the hell are you doing, Price?" Goss snaps. A couple of the people Price had been whispering to turn and hurry away. "Where the hell are they going?"

"TL wants to get some of your weaker crew members up to the roof," Price says quietly. "We might be able to give them a chance to survive until a different Team gets here."

"A different Team? Is that what she said?" Goss asks.

"No, not exactly," Price replies. "But why else would she want people on the roof if she doesn't think they'll get rescued?"

"You really think another Team is coming?" Goss chuckles. "Have you been up top? Have you seen what is out there?"

Price shakes his head.

"Well, I have, Mate," Goss says. "If those Zs get through the bay doors, then being on the roof won't make a damn bit of difference except to hold off the inevitable. This warehouse gets breached and we are all goners, Price."

"Jesus, Goss," Price says, looking around at the faces of the people who have started to take notice of their conversation. "Shut the hell up."

"I don't need some snot telling me what to do," Goss says. "And I don't need you trying to sugarcoat the fact that your TL has already given up."

"What? I didn't say she—"

"Doesn't matter," Goss says. "Moore is wrong once again. If she's sending people up onto the roof then it should be the strongest, the ones who can hold out and maybe, just fucking maybe, wait long enough for this herd to pass by."

Price shakes his head. "What good will that do?"

"It means a few of us can live," Goss says. "Then we slip away from the herd and get the hell out of Denver."

"And go where?" Price asks. "Are you just going to run around the wasteland?"

"Maybe," Goss says and shrugs. "Better than being trapped in here." Goss turns around and looks at a few of the crew. "You, you, you, and you. With me. Spread the word to our best and tell them we're retreating to the roof."

"Hold the fuck up!" Price shouts, his M-4 at his shoulder. "No one is doing anything even close to that! TL Moore has given orders for the weaker of you to go up top! That's all! No one deviates from their duties until she says otherwise!"

"Or what?" Goss asks. "You start shooting? Is that it, Price? You going to shoot us? All of us?"

"Yes. I mean, no," Price stutters. "I don't fucking know!"

The carbine shakes in his hands as he aims at the crew members who have started to line up behind Goss. He tries to look them in the eyes and all he sees is anger and fear. And hatred. Hatred directed at him.

"Back off! You need to listen to me! You need to listen to TL Moore!" Price shouts. "DTB2 is here to help you! It's our job! If you listen, then maybe we can all—"

A man lunges past Goss and tries to go for Price's carbine. The M-4 barks and the man falls backward, a hole in his chest, wide open and bleeding.

"Oh, shit," Price whispers. "I didn't mean to!"

It's too late. The crew members, led by Goss, rush the Mate and are on him. He goes down under a pile of angry faces, enraged fists pummeling him before he can even get his hands up to defend himself.

"Stop!" he cries out. "What are you doing?"

His words are cut short as a boot slams into his mouth, shattering his teeth. His M-4 is pried from his grip and there isn't a thing he can do about it. The world is nothing but crazed faces and pain. Price tries to curl up into a ball, protect himself from the attack, but someone grabs his legs and pulls them straight as someone else kicks him in the gut over and over.

"We take the roof for ourselves!" Goss yells, holding Price's M-4 over his head like a hard-won trophy. "We can survive up there, and we don't need this damn Team's permission!"

There are several shouts of agreement, but more shouts of just rage as Price is beaten to death before everyone's eyes. Eyes that are filled with pure hate, mixed with delirious panic.

"Come on!" Goss shouts as he starts running to the far wall of the warehouse and the doorway he's already been through once this evening.

————

"Where is everyone going?" Moore yells over at Billy. "What the hell is happening?"

Billy reaches out and snags the arm of an older man, yanking him to a full stop. The older man's eyes are wild and swim in his head.

"What's going on?" Billy asks. "Was there a breach on the other side?"

"We're getting to safety," the man growls. "Gonna hide on the roof until we can get away. Nothing but death down in here."

"What?" Moore yells. "No! You can't survive up there! Not everyone!"

"That right?" the older man snarls. "Not everyone? Who then? DTB2? Is that it? Goss was right! You were gonna take the roof and save yourselves!"

"Goss was what?" Moore snaps. "Jesus. That stupid asshole."

The older man breaks free of Billy's grip and runs away toward the crush of the mob heading to the stairwell. Billy starts to go after him, but Moore waves him off.

"Let him go," Moore says. "It doesn't matter if they're on the roof or down here. It's all over now."

"What? Why?" Billy asks. "We can fight this out, TL. We're DTB2! We can do this!"

"We could have before," Moore says. "Maybe. But not now.

Come on. We go find the others and we get gone. This mission is a failure and there's nothing we can do about it. Time for self-preservation."

"TL, you can't mean that," Billy says as he watches the crew members rushing by him. "These people…"

"Are already dead," Moore says. "You want to join them?"

"No," Billy replies.

"Then we find the others and get out," Moore says. "I have an idea of how. Meet me by the northwest corner ASAP. We have one shot and one shot only."

Moore waits for Billy to acknowledge her, which he does slowly like his head doesn't know how to nod anymore.

"Go," Moore says.

"But, sir," Billy responds. "Everyone counts…"

"And we always remember," Moore says. "But only if someone is left to do the remembering."

Billy's nod gathers strength and he gives a brief salute. "Yes, sir."

Moore watches him run off and then looks toward the northwest corner of the warehouse. She has to go through the whole mob to get there. And from the angry looks shot her way, she's not sure how easy that will be.

———

Goss slides to a stop as he sees Moore shoving people out of her way.

"Where's she going?" he says to himself, the M-4 gripped in his sweat-slicked hands.

He looks over his shoulder at the doorway to the stairwell and the cluster fuck it has become as dozens of people try to shove through at the same time. Fists start flying, and the scene devolves into an angry brawl in the amount of time it takes Goss to blink twice.

"Fuck," he mutters, then zeroes back in on Moore. She's

reached the edge of the mob and turns left, her eyes not even glancing back toward the stairwell. "Someone has a better plan."

———

The bay doors by the loading dock where Spence took her own life bend, bend, then buckle completely, their edges tearing right out of the floor to ceiling tracks. Zs, hundreds of them, push around the warped and twisted doors, shoving their way into the warehouse like the crew members trying to shove their way through the doorway to the stairs.

Except the Zs don't have a stairwell to bottleneck them. They have a wide-open warehouse with plenty of space to spread out in. And spread out they do. The hundreds shamble, stumble, lurch, and even run toward the sounds of the panicked mob that is so busy trying to get to the roof that they have forgotten why they are fleeing in the first place.

But, as the Zs reach the back of the mob, the crew members are quickly and painfully reminded.

Screams fill the warehouse as Zs tear into flesh, ripping at throats, clawing at arms and legs, biting down on any exposed skin they can find. Blood begins to spray everywhere, splattering against the rest of the mob, turning their angry panic into one of complete and total insanity. That insanity is matched by the Zs as the smell of fresh meat and blood sends them into a frenzy that becomes a scene of total horror.

Men and women are torn apart as the Zs push into the mob. Limbs are ripped off, faces shredded. Geysers of blood shoot up and out as veins and arteries are opened. The brave try to fight back, the desperate push on. None of them succeed as all fall under the overwhelming number of Zs that continue to stream through the open bay doors.

———

Moore reaches an office door and grabs the knob. But before she can turn it, the wind is knocked out of her as she is tackled to the ground. Her M-4 clatters away, skidding across the concrete, just out of reach. She starts to scramble for it, ready to fight off the Z that has taken her down. Until she looks to the side and realizes the body that rammed her isn't one of the undead.

"Goss! You fucker!" Moore yells as she kicks at the man, trying to get some space between them so she can retrieve her M-4.

But it's his M-4, the one he stole from Price, that she encounters first as the butt slams into her forehead, knocking her briefly senseless.

Goss picks himself up and turns to the office door. He grabs the knob and twists it, throwing the door open to reveal a good-sized administrative office. And a set of boarded-over windows on the far wall.

"You sneaky bitch," Goss mutters as he hurries into the office and over to the boards. He sets the M-4 aside and works his fingers under one of the boards, pulling at it, testing to see how secure it is. "You double-crossing, sneaky bitch."

He gets a good grasp and pulls, popping a couple of old, rusty nails. The boards must have been put up a long, long time ago for the nails to snap as easy as they do. Maybe someone had thought the warehouse would be a good refuge early on when the Zs first started to rise. Goss becomes paranoid and spins around, looking for signs that maybe someone is still in the office with him.

But no one is there. Not even a trace that people had ever used the office as a place to hide.

He goes back to working at the boards, pulling, tugging, bracing a foot against the wall so he can get some leverage on the old plywood. It takes him a minute, but he gets one board off and stands there and stares at what he sees outside.

"No," he whispers.

Then he feels the cool steel of a 9mm muzzle against his temple.

"You are one of the dumbest people I have ever met," Moore

says, her finger on the trigger, her thumb cocking back the hammer. "The plan was to stay down, stay quiet, and hole up in here until it was clear enough to get away. But you had to ruin that by yanking at a board. How'd that work out?"

Goss's eyes turn to look at Moore, but he doesn't answer. She nods.

"Exactly, asshole," Moore says.

Her own eyes move toward the exposed window and the thousands of Zs that swarm around the backside of the warehouse. So far none of them have directed their attention at the office and the two people standing in plain sight, but Moore knows it's only a matter of seconds.

She decides to hurry that process along.

"You get to be one of the lucky ones, Goss," Moore states. "Even though you don't deserve it."

"Lucky ones? What does that mean?" Goss asks just as Moore pulls the trigger, sending his brains flying across the office to splatter on the far wall.

The sound of the gunshot instantly draws the attention of the closest Zs outside the window, and dozens and dozens of undead heads swivel to meet Moore's gaze. She holsters her 9mm and picks up the M-4 Goss had set down. She puts it to her shoulder, takes aim, and opens fire.

Z heads burst open as each round finds its mark. Moore doesn't stop until the magazine is empty. She is busy pulling a fresh one from a pocket on her vest when the rest of DTB2 hurry into the office. They all glance at Goss's corpse, then at the shattered window.

And the Zs struggling to work their way in through the frame.

"TL?" Billy asks.

"Time to go out with honor, Mates," Moore says. "Take as many down as you can."

"We can go this way!" Santiago says. "The Zs are distracted!"

Moore opens fire again, obliterating the skulls of the Zs squeezing past the window frame. Their corpses clog the hole, and the wall begins to groan from the pressure of the thousands behind them.

"TL!" Santiago shouts. "We can get out!"

Moore looks at the man, then at Billy. The other Mate nods and gestures for her to follow. She hesitates for a second and then sprints from the window as the wood around begins to splinter and crack.

Outside the office, Moore sees how the Zs have become distracted.

Thousands pour into the warehouse, all following a direct line of their undead brothers and sisters to the doorway and the stairwell leading to the roof. Moore says a quick prayer for the people lost but is also silently thankful that their sacrifice means her escape.

Everyone counts, especially a Team Mate who can live to fight another day.

The three Mates stay close to the far wall, keeping the rows of shelving between them and the stairwell door. They make it halfway down the wall before their way is completely blocked.

"The other bay doors," Moore says. "They've already breached them."

"Come on," Santiago hisses. "There's a side door this way."

He pulls on Moore's arm as Billy leads the way down an aisle and then suddenly cuts left into a gap between two sets of shelving. Moore nearly kicks herself for not knowing about the single door emergency exit that is tucked away out of sight. It is bad leadership on her part for her Team not to have found it earlier.

She removes Santiago's hand from her arm and sets her M-4 against her shoulder.

"Okay, once we are out, we run," Moore says. "We don't look back, we don't try to stay together, we don't do anything except run and stay alive. Head to the Stronghold and warn everyone. Understood?"

"Yes, sir," Billy and Santiago say.

"Good," Moore nods. She puts a hand on the door handle, a

long bar in the middle of the metal surface, and smiles at her Mates. "Ready?"

"Ready," Billy says, M-4 up.

"Ready," Santiago echoes, his M-4 up as well.

Moore shoves against the handle and the door starts to swing open, then sticks. She puts her shoulder against it and shoves. It flies open, spilling her onto the cold concrete outside. A few thousand Zs all turn and look at her.

"Go!" Moore yells as she gets into a crouch and starts firing, aiming for the legs of the Zs closest to her. "Now!"

Billy and Santiago sprint from the warehouse, their carbines barking fire along with Moore's. They take off to the side of the warehouse and keep running as Moore gets to her feet. A line of Zs starts to break off and head their direction, but Moore stops them with several well-placed shots and some deliberate words.

"HEY!" she screams. "HEY! COME GET ME, MOTHER-FUCKERS!"

The Zs switch their focus back to Moore and she waves her hand over her head while firing her M-4 one handed, blindly sending bullets into the massive herd of Zs.

"COME ON!" she screams and backs toward the open door. "OVER HERE!"

The herd comes for her, rushing as fast as the shambling monsters can move. Moore empties her magazine, loads another, empties that, loads another and empties that one before she is out. Hundreds of Zs litter the concrete, creating obstacle piles for the herd. They trip and stumble, adding to the blockade of undead flesh, and Moore smiles.

"That's right, assholes," she says. "That's what a Mate can do."

Then several figures crawl quickly over the pile and jump to the ground, landing not quite gracefully but with enough stability not to topple over.

"Oh, shit," Moore says as the fast Zs sprint at her.

She rushes back inside and pulls the door closed just as the Zs reach the warehouse. Bodies slam against the metal, the sound ringing out around her. Moore keeps backing up until she is up against the shelving directly across from the exit, her eyes locked onto the door that shakes and rattles with the impacts of the angry Zs.

Moans from her right get her attention and she pulls her 9mm, spinning about to see at least twenty Zs coming her way. More moans from her left cause her to spin that way and she sees double the number heading right for her.

Cut off, Moore places the muzzle to her temple, laughing at the irony of it all. She closes her eyes and pulls the trigger.

The gun clicks empty.

"What? No!" she yells and is answered by the moans of the Zs that have her boxed in.

But above their moans is another sound. A loud groaning. Not the groaning of Zs, but the groaning of stressed struts and trusses.

Moore looks up just as the ceiling gives way and thousands of undead bodies, mingled with several recently alive bodies, collapse down on her. She gives one last scream before the tons of materials crush her, killing her instantly.

———

Billy skids to a halt as the night erupts with the sound of the collapsing warehouse. Santiago is up ahead a few feet and he stops as well. They both turn and look back as sparks from the barrel fires inside the warehouse lift up into the night.

"Come on," Santiago says, jogging back to get Billy. "We have to get to the Stronghold."

"I know," Billy says. "It's just…"

"Yeah, she knew what she was doing," Santiago says. "We always remember."

.

FIVE
AVENUE OF NIGHTMARES

The sound of a building being slowly crushed by the weight of hundreds of thousands of Zs is not something Val expects to ever forget. It isn't a massive sound that happens all at once, but a slow build of glass shattering and concrete crashing to the ground.

The beginning is sporadic, the occasional groan of a five-story structure stressed past a point it was designed to endure. The groans increase until a window pops, then another and another. The glass hitting the ground below does not sound like a poetic tinkling but like a headache-inducing stab of sharpness.

Then the weak points of the facade crumble. Hunks of old plaster, gutters, ledges weakened by a century of wear and tear without any maintenance. The impacts are sometimes loud cracks, like a gunshot—sometimes wet *thunks* as they hit the undead below and a skull explodes or shoulder is torn apart.

The images of the building falling apart, quickly eroding by a force of nature that has plagued the planet for over a hundred years, fill Val's mind. She can see the shards of glass, the chunks of concrete, rain down on the herd that continues to push its way into Denver. She shakes her head and stands, stretching her tired and sore muscles as she walks over to Cole.

"How did there get to be so many?" Cole asks, binoculars pointed east as the sky behind him slowly lightens, turning a deep purple, then bright pink. "We're a century past Z-Day. How can all of these still be around? What the fuck have they been eating?"

"Everything," Sister says, squatting in a corner of the roof, her leather pants around her ankles.

Cole glances over and doesn't flinch. Watching a Team Mate drop trou to take a piss is not something unusual. Modesty goes out the window when your job is to kill anything that is a threat to the Stronghold.

"There can't be that many people left," Val says.

"Not anymore," Sister says as she stands and pulls her pants up.

Val can't help notice the woman has more radiation sores on her legs. Not to mention dozens of nasty-looking scars. Sister catches her noticing, but Val doesn't turn away.

The rest of DTA and DTB1 are stationed at various points on the building's roof. Except for Alastair who is one floor down, keeping an eye on the wounded and sleeping Tiny D. As the sky continues to brighten, the landscape that is the Denver wasteland becomes more and more visible. As does the destruction that is occurring across the broken city.

"Smoke to the northeast, northwest, and due south," Shep announces. "The northeast one matches up with the glow we saw last night."

"The city is burning," Stanford says, yawning from the spot where he's crouched next to the roof's edge. "We've had burns before, but this is gonna be too much."

"If the Zs don't get us, then the fires will," Diaz says. "It's a race to the death. Ours."

"Nice," Carlotta scoffs. "Not a morning person, Diaz?"

"Not on mornings like this," Diaz says, nodding his chin toward the dark masses of Zs that fill the Denver streets a few miles away. "Not with all those tourists fucking up our city."

"Tour-whats?" Tommy Bombs asks.

"Tourists," Diaz says. "I read about them in some book about those things that people used to go to. They had rides and costumes and shit."

"Amusement parks," Val says. "I read that book too. They looked like hell."

"Yeah, well, people who went to them were tourists," Diaz continues. "They'd come from all over and *tour* the parks."

"Good for them," Carlotta says. "People had too much time on their hands pre-Z."

"They had too much everything," Sister says. "They wasted it all. They wasted the world. Idiots didn't know what they were doing."

"She's not much of a morning person either," Carlotta says.

"Hey," Lang says as she snaps her fingers and points to the west. "I've spotted another Team."

"Stay put," Cole says to the other Mates. "Let me check it out."

"Me too," Stanford says. "TL and all that shit."

"Not a contest, kids," Val says.

The Mates keep their posts but shoot wary glances over at Cole, Stanford, and Lang as they stare out at the western part of Denver.

"Too hard to tell from here," Cole says, putting his binoculars to his eyes, then lowering them almost as quickly. "Maybe when the sun comes up more."

"We going to the next pyre station?" Lang asks. "Or straight back to the Stronghold."

"Straight back," Stanford says. "The pyre stations are empty by now. Or they better be after we had that first one send the signal. Any of the sentries or Runners who wanted to stick around are on their own."

"Runners better be fast," Sister says, startling the three as she comes up behind them.

"Need to put a bell on you," Stanford says.

Sister gives him a look that is a mix of sadness and amusement. "Yes. I've been told that before. Can't sneak up on Zs and crazies with a bell on."

"Can't sneak up on exhausted Mates either," Stanford replies and shrugs.

"We need to get moving again," Cole says. "Whatever Team that is, they should have seen the pyre color to fall back to the Stronghold. Denver is lost and we have to regroup."

"Maybe they're cut off," Lang suggests. She has Cole's binoculars and is studying the area she saw the Team in. "I see barricades and small bits of smoke. Not big fires, but small burns. Someone is steering them and killing visibility at the ground level."

"A hunt," Sister says, almost giddy. "The cannies are hungry. All their food is gone. They got lucky a Team came by."

"They got lucky?" Cole snaps, turning on the woman. "Those are our Mates down there! There is nothing lucky about a bunch of psycho cannies hunting them down!"

"Then we go help them," Stanford says. "We get behind the cannies and kill all the fucking freaks."

"We have to get back to the Stronghold," Cole says. "That is the mission now. We take this crazy old chick back there, then Commander Lee can tell us what our next op is."

"So, we leave our people behind?" Stanford asks. "That's cold, Cole."

"Cold Cole," Sister snickers.

"Ford just doesn't want to deal with his mom," Val says from her post. "That's why he wants to delay heading home."

"Exactly," Cole says. "So we are going—"

"But he's right," Val continues. "Whatever Team it is, we have to go help them." She looks at Sister. "What do you think? You think we can get there and save our friends before the herd hits us?"

"No," Sister says. "But we should do it anyway. Never pass up a chance to save friends and kill cannies, I always say."

"Is it? Is that what you always say?" Stanford asks, sneering.

"Yes," Sister replies. "It is. I also say wipe front to back. You want to hear more sayings?"

"Nope," Stanford says. "I'm good."

"Cole?" Val asks.

"I'm thinking," Cole says. He looks about the roof and sees all eyes on him. "Fine. We go help them." He points a finger at Sister, then one at Val. "But if things go sour, you get her up to the Stronghold. She may be full of shit like Ford says, but that's not our call. Commander Lee can decide if she's lying and put a bullet in her head herself."

"Maura wouldn't do that," Sister laughs. "We go way back. Way, way back."

"My condolences," Stanford says. "So, are we doing this now, Cole? Or do you need us to get in a circle and hold hands for a pep talk? Come on DTA TL, oh mighty one, what's the situation?"

"The situation is you are incapable of being anything but an asshole," Cole says, "and we are moving out. Diaz? Go help Al get Tiny D down to the first floor. We'll clear the street."

"Roger," Diaz says and takes off through the roof access door.

Cole turns and meets everyone's eyes.

"We move hard and fast," Cole says. "Don't slow down because of Tiny D. We get there, kill some cannies, if that's what's there, rescue that Team, and then book it to the Stronghold. No more delays. I want us bunked down in the Team barracks tonight, not hiding in the foothills on the Turnpike. Am I clear?"

"Loud and clear," Stanford says. "DTB1! What he said."

"Let's move," Cole orders. "Now!"

———

The man is built like a gorilla. Nothing but muscles on muscles, thick hairy arms, short powerful legs, a chest like a barrel and a shout that can shatter eardrums. The man is busy using that shouting skill to get his Team in place and ready for the attack they all know is coming.

"Crumb! Watch our six! Fitzpatrick! You're with me! Pickering, you have our three, and Gane, you have our nine! Nothing gets through!" Gary Hoffman, Denver Team Beta Three's Team Leader, yells. "Fuck these crazy freaks! We hold this position and do not give them an inch!"

"Shadows on our six, TL!" Team Mate Peter Crumb shouts. Short and skinny, Crumb has had to fight hard to earn the respect of his Mates. The fact he's a crack shot with a pistol certainly helps. "I count five!"

"Keep them off us, Crumb!" Hoffman yells.

"Roger that, TL!" Crumb replies. He holds his 9mm in his right hand with his left cupped underneath both, keeping the pistol steady. "Counting seven now!"

"Shit," Hoffman mutters. "Fitz?"

"I don't see a thing ahead of us, sir," Team Mate Gina Fitzpatrick replies. "You want me back with Crumb?"

"Not yet," Hoffman says. "They may be saving the big wave for us here and those back there are only distractions." He glances over his shoulder at the other Mates of DTB3. "But be ready to fill any gaps if they come at us from the sides."

"I can't see shit through this smoke, TL," Team Mate Basil Pickering says. "We're sitting ducks here, sir."

"I'm aware of that," Hoffman barks. "But nothing we can do. These crazies set the trap and we walked right into it. Our only option is to fight our way out."

"Then shouldn't we be moving?" Team Mate Nian Gane asks. He looks at Hoffman and frowns at the sharp glare he receives. "With all due respect, sir."

"You want to respect me? Then do your job and shut the fuck up," Hoffman growls.

The growl is barely audible, but the words reach Gane nonetheless. He nods and turns back to face the left side of the group.

"TL, I think we should listen to Gane," Fitzpatrick says.

The woman has long, muscular arms on an almost petite torso that sits on two tree trunks for legs. Her bottom half looks like she could take on a hurricane and stay standing. She braces those legs as a scraping sound is heard from the smoke a few feet in front of her.

"You were saying?" Hoffman whispers. "Get ready."

The members of DTB3 stand there, the tension in their bodies humming like live electricity, their senses on high alert. Five seconds ticks off, ten seconds. Twenty, thirty, fifty, a minute.

Then the first one comes screaming from out of the smoke on the right side. Team Mate Basil Pickering fires twice with his M-4, once in the head and once in the chest, and the figure drops to the ground, skidding a couple of feet before coming to rest just out of toe-nudging range. Pickering ignores the man's corpse and keeps his eyes on the direction it came from.

A second shadow emerges from the smoke, a short woman without any hair or skin on the top of her head. The exposed flesh is streaked with black and green and oozing a yellow pus that drips down off her head, coating her ears and the side of her neck. Pickering gulps, but doesn't hesitate, and fires. Two bullets in the forehead and the mutilated woman collapses onto the first corpse.

"Coming my way!" Gane yells before he opens fire on the four shadows that rush him.

He drops three before the fourth gets by his M-4's rounds and launches himself into the air. The crazy man is screaming at the top of his lungs, both hands slashing wildly with rusty knives that look like they haven't seen a sharp edge in years. That's all the observation Gane gets before he's rammed in the chest by the man and tumbles backward hard onto the broken concrete.

"Gane's down!" Fitzpatrick yells.

"Take his place!" Hoffman orders. "I got this position covered!"

Fitzpatrick rushes over to help Gane. She slams the butt of her carbine down onto the back of the attacker's head, cracking the man's skull and knocking him cold. He collapses onto Gane and the Mate looks up at Fitzpatrick, his eyes wide and full of pain.

"I caught one," Gane whispers, coughing up a mouthful of blood.

"Shit," Fitzpatrick hisses.

She starts to reach for the brained corpse to pull it off Gane, but footsteps get her attention and she whirls about, her M-4 up and firing the instant she sees the three women sprinting at her. The middle one falls, her chest ripped apart by the carbine's slugs, but the other two get by and come at Fitzpatrick with long hunks of rotten wood in their hands.

"Really?" Fitzpatrick mutters as she ducks a swing from the first woman, drops to one knee, and jams the barrel of her carbine right into her belly. She pulls the trigger twice, then rolls backward as the second woman takes a swipe at her. Fitzpatrick comes up firing, shredding the second woman's kneecaps. "Fuck you."

The two women drop, screaming and crying, their hunks of rotten wood forgotten as their hands go to their wounds. The first woman sits on her ass, rocking back and forth as she struggles to push her intestines back into her midsection. The second woman just screams, her hands fumbling at what is left of her knees.

Fitzpatrick stands and puts a bullet in each of their heads, silencing the wails of agony. Gunfire erupts, and she spins about to see Crumb emptying his 9 at the shadows that refuse to engage him and instead dodge back and forth in the cover of the thick smoke.

Thick smoke that is making it hard to breathe.

"Tighten up!" Hoffman orders. "We go back to back and try to push our way out!"

"Which way, TL?" Crumb asks as he ejects his spent magazine and slaps in a fresh one. "My way is not an option."

"This way," Hoffman says. "I don't see them up ahead."

"Gane isn't going anywhere," Fitzpatrick says as she pulls the corpse off her Team Mate.

The man's eyes flutter open but don't focus. Fitzpatrick makes a hushing noise, telling him to relax and be quiet, as her eyes lock onto the hilt of the knife that is embedded in the man's chest. Blood bubbles up around the part of the blade that's visible.

"It's in his lungs, sir," Fitzpatrick says.

"Do it," Gane whispers, blood trickling from the corner of his mouth. He coughs hard and the bubbles on his chest grow, then burst. He slowly shakes his head. "Do it."

"TL?" Fitzpatrick asks, her voice shaky.

"Do it," Hoffman says, echoing Gane's request. "We can't take him with."

"Everyone counts," Fitzpatrick says, tears in her eyes as she stands and places the barrel of her M-4 to Gane's forehead.

"We always—" Gane starts to say, but is cut off by the loud crack of Fitzpatrick's carbine.

"Here they come again!" Pickering yells, opening fire.

"Mine too!" Crumb shouts, his 9mm barking as well.

"Fuck me!" Hoffman yells, his M-4 letting loose with a barrage of bullets as the open way before him is suddenly filled with screaming, running crazies. "Give them everything you've got!"

Fitzpatrick is able to get turned around just as four men rush at her. None of them have weapons, only long, nasty, pointy fingernails on the ends of gnarled hands. They flash their sharpened teeth and foamy spit drips from between their lips. Their snarls are more like wild animals than human beings.

That's when Fitzpatrick notices something in the crazed men's eyes. The complete lack of life. They aren't men anymore.

"Zs!" Fitzpatrick yells. "Some of them are Zs!"

She backs up quickly, her M-4 unloading on the undead men. Knowing what she's up against now, she takes the Zs out at the legs first, dropping them onto the other corpses that have started to pile up. Fitzpatrick winces as one of the Zs begins to rip into the still-warm flesh of Gane's corpse.

"No, you don't," Fitzpatrick says. "I don't want to always remember that."

She puts a bullet in the head of the Z trying to munch on Gane.

The three others crawl towards her, fighting each other to get to her live body first. She stays just out of reach, enraging them.

"Fitz! Put them down!" Hoffman yells as he reloads. "Stop fucking—!"

His words are cut off as he screams in pain. A long spear made from a rusty metal pipe sharpened at one end sticks out from his chest and back. Blood pours from the hole in the pipe spear, falling to the ground behind Hoffman like a macabre version of those desktop bamboo fountains from pre-Z.

Not that Fitzpatrick has ever seen one of those bamboo fountains. She hasn't seen a man impaled by a pipe spear either. What she has or hasn't seen before are not thoughts that rush through her mind as she moves to her TL and reaches for the falling man.

Hoffman tumbles over backward and blood geysers up out of the dull end of the pipe, shooting a good six feet in the air before coming down to coat him and Fitzpatrick as the woman skids to a stop and drops to her knees next to the dying man.

"TL!" Fitzpatrick yells.

"Fitz! Leave him!" Crumb yells, running over to her and grabbing her shoulder. "Come on! Pickering has punched a hole!"

Fitzpatrick looks into the glazed eyes of her TL and shakes her head. Before she can say anything, Crumb puts a 9mm round in his temple, sending the TL's brains spraying out to the side. Fitzpatrick chokes back a scream and looks up at Crumb.

"Had to be done! Now come on!" Crumb yells, pulling her to her feet.

She staggers a second and gets her bearings, then brings her M-4 up and hurries along with Crumb after Pickering. They pierce the thick smoke, coughing and gagging from the fumes, but do not slow down. Angry shouts and screeches follow behind them, both man-made and Z-made.

The dim outline of Pickering's form can barely be seen as they sprint down what looks to be an alleyway. The old rusted husks of dumpsters line the cracked and crumbling brick walls of the two-story buildings on each side. Much of the brick from the facades has fallen off, leaving random piles of debris strewn about, ready and waiting to snap the ankles of the unwary.

But both Fitzpatrick and Crumb see the piles, dodging around them as they continue to follow after Pickering. The smoke begins to thin and they see their Mate slow, then stop suddenly. He lifts an arm and clenches his fist, crouching low. Fitzpatrick and Crumb reach him, crouching down next to the man.

Fitzpatrick is about to ask what he sees, but a strong gust of wind clears the smoke away for a couple seconds and the words choke in her throat, along with a terrified gasp.

Thousands upon thousands of Zs fill the streets before them. The alley has led them to the edge of a small hill, and out before them, visible since the buildings for several blocks have collapsed and crumbled into piles of nothing, for as far as they can see, are Zs. So many Zs.

"They are between us and the next station," Pickering whispers. He points and indicates a water tower about a mile away. "The pyre is out, which means they've been told to get the hell out of Denver."

"We should do the same thing," Crumb says.

"That would be nice," Pickering replies, then shows them his hand. The glove is coated with blood. "But I'm not making it up the Turnpike. We get to that station, grab you two some supplies and ammo, then you leave me while you two head for home."

"Leave you?" Fitzpatrick whispers. "We leave you up there and you're dead. There's no way we'll get back into the city to rescue you. Look at all the fucking Zs!"

"I see them, Fitz," Pickering replies. "I didn't say you'd come back to rescue me. This isn't a knife wound."

He twists and angles his body, showing his Mates where he's been wounded. And by what.

"Fuck," Crumb says. "How the hell did one get in close enough for a bite?"

"I don't know," Pickering says. "I thought I had them all, then shit went bad. I looked down and the bastard had my leg. I put one through his head, but it was too late."

"Pickering, man, I'm sorry," Crumb replies.

"Shit happens, brother," Pickering says. "We're Mates, so shit just happens worse to us."

"We'll get you to that water tower," Fitzpatrick says. "I'll carry your ass on my back up that ladder if I have to."

"Thanks," Pickering says. "It's bullshit, I know. You two should just ditch my soon-to-be-undead ass, but I don't want to die down here on the ground where the Zs can get me. I'm being selfish asking this of you."

"That's a bunch of crap," Crumb says.

Pickering gives them a weak smile. "I'll take care of myself up there when I know it's time. The key though is to get you two enough ammo for the sprint to the Turnpike. No way you can get through this shit hand-to-hand."

The sound of feet on brick gets their attention, and they whirl around to see several men and women running at them down the alley.

"Shit," Crumb says.

The three Mates turn and open fire, tearing into the crazed attackers' bodies, sending them flying against the old dumpsters and falling to the piles of building crumbs.

Fitzpatrick stands and helps Pickering to his feet. Crumb starts to move to the wounded and dead crazies, but Fitzpatrick clamps her hand on his shoulder.

"We need to put them down before they change," Crumb says.

"Don't bother," Fitzpatrick says. "Won't make a difference if a few more join the herd."

"Yeah, speaking of," Pickering says. "Those gunshots have brought us some attention."

Fitzpatrick and Crumb turn back to the insane amount of Zs and see a horde branching off from the main herd, heading right for them.

"Shit," Fitzpatrick says. "That's our one avenue to get to the water tower."

"You find a new one," Pickering says as he unbuckles his vest and lets it fall to the ground. He tosses his M-4 on top, as well as his 9mm. "Get to those supplies, then bust ass up the mountain, got it?"

"Wait, what?" Crumb asks, but it's too late.

Pickering takes off at a running limp, his hands over his head, waving back and forth.

"Hey! Come on, you undead sons of bitches! Meal time!" Pickering shouts at the top of his lungs. He heads off in the opposite direction of the water tower. "Look at me! Free food! Come and get it, boys and girls!"

"God dammit," Crumb snarls. He checks his 9mm, then reluctantly reaches down and grabs extra magazines from Pickering's dropped vest. He fishes out the two M-4 magazines and tosses them to Fitzpatrick. "You want his carbine too?"

"No," Fitzpatrick replies, tucking the magazines into pockets on her own vest. "Mine'll be enough."

"Nothing is going to be enough against that," Crumb says, nodding toward the gigantic herd of Zs that swarms over Denver.

"No, not against that," Fitzpatrick agrees. "But it may be enough to get us the fuck away from that. Come on."

She starts running, careful to keep low and as much out of the line of sight of the edges of the herd as she can. Crumb mimics her posture, following right behind.

———

"Hold," Val hisses.

DTA and DTB1 all come to a stop. None of the Mates look happy about the pause in their forward progress, especially since they are long past getting ahead of the Z herd and have only been maintaining a delicate invisibility for several blocks now.

"What is it?" Cole asks, moving up next to Val.

"Listen," Val says.

They wait, but all that can be heard is the droning sound of hundreds of thousands of undead feet shuffling along the cracked asphalt of Denver's roads.

"Val," Cole growls.

"Listen," she insists.

After a second they all hear it and turn toward the sound.

Someone is shouting, deliberately drawing the Zs his way. Which happens to be right towards the two Teams.

"Shit," Cole says. "What is the idiot doing?"

"I'd say he's saving someone's ass," Stanford says. "Getting them to follow him instead of the other person or persons. More brave than idiotic."

"You'd know one of those things," Val says.

"Ha ha," Stanford replies.

"What do we do?" Val asks Cole. "We're going to intersect with who knows how many Zs."

"Shit," Cole grumbles.

"We could take out the dipshit," Stanford suggests. "Let the Zs swarm on him and then slip by while they eat."

"Have you lost your mind?" Cole asks. "That's probably a Mate out there!"

"Calm down," Stanford says. "The guy is already dead. No way he's getting away from the Zs. Not while he yells for them to follow him."

"Maybe he sees someplace he can hide and is heading that way," Val says.

"Maybe," Stanford says. "But I doubt it."

"Jesus, Ford," Cole says. "You're a cold motherfucker when you get your heart broken."

"Better a cold motherfucker with a broken heart than a dead asshole with his guts feeding a bunch of Zs," Stanford says. He glances around and eyes a less-than-stable fire escape across the street on the alley side of a building. "I'll do it. I'm the best shot."

"Ford!" Cole nearly shouts, then clamps his mouth shut as the Mate sprints across the road and into the alley. "Fucking asshole."

"Come and get it!" the shouting voice calls out.

"He's getting closer," Val says.

They watch Stanford grab the fire escape ladder and haul himself up onto the first grate. The whole structure wobbles and shifts and he freezes in place. Once it stops moving, he carefully makes his way up the three flights of metal stairs until he is at a ladder bolted to the side of the building.

"I'm still not cool with this," Cole says. "Killing another Mate..."

"Everyone counts, Cole," Val says. "But sometimes they count in ways we don't think of."

"You sound like that Sister chick," Cole says. "And I'm not cool with that."

Stanford stands on the roof of the building across from them and puts his M-4 to his shoulder. He waits for a few seconds as the sound of the yeller gets louder and louder.

Val peers around the corner of the alley the Teams are in and sees a man come limping quickly down their street. A thousand Zs easy are close on his ass, but even with the limp, the man is moving fast enough to stay ahead.

"Oh, fuck me, it's Pickering," Val says and looks at Cole, her eyes wide.

"Makes it real now, doesn't it," Cole says just as a shot rings out.

Pickering staggers and looks down at his chest, then up toward the building where Stanford is standing. Another shot rings out and half of Pickering's head is obliterated.

Val turns and gags, trying to keep her gorge down. Cole pats her on the shoulder until she straightens up. She takes a couple of deep breaths, looks at him, then looks back into the alley at the rest of DTA and DTB1. Stone-cold faces and hard eyes look back at her. They nod, she nods back.

"Ford did what he had to," Val says.

"Yeah," Cole replies.

It's his turn to look back at the Teams, and he raises a hand then points two fingers out of the alley and down the street, away from the Zs that are swarming over the cooling corpse of fresh meat.

"We don't stop again," Cole says. "A man died so we can keep going. A *Mate* died. We do not slow down or rest until we're on a fucking trolley and heading up the mountain to the Stronghold. Got it?"

They all nod.

"Go," he orders.

———

The sound of the gunshot makes Fitzpatrick slow down and cock her head. She looks over at Crumb and he shrugs.

"Could be someone else," Crumb says.

"I don't hear Pickering yelling anymore," Fitzpatrick responds. "Someone shot him."

"Or he couldn't keep going and shot himself," Crumb says. "He left his magazines but kept his 9."

"I'd like to think it's that," Fitzpatrick says. "But if it's the other, I'm going to find a motherfucker and blow them away."

"Let's live through the next few hours before we plan any revenge," Crumb says as the two Mates keep sprinting in the direction of the water tower.

———

Stanford hangs off the bottom of the fire escape ladder for only a second before dropping to the ground. He checks his carbine, making sure it is snug to his back, peeks out at the road and the herd of Zs still feasting on Pickering's body, then gets ready to sprint after DTA and DTB1.

He gets ready but doesn't start sprinting right away. The

sound of metal groaning and tearing stops him, and he looks up at the fire escape above him.

"Are you fucking kidding me?" he says to himself as he watches the topmost grate start to pull away from the brick building, its rusted bolts finally giving up. "Shit!"

Stanford runs as fast and hard as he can away from the alley as the entire fire escape begins to collapse to the ground. The sound of metal tearing is deafening, like knives shoved into Stanford's ears. The impact of the fire escape onto the dumpsters and asphalt in the alley is louder than the worst thunderclap. Stanford can feel the impact through his boots as much as he hears it through his assaulted ears.

DTA and DTB1 turn to look back at him and he waves his hands, gesturing for them to keep going, but a hell of a lot faster. Everyone's eyes go wide and they do just as his gestures suggest.

Stanford is actually surprised at how fast Alastair and Diaz are moving with Tiny D's stretcher. They're barely lagging behind the main group. Diaz glances back once more and catches Stanford's eye, then looks past him and shakes his head before turning forward.

There is no need to even look over his shoulder. Stanford knows exactly what Diaz saw. He can feel the thousands of undead feet vibrating the broken street just as well as he had felt the fire escape hitting the ground.

"I fucking hate Zs," Stanford says. "I really fucking hate Z herds."

He digs deep and picks up speed, hoping to catch up with the Teams before the Zs catch up to him.

———

The water tower looms above Fitzpatrick and Crumb, its bulbous top shining bright in the early morning sunlight. The glare causes Fitzpatrick to put a hand to her eyes. Once shielded, she has a better view of the ladder attached to one of the legs of the tower. And also at what hangs from the ladder.

"Holy shit," Fitzpatrick says, whipping her M-4 up and spinning about, looking for the attack she is sure is coming.

"What?" Crumb asks, then glances at the ladder. "Oh, fuck. That's Tally Jones. She's with DTB4."

"She was," Fitzpatrick says. "Until the cannies got to her."

"Cannies?" Crumb asks. "We don't know it was cannies."

"Did you see the teeth on those crazies back there?" Fitzpatrick replies. "Sharpened, man. Cannies have moved in and taken over."

"Crap," Crumb says. "The Zs must have driven them out of the waste and deeper into the city."

"Food source is gone," Fitzpatrick says.

Crumb stares up at the top of the ladder and the second body partially draped over the edge.

"I think that's Simon Torres," Crumb says. "Man, his family has been in the Stronghold since almost day one. He's the last of that line."

"Bummer," Fitzpatrick says, looking quickly to confirm. "Yeah, that's him. What are you thinking, Crumb?"

"That dead Mates have gear we need," Crumb responds. "It's a shitty thought, but we made it this far. It'd be stupid to let Pickering's sacrifice go to waste."

"I'll cover while you rummage," Fitzpatrick says.

"Seriously?" Crumb asks. "Thanks."

Fitzpatrick doesn't respond. The sound of Zs is everywhere, and she is busy moving her M-4 back and forth, back and forth, waiting for the first group of Zs to come at them. Lucky for them, the water tower is surrounded by a concrete block wall with traces of old razor wire at the top. The chain link gate that had been at the entrance to the enclosure is torn from its hinges, making it useless, but at least the one entrance makes a perfect bottleneck if Zs decided to get curious.

It also means only one exit if things go bad.

A heavy whump makes Fitzpatrick jump, and she spins about.

"Sorry," Crumb says from the ladder. "Only way I could get by."

"A warning next time, please," Fitzpatrick replies.

Fitzpatrick can hear Crumb moving about far above her, his boots clattering on the metal walkway as he scavenges for supplies.

"No other bodies up here," Crumb calls down quietly. "They either got away or were taken away."

"Let's pray for the former," Fitzpatrick replies.

"Food too or just ammo?" Crumb asks from above.

"Food too," Fitzpatrick replies, her stomach growling at the thought of something to eat.

DTB3 had been on its way back to the Turnpike and the system of trolleys that carried people up and down the old highway from Stronghold to Denver and back again. Standard procedure is to carry as few rations as possible to keep weight down. They had all timed it perfectly so the last of their food was gone on their last night of deployment into the Denver wasteland.

They would have been on a trolley by now, but those plans obviously changed.

"Not much here," Crumb says. "Some apples. A pack of protein crumble. Oh, wait, here's a—Fuck!"

There're six gunshots in rapid succession, then Crumb's agonizing scream. Fitzpatrick looks up in time to dive to her side and avoid the falling body of her Team Mate. Crumb's head explodes as it hits the pavement. His torso is a mess of blood, bone, and pulpy flesh, obviously torn apart by the gunfire Fitzpatrick had heard.

Her carbine pointing up at the water tower, Fitzpatrick knee walks backward until her back bumps against the concrete wall surrounding the water tower. She keeps her eyes and weapon trained on the walkway, waiting for a sign of the shooter.

There's a scrape of boot on metal, and she is about to pull the trigger at where she thinks the sound is coming from, but a different sound gets her attention. A few feet to her right are the broken chain link gate and wall opening. The gate rattles and shakes as it is bumped aside by the Zs that shamble their way into the enclosure, drawn to the sounds of the gun that killed Crumb.

Fitzpatrick has a brief irrational thought, one of those that pops up in times of trauma, that maybe the fall had killed him, not the bullets, but the thought flies away as survival instincts kicks in.

She has nowhere to go.

The wall is ten feet high. Higher than she's able to scale. Maybe if she gets a running start?

She sprints across the enclosure, dodging the legs of the water tower, and throws herself up and at the far wall. Her hands scramble for purchase, her boots dig for holds, but the concrete is old and crumbly, coming loose in her grip, sending her falling back onto her ass.

Fitzpatrick picks herself up and spins about, her M-4 back in hand.

"They're gonna eat you up," a croaky voice says from above her.

Fitzpatrick looks up to see a woman's weather-cragged, sharp-toothed face grinning down at her.

"You dead," the woman cackles, causing some of the Zs to take notice and angle their putrid necks so they can look up at the food far out of reach.

One shot. That's all Fitzpatrick fires, and the woman's brains explode out the back of her head.

Without hesitating, Fitzpatrick sprints toward the water tower ladder and leaps at it just like she leapt at the concrete wall. But this time she's able to grab on and scrambles hand over hand all the way up until she is standing on the water tower's walkway and looking down at the enclosure that is quickly filling with Zs.

Her first thought is she is totally fucked. Her second thought is Crumb had said there were apples. She is starving and thirsty. Apples are perfect for satisfying both.

She looks about until she finds the pack with apples, pulls one out, inspects it for rot, finds none, and takes a huge bite. Then she looks over at the body of the woman she had shot and sneers.

With just a few nudges from her boot, all the while still chomping on the apple, Fitzpatrick is able to get the dead canny's body loose from the walkway. It tumbles end over end, splatting hard on the concrete right next to the pile of Zs munching on Crumb's corpse.

The Zs pounce on the flesh, ripping into it like Fitzpatrick is ripping into the last of the apple.

She throws the core down into the horde and then takes a deep breath. She looks up and out at the city around her and that breath is nearly knocked from her.

"Jesus Christ," she whispers as she sees the dozens and dozens of columns of smoke that dot the landscape where fires burn and rage through the dead city.

She also sees the grand ocean of Zs that march from the East, stretching all the way to the horizon.

"This can't be," she says. "There's no way there can be this many. How? How?"

The word echoes in her head as she remains glued in place, unable to tear herself from the cataclysmic scene.

SIX

MIDNIGHT TRAIN TO BOULDER

"That's Fitzpatrick," Cole says, lowering his binoculars as the Teams dash into a tight alleyway between what used to be a burrito shop and a hair salon so many, many years before. "She doesn't look too hot."

"Can we get to her?" Carlotta asks.

"Not after the mess Ford made," Cole says. "That whole part of the city is cut off for good."

"Fuck you," Stanford grumbles.

"I was just yanking your chain, man," Cole says. "Calm the hell down."

"You have to admit that was pretty epic, TL," Tommy Bombs says. "If anyone was going to bring a fire escape down only yards from a few thousand Zs, it'd be you."

"Thanks, Tommy," Stanford says. "Your confidence in my ability to fuck up is second only to my mother's."

"I was only kidding," Tommy Bombs replies, looking hurt.

"Leave the crab alone," Cole says, patting Tommy Bombs on his shoulder. "Head up front and let Val know we need to cut over at 80th and double back to the Turnpike."

"Got it," Tommy Bombs says.

He nods to Stanford but only gets a frown, then he's off,

squeezing past Alastair and Diaz, with the stretchered and semi-conscious Tiny D between them, past Lang and Shep, and up to where Val and Sister stand at the far end of the alleyway.

"Cole says to cut over at 80th to the Turnpike," Tommy Bombs says.

"Yeah, that's not happening," Val says. She points at the open land between them and a long-abandoned subdivision. "The herd is already at the Turnpike. Look at the trees."

Tommy Bombs stares out of the alleyway at Zenobia Street and the subdivision on the other side. Dozens of Zs are shambling this way and that. Not nearly a herd, but enough to make a decent horde if they grouped together.

But those aren't the problem. The problem is exactly as Val says it is. The huge oaks and massive fir trees that tower over the crumbling houses sway back and forth. They look like a strong wind is going at them except for one problem: they are swaying in different directions.

"There have to be thousands over there already," Val says. "Listen. You can hear them pushing past the houses too."

Tommy Bombs does listen, he does hear the creaking and groaning of the old structures, he does realize that cutting over to 80th Street is not happening.

"What do I tell Cole?" Tommy Bombs asks. "Can we go another way?"

"We keep going up Sheridan and cut over at 88th," Val says. "Or where 95 crosses over the Turnpike. Whatever is safest. But 80th is out of the question."

Sister grunts.

"What?" Val asks. "You have something to say?"

"Already too many Zs," Sister says. "Won't be better up ahead." She looks over her shoulder and her eyes focus on the stretcher. "We're too slow."

"You have a better idea?" Val asks.

Tommy Bombs looks back and forth from one woman to the other.

"Guys, I have to tell Cole something," he says. "Don't leave me hanging."

"What's your idea?" Val asks.

"We drive," Sister says. "Take a truck up the mountain cross country. Skip the Turnpike until we're away from the herd."

Val and Tommy Bombs stare at her like she's started speaking a foreign language.

"Did you say drive?" Tommy Bombs asks. "A truck?" He looks at Val. "She said drive a truck, right?"

"Yeah," Val replies. "She did."

"What?" Sister asks. "You've never driven a truck before?"

"No, I have never driven a truck before," Val says. "No one has. There's no fuel for trucks or cars or anything with a motor. That's why we have the trolleys."

"No fuel?" Sister laughs. "Bullshit. Plenty of fuel. Big barrels of it at each safe house."

Val tries to form a reply, but her mouth just opens and closes. Tommy Bombs, not always the best conversationalist due to his constant stutter and shaking when not in a combat situation, comes to her rescue.

"We don't have safe houses," Tommy Bombs says. "We have pyre stations throughout Denver, but nothing called a safe house."

"Sure you do," Sister says. "I've been keeping them maintained for years. There are two between us and Boulder. One at 108th and one at the Omni. I sleep in that hotel sometimes. It's fancy."

"She's lost her mind," Tommy Bombs says.

"We've been up and down the Turnpike our whole lives, and every house and structure between here and the Stronghold has been searched and double searched," Val says, finding her voice again. "There are no safe houses, and there are sure as shit no working trucks with fuel that hasn't gone bad."

Sister eyes Val for a second, then turns her attention on Tommy Bombs.

"Have you been in every house and structure?" Sister asks.

"No," Tommy Bombs replies. "None of us have literally been in every house and—"

"So you can't say what's in all the houses, can you?" Sister pushes.

"Uh… no?" Tommy responds, his answer sounding like a question. He looks to Val for help.

But Val doesn't help. A light goes on in her eyes and she smiles.

"I've never been in the Omni," Val says. "Every patrol I've been on has always shown it as inspected by the previous Team."

"Ever talked to a Mate who's been in there?" Sister asks, her smile wide and beaming.

"No," Val says. "It's never come up."

"I thought Big Nails had been caught in a threesome there by his TL a few years back," Tommy Bombs says.

"That story screams rumor mill," Val says. "I've seen Big Nails. He's not threesome material."

"Shit," Tommy Bombs says. "What else don't we know?"

Sister laughs loudly, then clamps her hands over her mouth. "Sorry. Sorry," she apologizes. "There is so much you don't know it's just too fucking funny. Hilarious."

"Will the truck fit us all?" Val asks.

"I've never seen a working truck before," Tommy Bombs says like a kid who's just been told about ice cream. "Is it loud?"

"Yep," Sister says. "Which means once we get going, we can't stop. It'll bring the Zs after us faster than a canny hearing a baby cry."

Val and Tommy Bombs grimace at the image but say nothing.

"Go tell Cole we have a new plan," Val says to Tommy Bombs. "We're following Sister to the first safe house and catching a ride there."

————

Half of the exhausted Mates stand at the door to the old garage, their eyes nearly bugging out as they stare at the machine housed within. The rest of the Mates rest on the floor of the empty kitchen, all trying to catch some shut eye before they move out.

"This ride could kill her," Alastair says quietly as he stands next to Cole.

He looks back over his shoulder at Tiny D looking gray and wan on her stretcher. Diaz sits next to her, his fingers on her wrist, his eyes watching the hands on the face of his watch. Alastair turns back to the insane-looking machine before them and shakes his head.

"This ride could kill us all," he says.

"I'll take could over will any day," Cole says. "And those Zs outside will kill us for sure. One by one or all at once, we get stuck in that herd and it's all over."

"What the hell fuel does it run on?" Shep asks, standing just inside the four-car garage that houses only the one vehicle. Sister is off to the side, hand pumping a golden liquid from a steel barrel, through a plastic hose, and into the truck's fuel tank. "Diesel went bad decades ago."

"Cooking oil," Sister replies. "All that hemp y'all grow. Them seeds is handy for more things than frying up those fritters y'all eats."

"Why is she talking like that?" Cole asks Val.

"I don't know," Val replies. "Why are you asking me?"

"I'm just shit fucking with you," Sister says as she finishes with the pump and sets the hose aside. She puts the cap on the gas tank and gives it a twist, then snaps her fingers and points at the garage doors. "As soon as I start this up, we'll need to open those doors and go. Don't bother closing the doors. No one's coming back here for a long, long time."

"Uh...you can drive this thing?" Shep asks. "Like actually drive it without killing us?"

"Me? Yeah, I can drive it," Sister says. "I'm an excellent driver.

An excellent, excellent driver." She snickers. No one joins her. "Never mind. Go get everyone. Time to go."

Stanford hurries to the garage door and pats Cole on the shoulder. "Zs are filling the street. Time to go."

"That's what I just said," Sister responds. She opens the driver's side door and climbs up into the truck. She holds on to the door, letting it swing back and forth as she rests her chin on top. "We can fit five in the cab and the rest in the bed. Tiny D will need to be in the back so she can lie down. Don't worry about the Zs. The cage will hold. I've tested it."

"The cage will hold," Stanford scoffs. "She's tested it. Great."

The truck: a huge double cab, duel-wheeled thing with an iron-barred cage welded to the bed. Welded to the body are large saw blades sticking out by at least a foot. The front has an iron wedge attached to it and the back is nothing but long, sharp spikes.

Cole shakes his head. "This is insane."

"I agree with Cole," Stanford says.

"We don't have a choice," Val adds.

"Tiny D is gonna die if we don't get going," Diaz announces.

"More Zs!" Tommy Bombs says, running from the front room and into the kitchen. He slides to a stop when he sees what's beyond the door to the garage. "Holy shit."

"Time to go," Sister says. "Don't make me honk the horn."

"The what?" Cole asks. "Forget it, I don't care. DTA! Load up!"

"DTB1!" Stanford calls. "Do the fucking same!"

"Time to hit the road," Sister says. She points to the garage doors. "Get those open then hop on in, Mates."

Val and Shep hurry to the garage doors and lift them up, opening the space to the insane world outside. Instantly, the Zs that fill the street turn their attention to the noise and begin to shamble in the Teams' direction. Both Val and Shep lift their M-4s to fire, then nearly scream as the loudest noise they have ever heard erupts behind them.

"Holy shit!" Shep cries as he turns and watches the truck

shake and shudder, its V-12 engine coughing smoke out of the two tailpipes just under the tailgate.

"It's like it's alive!" Val shouts. "Come on!"

The two Mates run back to the truck and help Alastair and Diaz lift Tiny D's stretcher into the bed, then jump up inside the cage, slamming the tailgate and the cage door closed behind them. They secure a set of heavy pins and Val slaps her hand on the side of the truck.

"Go!" she shouts.

Before the word is even out of her mouth, the truck whips into reverse, speeds down the long driveway of what would have been considered a McMansion pre-Z, and out into the street, crushing several Zs as Sister whips it around, puts it into gear, and races away from the full herd that is only a block away.

Val looks at the rest of the Mates in the bed with her and shakes her head as Sister rolls down the driver's side window, which is protected by a grate of metal just like the rest of the windows, and howls.

"She's having fun," Val says. "The crazy woman is having fun."

When Sister said she'd take them off road, she did not mean through residential backstreets and old highways. She meant off road, away from the natural paths Zs tend to follow.

Val looks over at Diaz as the big man presses his head to the bars over the tailgate and spews vomit in the dusty wake of the big truck.

"This is not like being in a trolley!" Alastair shouts over the roar of the truck's engine.

"No shit!" Val replies.

"How the hell did she learn how to drive?" Alastair yells.

"I don't know!" Val responds, spitting dirt and grit between her words. "How did she get this thing to run? Autos haven't worked in decades!"

"Sister seems to know shit none of us know!" Diaz shouts, leaning back and wiping his mouth. "She ain't right in the head!"

"No shit!" Alastair yells.

The truck hits a hard bump and Tiny D's stretcher bounces a bit, causing the wounded woman to moan loud enough for everyone to hear even over the diesel engine that roars in front of them.

"She's going to kill us trying to save us!" Val yells.

"Not if they don't first!" Shep shouts from his spot by the cab. He points through the cage at the dark mass just ahead.

"Zs? How the hell did so many get ahead of us?" Alastair asks.

"Are they being herded?" Diaz asks.

"I don't think so," Val says. "I think they've just finally made it here. Sister said the East Coast is gone and the Zs are moving west. It's a natural migration."

"Nothing fucking natural about that," Diaz says.

The cab window slides open and Carlotta looks back at everyone.

"You're going to want to hang on," Carlotta says. "Sister is driving straight through."

"She's what?" the Mates in the truck's bed yell at the same time.

"Yeah, she's going through them," Carlotta says. "She's pretty sure she can do it."

"Pretty sure? Pretty sure!" Diaz shouts. "Fuck that!"

"Just hang on," Carlotta warns. "She isn't slowing down."

The window slides shut and the Mates all look at each other, then up at the herd of Zs getting alarmingly closer and closer.

"A hand on the cage and a hand on the stretcher," Val says. "Otherwise Tiny D is going to get tossed to death."

"We're all going to get tossed to death!" Alastair yells as the truck closes the distance on the Z herd.

Everyone grabs onto the cage and Tiny D's stretcher, their eyes locked onto the mass of undead rushing at them. Or them rushing at it. Doesn't matter, because in less than a couple of seconds they are in the thick of it, impact after impact rocking their world.

To all of their surprise, the truck doesn't slow down. It rams the herd and just keeps going, the wedge on the front making an instant path while the saw blades and spikes slice and dice the Zs in half and more.

Black blood sprays up into the air, covering the cab and splattering the Mates in the open-air bed. The truck shudders and bounces as bodies are crushed under the heavy-duty tires. The sound of the herd moaning and hissing at the meat just out of reach is almost as loud as the breaking of the undead bodies. Almost.

Sister cuts to the right and slices a diagonal line through the herd, aiming for the hint of a road off to the northeast. There's a hard *thunk* and a *thump whump whump* and the truck suddenly begins to pull to the left, aiming back the way they were headed.

"What is that noise?" Alastair yells.

"I think it's one of the tires!" Shep yells, pointing to the front driver's side. "The truck is dipping down that way!"

The *thump whump whump* continues for a few moments, then the truck straightens out and the noise diminishes but doesn't go completely away. Sister gets the truck aimed in the right direction again and the vehicle picks up speed, ripping through the herd at a speed that makes the hardened Mates want to close their eyes. Which isn't a bad idea, considering the spray of Z guts and gore coming up over the hood and sides of the truck.

There's a whack and thud then the truck is back on pavement, albeit broken and cracked pavement, and it races around the edges of the Z herd, aiming straight at an on-ramp that has been cleared of old vehicles.

"The Turnpike!" Val yells. "She's taking us back onto the Turnpike!"

"Good!" Diaz shouts. "Maybe we can get out of this nightmare thing and use a trolley like sane people!"

"Dude, we're DTA!" Alastair laughs. "We don't do what sane people do!"

"Second that for DTB," Shep says as the truck hits the on-ramp and races up to the Turnpike and a clear shot to the Stronghold.

Except there is no clear shot.

When they get onto the Turnpike, all they see are bodies. Bodies of what they think are friends and neighbors. Most are so horribly mutilated it's almost impossible to identify them as human beings, let alone as individuals who can be recognized.

The truck comes to a quick stop and the doors open, the occupants of the cab stepping out quickly, carbines up, eyes alert.

"What the hell?" Cole snaps. "The Z herd isn't here yet. What did this?"

"Cannies," Sister says. "They're on a frenzy."

"A what?" Stanford asks.

"A frenzy," Sister says. "It's what cannies do when they get panicked. They find people and then just kill, kill, kill, until no one is left alive. They eat some while they kill them but mostly leave the bodies behind and come back for the meat once they've murdered everyone they can find."

"Why the fuck would they do that?" Cole asks.

"Why do cannies do anything?" Sister responds. "They are insane. The meat makes their brainpans get all whoo hoo and shit. Someone I knew a long, long time ago explained it to me. He said it was prions. Little sparky things of whatever in your head that begin to breakdown and go all nutso when you eat other people. He said it was probably what made me different. But then we found out about—"

She stops mid-sentence and cocks her head.

"Listen," she whispers. "Hear that? People need help."

"Jesus, how are there any people left alive?" Alastair whispers, and he and the rest from the bed climb out and join the other Mates. "That's Brenda Lighton there and Mark Velasquez over there. They're heads of two different reclaim crews."

"De'Andre Talbot is there," Val says, nodding in a specific corpse's direction. "He's Reclaim Crew Six's foreman."

"Shit," Cole says. "Shit."

"Quiet," Sister hisses.

She waits in the road, her head moving slowly back and forth. To all the Mates, she looks uncannily like a Code Monkey, the way she angles her ears toward whatever sound she is listening to.

"We drive," Sister says. "Guns up and ready. You have a clear target, take it. Do not hesitate. Zs are easy to take on in this thing." She pats the side of the truck, avoiding the sharp saw blades. "But cannies can climb and will climb. If they have weapons, they'll gut you inside that cage where you sit."

"Then we don't fucking sit," Diaz says. "We fight."

"Good plan," Sister says and hurries back to the driver's side and climbs into the truck. "Come on!"

Everyone barely has time to hustle back into the truck and shut the doors and tailgate before Sister is flooring it and the truck is racing around the piles of bodies, heading northwest and up the Turnpike once again.

They go almost a mile before the Mates in the bed start to look at each other like maybe Sister isn't as sharp as she thinks she is. Then they come around a long curve and see at least two dozen cannies surrounding a set of trolleys locked in at the switching station. None of the cannies are looking at the trolleys; instead, they are facing right at the truck.

"This thing doesn't exactly sneak up on folks," Alastair says.

Diaz struggles with a hatch in the top of the cage until Val reaches up and shoves the latch aside.

"You cool?" Val asks.

"I'm cool," Diaz says. "My head is fucking spinning from all this shit though."

He pushes the hatch open and stands straight up, his M-4 to his shoulder and aimed right at the cannies. The truck's doors fly open and the rest of the Mates follow suit, their M-4s up as well as they take aim at the cannies.

"I can make this easy or hard," Cole calls out. "You put those weapons down and step away from the trolleys and you may get to live. Anything else means you fucking die."

The cannies don't respond. They don't drop their weapons—a mix of blades, chains, spiked bats, lead pipes, boards with nails, anything that can crush a skull and take down prey or keep a Z away. They don't step away from the trolleys. All the cannies do is stare.

"Do you think they can't understand us?" Stanford asks. "Maybe they're all deaf. You know, like how the Code Monkeys are all blind?"

Cole fires his M-4 over the cannies' heads and several flinch at the report.

"Nope. Not deaf," Cole says. "Just crazy."

"How many are we looking at?" Diaz asks from his position in the bed. "Eighteen? Twenty?"

"More than that," Shep says. "I'd say twenty-five, at least."

There's a cry for help, faint and weak, from behind the cannies. One of them turns and bangs a pipe against the trolley bars and the voice stops instantly.

"We risk hitting any survivors in the trolleys if we open fire," Carlotta says. "How are we doing this, TL?"

"Cole? Ideas?" Stanford asks. "We're great shots, but that's a lot of lead heading right at our people."

"I have this," Sister says.

"What the hell?" Cole yells. "Hold on!"

Sister ignores him and walks toward the cannies, her hands raised, her movements slow and obvious.

"Howdy," she calls out. "Who's the head honcho around these here parts?"

The cannies look confused at her question. The Mates look just as confused.

"Who's the boss?" Sister asks, shaking her head. "Ain't none of you watched one of them old western movies? Any of you seen a movie at all? I used to love watching movies."

"What the hell is she talking about?" Alastair asks Val as the Mates climb out of the bed of the truck and stand with the others, carbines ready.

"Not a clue," Val says. "They haven't shown a movie in the Stronghold since we were kids."

"Listen up, flesh eaters," Sister says. "I need to have a chat with your person in charge." She says the words slowly, carefully, like she's talking to children. "You have some of my new friends' friends in those trolleys. We need them back without any more harm coming to them. I am guessing that the only way to make that happen is to talk to your boss."

The cannies only stare, but a few start to grip their weapons hard enough that the sound of knuckles cracking is like gunshots. Sister holds up a hand, making sure the Mates don't open fire.

"I'll ask one more time, then I start getting pissy," Sister says. "None of you want me to get pissy."

She pats the machete on her hip, something she picked up in the garage where she'd kept the truck. She nods her head at, but doesn't move a hand toward, the 9mm on her other hip.

"I get stabby and shooty when I get pissy. I'd like to avoid the stabby and shooty and just help those folks in the trolleys. Then we'll be on our way and you all can deal with the gigantic herd of Zs coming up the mountain."

No one responds.

"Dammit," she sighs. "I didn't have to tell you about the herd. Although I bet y'all already know it's coming. That's why you're pushing through Denver, right? Because the herd's moved you out of your holes and hiding places? Herds'll do that. Yes they will."

Still no response.

"Jesus, do you want to die?" Sister asks. "Some of you have to know who I am. Sister? You've heard of Sister, right?"

More than a few eyes widen and a couple of heads turn to look at a very tall man dressed in a long, tattered duster with a wool cap pulled down over his ears. He growls and glares at Sister, then takes a step forward.

"You ain't Sister," the man says, pointing a sharpened steel rod at her. "Sister is dead. Been dead a long time. My mama told me stories about Sister, the canny killer. The woman Zs fear. She's a nightmare story. The boogeyman."

"Boogey*woman*," Sister says. She pats her chest. "I got boobies."

"This is getting weird," Cole says to Stanford.

"Getting?" Stanford chuckles, shaking his head. "It's like we stepped into some alternate reality a couple days ago and—"

"Do you mind?" Sister snaps, looking back over her shoulder at Stanford. "I finally get them to talk and you two start up? What the hell, Mates?"

"Uh… sorry?" Stanford replies.

"Apology accepted," Sister says and returns her attention to the canny leader. "My friends aren't the brightest. Sometimes they don't know when to be quiet and let the adults talk. You get what I'm saying? Not easy being in charge, is it?"

"You ain't Sister," the canny leader replies.

"Okay, maybe not," Sister says and shrugs. "But say I am. There are twenty-five of you. I've taken more at once. If you've heard the stories then you know that half of you will be dead before the first of you raises a weapon to me. Also, if you believe those same stories, once I get to work, I spare no one. Can't risk it."

She claps her hands together and the cannies all jump, except for the leader. He just glares and glares, his eyes burning with hatred and violence under the edge of the wool cap.

"Last chance," Sister says. "You all get to walk away alive or you get to deal with me. That means you all die. Because I could give two shits if you believe who I am or not because I know who I am. I am Sister and I am out of fucking patience, you stupid shit fuckers."

"These cages have wheels already," the canny leader says. "Food stays in the cages. We take the cages with us. You fuck off."

The canny leader adds a snarling upper lip to his perma-glare.

Sister gives him a look that clearly states, "Really?"

"You ain't Sister," the canny leader says and motions for his people to start walking forward. "Kill the bitch. Kill her hard."

"Okay," is all Sister says.

The machete is off her hip and flying through the air before anyone even realizes she's moved. The canny leader staggers back, the weapon suddenly sticking out of his chest. There was barely time to blink from throw to impact.

"I'm going to want that back," Sister says as she casually walks toward the cannies. "Val back there took her blade back from me, so the machete is all I've got."

She pulls her 9mm but doesn't point it at the group. She lets her arm hang at her side, loose and easy like nothing has just happened.

"I have fifteen rounds in this pistol," Sister says, then looks down at the 9mm. "Or is it seventeen? Not sure what kind I have in my hand. Could end up that two of you get lucky and don't die. By bullets. Don't die by bullets. I want that clear, because no matter what, y'all are going to get dead. Dead, dead, dead."

The cannies stand there, some staring at the fallen corpse of their leader, some staring at Sister. None of them move a muscle.

Sister raises her pistol and then all hell breaks loose.

"Three, two, one, die!" Sister yells as she starts squeezing the trigger.

As the cannies rush her, their stupor over and bloodlust restored, Sister takes careful, quick aim. Fifteen cannies drop from perfect head shots before her pistol clicks empty. Then they are on her.

She ducks the first three that swing at her. She comes up and grabs a canny by the arm, snapping him over her knee as she takes the chain from the man's grip. The canny screams as his arm points down in a direction it was not meant to point, but that scream ends fast as Sister whips the canny's own chain against his temple, silencing him forever.

She spins about and takes the legs out of the other two before she turns back to the six that are left. Six. That's it. The leader down, fifteen with holes in their heads, one brained by his own chain, and two with knees that will never hold their weight, leaves six standing cannies, armed and enraged.

Four rush Sister head on and she snaps the chain out, destroying half of a man's face before snapping again and crushing another man's windpipe. Those two men fall to their knees, one suffocating slowly while the other screams and holds his hands to his mangled face.

Sister spins the chain around in her hand and looks at the other two who try to get in close to her. She shakes her head and wraps the chain around one's wrist, nearly breaking the woman's hand right off. She kicks out with her right leg and catches the other canny in the gut, winding him instantly. Sister spins the broken-wrist canny around and slams her into the winded one, sending both of them falling to the pavement.

The last two look at Sister. One of them pisses himself while the other just keeps muttering some prayer over and over. Sister keeps her eyes on them while she lifts a boot and stomps hard on the winded canny's head, popping it like a bag of Z guts.

The piss-pants canny screeches and turns to run, but only gets a foot or two before a shot rings out and his head is blown apart. The last canny, now on his knees as he mumbles his prayers, shakes his head over and over, his eyes clamped shut.

Sister whirls about and stares at Stanford as the man lowers his smoking carbine.

"Mine," she says, and Stanford actually takes a step back from the force of her voice.

"Sure. Whatever," Stanford says and holds up a hand. "My bad."

Sister walks up to the praying canny and grabs his chin. He whimpers but doesn't stop praying. She looks him over then shoves him hard, sending him ass first onto the broken pavement.

"You have five seconds to get up and run," Sister says. "I don't care where you go, just away from here. If you live then you remember that Sister is real. You tell your friends that I'm real. You tell them that cannies are done in this world." A deep sadness comes over her and she nudges the man with her boot. "Everything is done. Go. Get the fuck out of here."

The canny hesitates for only a second then glances around, looking for the trick. He finally stands up and starts running as fast as he can. He's off the Turnpike, over the edge, and lost from sight in a flash.

"Are we really letting him go?" Stanford asks.

"Yeah," Sister replies. "He's dead anyway. Too many Zs."

"Unless he heads west," Cole says. "If he lives getting over the pass and out of the Rockies then he could make it."

"Nope," Sister says. "The West is gone too. Nothing but Zs on the other side of these mountains."

"How the hell do you know that?" Stanford asks.

"How the hell do I know anything?" Sister replies. She taps her head. "Because it's my shit fucking job, that's how. And I am very good at my shit fucking job."

"You like saying shit fuck," Val says. "A lot."

"Yeah, I do," Sister says and smiles. Then she turns to the wounded cannies strewn between the slain ones. "You guys take care of these assholes while I open the trolleys. I'm done with cannies for today."

"Yeah, sure, no problem," Stanford says. "Anything else you need us to do? Maybe wash the truck later when we get back to the Stronghold?"

"Wash the truck?" Sister responds. "That's a waste of time and water. Don't be stupid. Stupid is dumb."

"Stupid is dumb," Stanford says and nods. "That's wisdom right there."

"Val, go help the crazy woman with the trolleys while we

clean up," Cole says. "DTA! Quiet the screamers and silence the corpses. I don't want a single one of the bastards getting up and walking his or her way up to our front door. Plenty in the herd behind us already."

"DTB1!" Stanford says. "Same orders. And drag the bodies out of the way so we don't have to drive over them."

The Teams get to work as Sister and Val walk up to the trolleys.

Basically heavily reinforced steel and iron cages on wheels designed to hold reclamation crews or the materials they scavenge, the trolleys are hooked to a series of heavy-duty steel cables that start and end at switching stations all up and down the Turnpike. Once a trolley reaches a station, a winch jock uncouples the trolley from one cable and then couples it to another cable that will take it down, or up, to the next switching station.

The trolleys in front of Val and Sister have seen their last days and are at their final switching station. The winch jocks in charge of the cables are nothing but fleshy smears across the gears and levers that move the vehicles. Those trapped inside the trolleys watch Val with hopeful eyes and Sister with wary eyes.

There are only four people trapped inside. Four alive, at least.

Blood drips from the edges of the first trolley as corpses empty their liquids from multiple stab wounds. Behind those corpses, using them to block the attacks, is a woman, cut and bruised badly, looking from Val to Sister and back.

"TL Henshaw?" Val asks, recognizing the TL from Denver Team Beta Four.

"Hey, Val," Henshaw whispers, her voice a hoarse crack. "Who's this?"

"You didn't hear my speech?" Sister asks. "I'm Sister."

"Yes, I heard," Henshaw replies. "But that doesn't tell me who the fuck you are."

"She's Commander Lee's field agent," Val says. "A spy sent out into the waste to check on the other survivor pockets."

"Former survivor pockets," Sister says.

"So she says," Val adds. "I'll tell you all about it as we drive up to the Stronghold. Let's get you guys out of there now first."

"Can we get out too?" a man asks from the other trolley. "I plan on never getting in one of these things again."

"Benji? No, sorry, Billy. Damn you twins. Hard to tell you apart," Val says as she looks over. She shakes her head and smiles. "And I always forget you're with DTB2."

"Was with," the other man replies. "DTB2 is gone now. We're all that's left."

"Shit, Santiago, I'm sorry to hear that," Val says. "Yeah, let's get you guys out of there. Sister? You got this one?"

"Latch is all shit fucked, but I can get it," Sister says.

"We shot the locks to keep the cannies from getting us," Henshaw says. "They still got most of us."

Sister only nods as she yanks a heavy pipe from a dead man's hands and then brings it down hard on the trolley's warped latch.

"But not all of you," Sister says. "So you win."

TL Henshaw cautiously steps out of the trolley and eyes Sister.

"Team Leader Allison Henshaw," Sister states.

"How do you know my first name?" the second woman snaps.

"I knew your great—" Sister starts to answer, then clamps her mouth closed. "I'm, uh, a spy. Yeah. That's how I know. Spy stuff."

"Val? We cool with this woman?" Henshaw asks.

"As cool as we can get," Val replies as she manages to break the latch on the other trolley.

Billy and Santiago climb out of the trolley. They stretch and then turn back to help the third man out. The third man is holding his arm close to his chest, a heavy, blood-soaked bandage wrapped around most of it.

"Bite?" Sister asks, shifting her focus to the third man.

"Yes," Henshaw says. "And he's coming with. We'll let Commander Lee and Dr. Terlington decide when he needs to be dealt with. I've lost too many people today to put him down out here."

"Okay," Sister says. "But he rides in back, and if he turns then he dies. Right, Val?"

Val scrunches her face up with a look of pure distaste but nods. "Yes. He can ride back with us and I'll handle him if he turns."

"Thanks, Val," Team Mate Scotty Kurowski says. "I appreciate that."

"Least I can do," Val says. "Sorry you got bit, Scotty. Sucks you went from gate guard to Mate and now have to deal with this."

"We all know the risks," Scotty says, shrugging. He flinches and takes a deep breath, holding his arm tighter to his chest. "I'm just glad I can say goodbye to some folks before I get the ice pick to the temple."

"Shut up about that," Val says. "Hamish will make that call."

"And ice picks are inefficient," Sister says. "You need a good blade or you risk not getting the job done."

She gives Scotty a thumbs up, then turns back to the Mates busy clearing the road.

"Come on!" she shouts. "I can hear the herd! We load up and move out in five!"

Henshaw starts to ask Val a question but stops as Val shakes her head.

"On the ride," Val says. "Trust me."

SEVEN
HOME IS WHERE THE HUEY IS

The guards at the main gate to the Stronghold stare with their mouths hanging open as the diesel truck rumbles up to them. The sight is so foreign that it isn't until the vehicle is halfway up from the former outer gate that they think to raise their weapons and hold out hands to halt the truck's progress.

On either side of the road that leads to the Stronghold's gate lay the ruins of what had once been the outer settlement of the survivor pocket that was Boulder, Colorado. Most of the residents had lived inside the secure walls of the Stronghold, but those with more independent spirits, or foolish spirits depending on who was asked, decided they couldn't handle being walled up and had populated the many neighborhoods that had surrounded the former University of Colorado campus.

But all of that was lost when the Code Monkeys sent a massive herd of Zs up the Turnpike as a deadly distraction to their own attack. In all fairness to the Zs, it was members of the Stronghold who had pressed the buttons, detonating hundreds of pounds of explosives set throughout the outer neighborhoods, burning all of the houses down to their foundations in order to stop the Z herd.

Now those foundations lay there, scorched and empty, skeletons of life and hopeful living.

The truck slows to a stop and the driver's side window rolls down. Sister unlatches the grate that protects her window and shoves it aside so she can lean out and give the guards a big, wicked smile.

"Those are some impressive hands," Sister says, nodding to the two men's outstretched palms giving her the universal sign for stop. "In the future, which there won't be, but could be, but probably not, you should lead with your weapons. Better safe than sorry when an armored and geared-out truck comes rollin' up on ya."

"Who are you?" one of the guards yells, taking Sister's advice and switching his focus from his hand to his rifle. "State your name and business or turn around and return the way you came."

"Oh, that way is no good," Sister says. "Whole shit ton of Zs blocking it."

"It's good, Trey," Val says as she shoves the cage hatch open and stands up. "She's with the Teams. Got our asses out of Denver."

"That place is lost," Alastair says, joining Val. Diaz gives a wave of his hand out of the cage but doesn't stand.

The passenger's side window rolls down and the grate is shoved open as well. Cole sticks his head out and gives a thumbs up to the guards.

"Let us in, boys," Cole orders. "We have to get to Commander Lee ASAP. We are on full alert as of this second."

"We're already on full alert," one of the guards, Trey, responds. "We all saw the line of pyres before they were snuffed out."

"You did?" Cole asks. He opens his door and steps out. The guards flinch and Cole frowns. "What the hell? If you saw all the pyres, then why are there only two of you on duty?"

"Commander Lee wanted all hands on deck," the other guard replies. "We're packing up the Stronghold. Getting ready to move."

"Move?" Cole asks. "Move where?"

"Into the real Stronghold," Sister says. "Lee knows it's over. She should have waited until I told her for sure, but she isn't wrong, so…" she shrugs and waves at Cole. "Get in and I'll drive us through."

"Real Stronghold?" Cole asks. "What does that mean?"

"You can't bring that in here," Trey says.

"Want to watch me?" Sister smirks.

"No, I mean, there's nowhere for it to go," Trey explains. "The streets are being barricaded and blocked off. Commander Lee is expecting an attack soon after seeing the pyres. She wants to slow down the herd as much as possible. Says we'll need the time."

Cole looks at Sister. "Need the time for what? And answer my question, what is the real Stronghold?"

"Commander Lee can explain that," Sister says as she hops out of the truck. She tosses the keys to Trey and grins. "It's yours now. Feel free to drive it around until the Zs show up. It's fun."

"I… I don't know how to drive," Trey says.

"That's just stupid," Sister says. "Everyone should know how to drive. So many cars in the world. So many fun, fun cars."

The Mates unload from the truck, and Alastair and Diaz get back to carrying Tiny D's stretcher. The guards watch with dawning realization that the group is made up of the remnants from fractured Teams.

"What the hell happened down there?" Trey asks.

"Bad shit, man," Diaz says as they walk past him and toward the huge gate protecting the Stronghold from the horrors of the wasteland. "Really bad shit."

———

"I want Val with us," Sister says as she walks into the hospital room where Cole and DTA stand, all eyes on the sleeping form of Tiny D. "She needs to be part of this."

"And why is that?" Cole asks, his eyes going from Sister to Val and back. "She's not a TL. I think Stanford and I can handle the briefing with Commander Lee on our own." He looks at his watch. "She should be ready for us now if the council members have finally left."

"Val's mom died helping set this up," Sister says and walks out of the room.

Val's mouth drops open, but she snaps it shut instantly as she sees the look of confusion, then suspicion, on Cole's face.

"I have no fucking clue what she's talking about," Val says before Cole can even pose the question.

"You sure?" Cole asks. He studies her face. "You have a look, Val. I know that look. You may not know exactly what she means, but you know something."

"Jesus! Come on!" Sister snaps, ducking her head back in the room. "Bunch of old ladies in here, standing around jabbering and chatting. Pull your granny panties out of your ass cracks and let's get a move on, people!"

Then she's gone.

"You guys have fun with that," Alastair says. "Diaz and I have this. If anything changes, we'll send a Runner to find you, TL."

"Hamish will be by soon," Val says to Alastair. "Tell him I had to go talk to my aunt, will you?"

"Will do," Alastair nods.

"Don't know what you see in that nerd," Diaz says. "A Mate like you should get a real man."

"So everyone thinks," Val says, "and has no problem telling me. Hamish and I have been together most of our lives. I love the man, and he loves me. So shut the fuck up."

"Hey, just saying that he's not up to your standards, Val," Diaz says, his hands up. "But if you love soft men, then you love soft men."

"Fuck and you," Val says.

"Come on," Cole says, pulling at Val's arm. "I think I hear Sister freaking people out down the hall."

"Tell Hamish where I went," Val warns, her eyes deadly serious.

"No problem," Diaz says as Val and Cole leave. As soon as they are gone, he looks at Alastair. "We going to tell him?"

"Nah," Alastair replies, grinning from ear to ear. "Where's the fun in that?"

———

The scene in the streets of the Stronghold is one of controlled and organized chaos. Residents hurry in one direction pushing carts and wagons loaded with supplies and personal belongings. Every few yards, a volunteer stands trying to keep people from pushing and shoving, trying to keep the peace that threatens to shatter at any second.

"Where are they all going?" Cole asks.

"No idea," Val says.

"The real Stronghold," Sister says. "I already told you that. Pay attention. Don't be stupid."

"No, you said…" Cole starts to argue, then shakes his head and gives up. "Never mind."

"Keep moving, people!" a man hollers at the crowd. "Keep it moving! You'll get instructions when you reach the Gym! Don't get comfortable, because we'll be hiking after that!"

"Dad?" Val asks, stopping short as she recognizes the volunteer. "What the hell?"

"There's my little girl," Collin Baptiste says as he turns to his daughter's voice. "How is my Valencia Stella Baptiste today?"

"Are you high?" Val asks, getting close to her father so she can inspect his pupils. "You don't stink like hooch, so I know you're not drunk."

"Nope, baby, not high," Collin replies. "Just happy to help."

Val looks over her shoulder at Cole and he shrugs, nodding at an impatient Sister.

"Don't look at me," he says. "I'm going to get the nervous-looking killer over to Commander Lee. Meet us there ASAP. I don't think your aunt is in the waiting mood."

"You can say that for sure," Collin responds. "She's busting balls, cracking heads, and—"

"Tweaking nipples?" Sister asks. "Once you bust balls and crack heads then there's really just tweaking nipples left. Unless you break bones, but that's not a thing."

"And tweaking nipples is?" Collin asks. He nudges Val with his elbow. "So, who's your sexy older lady friend there, Val? I knew you were on a mission, but I didn't know it was to bring a fine piece like this back."

"Oh, my God, you are gross," Val says. "Maybe scratch your nuts and fart next time you want to be this disgusting."

"He's high," Sister says. "But not wrong. I am a sexy piece."

"Come on," Cole says to Sister. "We'll leave the Baptiste drama to the Baptistes."

"I knew a Baptiste once," Sister says. "He was a wonderful man. Great in the sack. We broke up because I had to keep leaving. But he found a really nice lady and that's how these two eventually came about. Ah, those were the days."

Collin's smile falters and he narrows his eyes.

"Who did you say this woman was?" he asks Val, his voice suddenly cold.

"Excuse me," a woman with a wheelbarrow full of blankets asks as she pulls up next to Collin. "Do you know if—?"

"Not now, Bitsy," Collin snaps. "Go ask someone that gives a shit."

"And there's my real dad," Val says. "Didn't take long for him to come back."

"Who is this, Valencia?" Collin asks. "Where the hell did you find this woman? She's not some wasteland trash you rescued, is she?"

"I could be," Sister says. "I've been called worse."

She sighs and rubs at her face. One of her radiation sores

breaks and a clear liquid starts to ooze from it. She swears and wipes the ooze from her cheek before turning back to Collin.

"Collin Baptiste, you disappoint me," Sister says. "You had promise when you were little. You had promise when you married Molly. You even had promise when Molly got sick. I thought you'd get stronger, use your life to help and be a proud member of your bloodline. I know some ghosts are rolling in their graves that an ass like you is even still allowed to live here. Keep your nose clean, or I'll make sure that when those doors slam shut and lock, you are standing on the wrong side of them."

"Who are you?" Collin hisses as if Sister didn't just give him a seriously condescending lecture. "Do I know you? I do, don't I? I've seen you before."

"Maybe," Sister says. "Probably. But it doesn't matter anymore." She points at the crowd of people moving, moving, moving past them. "Do your job and answer questions. Keep telling them to move along. Get them into the Stronghold and then pray I don't put a bug in your sister's ear and get you tossed out on your butt."

Sister grabs Cole and yanks him away from the Baptistes.

"I guess we're going now," Cole says, looking very confused and shocked. "Uh. Don't take too long, Val."

"Not planning on it," Val says. Once they are a few yards away, she whirls on her father. "You said you weren't high? She says you are. What are you on?"

"Maybe some fermented aspen bark," Collin answers. "Cranky worked up a batch last month and it was ready today so he let me have a taste. It's not strong, just enough to take the edge off."

"What edge, Dad?" Val snaps. "You work on the sanitation crew. Since when does digging latrine ditches count as an edge?"

"You don't know what's going on, Val," Collin says. "My sister is not talking to me. She's been hiding something big." He waves his arms around at the moving crowd. "And here it is. But none of us know what 'it' is."

"Well, I'm about to find out," Val says. "Get back to work and I'll come find you when I can."

"Sure thing," Collin says. "But before you go, answer my question. Who was that old broad?"

"I'm not sure," Val says. "But she's important. And tough as nails. The woman is a stone-cold killer, so if you run into her again, be nice and keep your stupid mouth shut or she'll slice your lips off. I'm not kidding, Dad. That woman will slice your fucking lips off."

A few people turn to look at the Baptistes and frown at Val's words.

"Sorry, Mrs. Hoffstein," Val says. "I got carried away."

"Just mind your own fucking business, people!" Collin snaps.

"Jesus, Dad," Val growls. "Listen, I have to go. I'll find you later. Try to be sober so we can talk. Things are moving fast, and I don't know what I'll be doing next."

"You'll be stepping through the Stronghold doors with me is what you'll be doing next," Collin says.

"Yeah, I don't even know what the hell that means," Val says. "We'll talk later."

"When we do, Val, you'll tell me all about that crazy-looking woman," Collin says, jabbing a finger in her direction. "I know I've seen her before, but I don't know where."

"She's nothing you need to be concerned about," Val responds. "Just do what you're supposed to do and try to stay out of trouble."

Collin gives her a wink and two very sarcastic thumbs up. Val flips him off and then turns to hurry after Cole and Sister.

———

Val knocks softly and opens the door before anyone can answer.

"Sorry I'm late," she says as she squeezes into Commander Lee's crowded office. "My dad."

"No more explanation needed," Commander Lee says from

her chair behind her desk. "You have already wasted too many words on my inebriate of a brother."

"Inebriate," Sister snickers from her place against the wall. "That's a funny word."

"Take a seat, Mate Baptiste," Commander Lee orders, motioning to the last open chair in the room.

The other chairs are occupied by Cole Wright, Stanford Lee, Allison Henshaw, and Oscar Santiago. Sister leans against the office wall behind them, looking amused.

"No one from DTB3?" Val asks. "We thought we saw Fitzpatrick on a water tower back in Denver, but there was no way to get to her."

"We haven't heard anything from DTB3," Commander Lee responds. "And TL Wright has already given me a full report. As have all the TLs. Take your seat, Mate Baptiste, and just listen. You are here because Ms—" Commander Lee clears her throat. "You are here because *Sister* has asked that you be here. But this is a meeting for TLs, so do not interrupt."

"Sorry," Val says and takes her seat quickly. "I'll only speak if I'm asked a question."

"Thank you," Commander Lee says. She takes a deep breath and slowly lets it out. "When I saw the pyres I knew it was time, so I have already had this discussion with the council. You've seen the residents packing and hauling belongings and supplies, so you know we're moving everyone to a more secure location."

"Which is?" Cole asks.

"The real Stronghold," Commander Lee says.

"I kept telling him that and he was all like, hey, what's the real Stronghold crap? And I was all like, hey, just chill and wait for Commander Lee," Sister says. She snorts and smiles as if she's said the greatest joke ever.

"Yes, well, the real Stronghold is an immense and secure bunker below Boulder," Commander Lee says. "While it has been commonly known that the former NORAD was housed in the Cheyenne Mountain facility, that is only partially true. There is an ancillary control room there where operations can be handled and commanded, if needed, but the main facility was moved."

"Secure bunker location for what?" Stanford asks. "And why the hell haven't we been there all this time? Secure bunker location is a lot better than open-air location with only a wall between us and the Zs."

"That is a good question," Commander Lee says. "And I am not surprised it came from you, Stanford."

"Why do I feel like that was an insult more than a compliment?" Stanford asks.

"The real Stronghold is secure for one reason only: because once the doors close, they stay closed for at least a century, if not longer," Commander Lee says, ignoring her son's second question. "This ensures that the Zs cannot breach the facility because of a lapse in judgment by, say, panicked or confused occupants."

"You mean so when the cabin fever nutjobs who will eventually lose their shit decide to go crazy and run out the front door, letting God-knows-what stumble through to kill everyone inside," Stanford says. He looks around the room at everyone. "In case the subtext wasn't clear."

"Thanks, Ford," Cole says. "I couldn't have guessed that for myself."

"I'm here to help, buddy," Stanford says.

"Which you are not doing," Commander Lee snaps. "Please be quiet, son, or I will remove you from your commission as Team Leader and give that to Mate Baptiste here."

"Val wouldn't take it," Stanford says. "She's the most loyal cousin a man could—"

"Like hell I wouldn't," Val laughs. "You're on your own, Mr. Foot-In-Mouth."

"Oh, the betrayal," Stanford says, then yelps as Sister smacks him upside the head. "Ow! What the hell?"

"Shut up and listen to your mother," Sister snaps, then yanks up her shirt to show everyone the oozing wound in her side. "I still have to drain this fucker and get Val's lover boy to stitch it up so I can kick more ass than all of you combined. You are slowing that down, dipshit. Knock it off."

"Okay. Sorry," Stanford mumbles.

"From what you all have told me, we do not have much time to get everyone inside the Stronghold and close those doors," Commander Lee says, moving on. "When the herd hits the walls and gate, it'll be only a matter of hours before the crush of their bodies breaches this sanctuary and the streets are filled with Zs. When that happens, we need to be inside and locked down permanently."

"Okay, so let's do that," Cole says.

"You think it's going to be that simple?" Henshaw asks him. "It's not. Why else would we be here?"

"Exactly, TL Henshaw," Commander Lee says. "It's not that simple. It should have been, but time has not been on our side. Or the effects of time. Specifically the effects of time on machinery and electronics built well over a century ago."

"The nukes won't launch on their own," Sister says. All eyes turn to her. "What? They won't."

"Why the fuck would we want them to?" Cole asks.

"So we don't have to go to Cheyenne Mountain and launch them ourselves. Duh," Sister says. "Keep up, Wright. Sheesh."

"What Sister is trying to say in her own unique way is that part of the plan, once everyone has been transferred safely into our new Stronghold, is for the nuclear arsenal of the former United States of America to be at our command," Commander Lee says. "An arsenal that we need to launch in order to cleanse the major cities, and quite a bit of the land, of the herds and herds of Zs that have overtaken everything."

"Everyone's dead," Sister says. "Except for just a couple of pockets that may survive the big booms and flashes. Other than those peoples, there ain't no more left. They're all Zs now. And Zs don't die. If we don't fry them, then when the doors open in a century or two, there will still be herds of Zs."

"That's not possible," Santiago says. "They'll starve."

"If only that were the case, TL Santiago," Commander Lee says.

"TL?" Val asks, then holds up a hand. "Sorry."

"Yes, Santiago has been promoted to TL," Commander Lee says. "Not that there is a Team for him to lead. But I figured he deserved the promotion before you are all deployed."

"Zs don't starve," the single-minded Sister continues. "They feed off sunlight when they can't feed off peoples. Good thing cannies can't do that, right? Right?"

"Yeah, right," Stanford says. He hooks a thumb back at Sister. "She's not sane, is she?"

"That is debatable," Commander Lee says. "But Sister's sanity is not the issue. What she said is 100% correct. The Zs are feeding off sunlight to keep going. We do not know how or why, but the phenomenon was documented back when this place was founded. It is why there are sometimes very fast Zs. They get an energy boost from the sun as well as from fresh food."

"So we have to push the button that makes the big missiles function," Sister says. "Because there's nothing worse than missile dysfunction."

She laughs hard and loud, then slowly quiets down when she realizes she's the only one.

"Miss-isle dysfunction? No one?" she says. "You people suck."

"The remote connection from the Stronghold to Cheyenne Mountain has been locked," Commander Lee says.

"The Code Monkeys have done all the hard stuff," Sister says. "They've got everything ready to launch. What they didn't have ready, they will by the time we get there. I made sure of that."

"Hold on a minute!" Cole snaps. "She's been helping the Code Monkeys?"

"No!" Sister exclaims. "Well, yes. But they don't know that. I just made sure they found the last of the launch codes in my coat." She sighs. "I miss that coat."

"We needed the Code Monkeys to do all the prep and get the nuclear missiles ready for launch," Commander Lee says. "We know they have been to the silos and made sure the missiles are ready. The next step was to make sure they had everything in Cheyenne ready as well. The only problem is they can't initiate the actual launch. We were going to do that from here, but we can't anymore. The Teams go down, deal with the Code Monkeys in Cheyenne, restore the launch connection, complete the mission, and come back here before we seal the Stronghold for good."

"Oh, that's all?" Stanford laughs. "Then sign me up."

"You're already signed up," Cole says. "You're a TL."

"I was being sarcastic," Stanford replies.

"Me too," Cole says.

"You two finished?" Commander Lee glares. "You leave first thing in the morning. Tell your Mates so they can say goodbye to loved ones. This isn't a suicide mission, but it is not going to be easy. Have your people tie up loose ends before they go so I don't have to do it for them once the Stronghold doors close."

No one responds. They all sit there and look anywhere except at Commander Lee.

"I still don't get why I'm here," Val says. "I mean, I'll go on the mission with all of the other Mates, but why am I in this room right now?"

"I wanted to make sure you knew what the stakes were," Commander Lee says. She sighs heavily and glances at Sister. "There is one more issue. The launch control switch can only be initiated by genetic marker confirmation. This is why the Code Monkeys can't launch on their own. We need your genetic marker, Mate Baptiste."

"You're related to Granny G," Sister says. "Her genetic marker is one of the ones needed to authorize the launch of a full-scale strike."

Everyone is slightly taken aback at Sister's tone of voice. The weirdness is gone. The affectations and strange dialect are gone. She sounds sane, serious, and like a woman who has carried a heavy load for a very long time.

"You said genetic markers. Plural," Stanford says to his mother. "Whose is the other one?"

"Mine," Sister says. "I'll be there with you the whole way."

"Great," Stanford replies. "But still one more issue."

"Got that covered," Sister says and gives him a thumbs up.

"You don't even know what I'm going to say," Stanford snaps.

"Yes, I do," Sister responds. "You want to know how we get to Cheyenne Mountain when there are a million Zs in our way, right?"

"Yeah, I'd like to know that too," Cole says, looking at Commander Lee. "That truck of hers is not going to be able to get us through the herd. Not as far as we need to go."

"Who said anything about a truck?" Sister says. "Whubba whubba whubba whubba."

"I have no idea what the hell that noise means," Cole says. "Commander?"

"That is where we are going next," Commander Lee sighs. "Sister? Please? That noise is giving me a headache."

"Man, you guys really suck," Sister says. "Like suck hard. The suckiest. So much suck."

"We get it!" Stanford nearly shouts. "Holy crap, you are annoying."

"Now you finally know how it feels," Val says and gives Cole a high five.

"Ha freakin' ha," Stanford pouts.

———

Sister lets out such a long and loud string of curses that even the battle-hardened and foul-mouthed Mates have to wince. After several uncomfortable minutes, Sister finally calms down, her face flushed and her hand at her side, clutching her wound that she insists is not a problem no matter how many people try to tell her to go see Hamish ASAP.

"You said it would be ready," Sister says, her eyes burning with anger as she turns to Commander Lee. "Why isn't it ready?"

"I have had my best mechanics and engineers on it," Commander Lee says. "Structurally it is as sound as it was when it was first built. The engines are proving to be tougher than we thought. They weren't designed to use hemp oil as a fuel source. My mechanics are afraid we'll gum up the engines if we keep trying to start them with hemp oil."

"Well, yeah, you'll gum up the engines," Sister says. "That's why you have to cut the oil with kerosene. I told you that."

"The kerosene you gave us was at least a hundred years old," Commander Lee says. "We checked a sample and it won't ignite properly either. It's too weak. My mechanics—"

"Your mechanics are idiots who don't know shit about heli-copters!" Sister yells. She presses her hand to her side harder and winces, bending over slightly. "Son of a cocking bitch."

"This is a real helicopter?" Cole asks, staring at the huge machine before them. It fills half the warehouse that sits on the edge of the Stronghold. The rest of the warehouse is filled with worktables and a massive array of spare parts, both clean and covered in gunk and grease. "Are we riding in that?"

"Not if we don't have fuel," Sister snaps. "Jesus shit."

"Hamish is on the way," Val says. "I sent a Runner to get him when I saw you wince on the walk over."

"You did?" Sister asks, looking at Val. "But I didn't wince."

"Yes, you did," Val says. "We all saw it but didn't say anything."

"Huh," Sister responds. "I'm losing my touch."

She points at the helicopter, what was once called a Bell UH-1, or Huey, and stands up straight, a thin sheen of sweat on her forehead.

"Get those drums of kerosene and mix them fifty-fifty with the biodiesel," Sister orders. "It is not ideal and may still cause issues, but I can get us down to the Cheyenne Mountain entrance at least."

"What about getting us back?" Henshaw asks. "Or are we not coming back?"

"Ideally, you will come back, and before we have to close the Stronghold's doors," Commander Lee says.

"But the mission is priority, and we will do whatever it takes to complete that mission," Stanford says. "Right, Mother?"

"It's your job," Commander Lee replies.

"Yay for gainful employment," Stanford says.

"Better than latrine duty," Val says. "Ask my father."

"Right. Ask your father about how he feels when he's safe and cozy inside the new Stronghold while we're getting eaten to death by Zs and cannibals," Stanford replies. "Oh, wait, you won't be able to ask your father because you'll be down in Cheyenne Mountain playing genetic push button with the crazy lady here."

"You done?" Cole asks. "Because the rest of us are ready to take our duties seriously and do whatever it takes to keep our friends, neighbors, and families safe."

"Thanks for the guilt trip, Cole," Stanford says. "But I know why we're doing it. I'm just not happy about it."

"Shut up," Sister says. "All of you. Not one of you knows about sacrifice. Trust me on that one. You are all just children playing at adult games." She points a finger at Commander Lee. "You too, Maura Lee. Children. You were taught the military life, taught that the Teams are everything, but I don't think any of you shit fuckers really knows why. I do. We are getting in this chopper and flying down to Cheyenne Mountain to save the human race. Not just your friends and families, but the whole damn species! So I don't want to hear one more whiny word about not coming back! We either do or we don't! Get used to it!"

She sits down on the concrete, her ass *thunking* hard against the pockmarked surface.

"Ow," she whispers. "Where's that doctor?"

"Here!" Dr. Hamish Terlington shouts as he runs into the warehouse. "But I don't see why she couldn't... have... been... brought to... me..."

Hamish trails off as he sees the helicopter.

"Wow. Does it work?" he asks.

Sister shakes her head. "It will once it's fixed finally. Same with me, Doc. Now get over here and stitch me up. I got a whirly bird to fly."

"Whirly bird?" Henshaw whispers to Val. "I can barely understand this woman half the time. She's supposed to save the Stronghold?"

"No, we're supposed to save the Stronghold," Val says. "She's supposed to save us."

"How do you figure?" Henshaw asks.

"I don't know," Val says. "Gut feeling."

"Hope that gut is better than hers," Henshaw says, nodding toward Sister.

The woman is glaring at Hamish as he lifts her shirt and starts scolding her for not coming to see him right away.

———

"Do you think we get to see the real Stronghold?" Val asks as she and Stanford walk through the almost-deserted streets toward her house.

"I doubt it," Stanford says. "We have to be back to the helicopter within the hour. Mom gave us one chance to grab up whatever belongings we want taken inside. You know, in case we do come back."

He laughs sourly at the thought and shakes his head.

"You know your mom loves you, right?" Val says. "She's just in a hard position as commander and mother to a TL. She wants you to come back. Shit, Ford, she wants all of us to come back. But we're part of the Teams, and coming back isn't always an option. That's the life we live."

"Yeah. You keep telling yourself that," Stanford snorts.

They reach Val's house and stop.

"Oh," Val says. "Now I get it. Sorry. I'll leave you two to talk."

"Don't bother," Stanford says, his eyes locked onto the man sitting on Val's porch. "I'll help get your stuff so we can go to my apartment next and get my crap. Fuck this guy."

"Seriously, Ford?" Benji Chase says as Val and Stanford walk up the steps. "You're just going to toss me aside because we had a fight? Toss me aside when you know we may never see each other again?"

"You said it was over, asshole," Stanford snaps. "I didn't toss anyone aside. You did."

"That's bullshit and you know it," Benji replies. "You're just scared because I mentioned the L word."

"Lesbian?" Val asks, then cringes from the glares she receives. "I'll be inside. Out in about five minutes."

She walks through the door and is glad to leave the two men as they start snapping and shouting at each other.

"Nothing like two queers going at it on your own front porch," Collin says, sitting in a chair in the front room, a jar of clear liquid in his hand.

"I thought you were helping get people to the Stronghold," Val says. "But I can see something more important came up."

"Sheriff Marsh sent me home when I yelled at Mrs. Van Duyn for running over my toe with her cart," Collin says, lifting the jar and tipping it slightly in her direction. "Want a sip?"

"No, thanks," Val says. "I'm just going to get a box of stuff together I want you to take into the Stronghold. Some stuff from Mom and some of John's old things."

"Why?" Collin asks. "That's just junk. Won't help us survive."

"Maybe it isn't about just surviving anymore, Dad," Val says. "Maybe it's about remembering so that when future generations want to know who they are, where they came from, they will have some answers sitting in a box."

"Only answer I need is here in this jar," Collin says. "And Bullet has assured me we'll have enough of this to last for years. Between my cart, his cart, and a few others, we're using our space allotment to keep the party rolling, baby."

"Great," Val says. "I couldn't be prouder."

The shouting on the porch reaches a crescendo, then stops abruptly. Val hurries to the window, smiles, then turns away, shaking her head.

"They making out?" Collin asks.

"Like teenagers," Val says.

"You going to get a little piece from your doctor boy before you head out?" Collin asks. "Might ease the tension."

"Great," Val sighs and moves toward her bedroom. "The last bit of advice I get from my father is to go bone my boyfriend before being sent on a suicide mission. I have to wonder if humanity may not be better just dying off. Especially if you're going to have anything to do with its future."

"Cheers," Collin says and raises the jar again.

———

"Mates! Listen up!" Kevin Ross shouts from behind the armory cage. "All essential supplies have already been moved! What I have for you is ammunition, as much as you can carry, one ration kit each, one box of glow sticks each, one set of NVGs each, and four frags each. That is it." He motions to the almost-empty shelves behind him. "Everything else is gone, so do not ask."

"Rappel gear?" Cole asks. "We were told to get that."

"Rappel gear? Why?" Kevin asks.

"In case we have to drop from the helicopter fast without breaking our fucking legs," Stanford says. "You know, the little things."

"Right. Sorry. I forgot about the helicopter. Not something I'm used to. No rappel gear," Kevin says. "Because no one told me to hold that back. It is already crated and moved."

"Why?" Val asks. "Are people going to do some rappelling in the new Stronghold? Is it that big?"

"You have no idea," Kevin says.

"No, we don't," Diaz says. "Because we haven't seen it yet."

"You haven't?" Kevin asks. "Oh. Well, yes, it's that big. Several levels and sectors. It's almost as big inside as the Stronghold here outside."

"Lucky you," Henshaw says.

"What do you mean?" Kevin asks. "Lucky for all of us. Plenty of room for the residents we have now and any future generations. It's what the place was designed for."

"You don't know?" Stanford asks. "He doesn't know."

"I don't know what?" Kevin frowns. "If there is something about this mission I need to know, then tell me now. Supplies are limited, but I don't want to send you guys down there without enough gear."

"We probably aren't coming back," Cole says. "Commander Lee won't say it outright, but this is a one-way trip."

"Fuck me," Kevin says, which surprises many there, since he rarely cusses. He holds up a hand and then disappears into the gloom of the armory shelves. "Hold on!"

"Because we would go where?" Stanford calls after him.

They hear a lot of grunting and muttering then Kevin shows back up, a very heavy-looking box weighing down his arms.

"A little help, please," he says.

Diaz and Alastair move through the armory door and take the box from him, carrying it back out to the waiting and curious Mates.

"Those are something I cooked up after the Code Monkey attack," Kevin explains. "Inside are containers with concentrated phosphorous strapped to a detonator and a half pound of C4."

"Jesus, why would you make this shit?" Alastair says, stepping away from the box as Diaz opens it and picks up a wrapped pack with a wired button protruding from the center.

"You have to prime the detonator," Kevin explains. "Press the button twice and then hold it for two seconds. Once you let go, you have about thirty seconds before the charge builds and the bomb goes off."

"Thirty seconds?" Cole asks. "What kind of range does this thing have?"

"The C4 will take out anything within fifty meters," Kevin says. "But it's the phosphorous that does the real magic. That will fly for half a mile easy with that much force. It'll set anything it touches on fire."

"Why the fuck would you make these?" Alastair asks. "Thirty seconds is not enough time to drop this and get clear. If the blast doesn't rip us apart, then the phosphorous will eat right through us."

"You said this was a one-way mission," Kevin replies. "I made these bombs as a last-resort option. They're meant for volunteers to run into a herd and rip it apart from the inside."

"One-way bombs," Cole says. "Thanks, Kevin. These may come in handy."

"Really?" Alastair says. "Fuck."

"Gear up, people," Cole orders. "We'll take everything to the helicopter and then grab a couple hours shut eye before dawn hits and we're off. Check and double-check your kits. I do not want any surprises out in the field, am I understood?"

"What he said," Stanford says.

"Ditto," Henshaw says.

"I do not think she can fly this thing!" Hamish shouts as mechanics hurry to push the helicopter out of the warehouse and into the dawn-lit parking lot. "As a medical professional—"

"You have to get paid to be a professional," Stanford says. "Which you don't."

"None of us do," Diaz says.

"We get ration tickets," Alastair says. "That's the same, right? I'm unclear on the whole getting paid thing."

"Old world problems," Shep says.

"As a doctor, I am saying that this woman is not fit to fly,"

Hamish explains, glaring at the Mates. "The wound in her side is not healing as fast as she says it is. With every exertion, she is making it worse. I have cleaned it out and stitched it up, but one more fight and she could tear it wide open."

"I'll be flying, not fighting," Sister says, her hands on her hips, her eyes locked onto Hamish. "The fighting starts when I land."

"Exactly!" Hamish nearly shouts. "Then who will fly the helicopter back here? Not you, because you'll be dead."

"Jesus, he doesn't know either," Cole says, then shuts his mouth quickly as he sees the look on Val's face. "Shit. Sorry."

"I don't know what?" Hamish asks. No one responds as all eyes turn to Val. "I do not have much time, people. I have patients to move and supplies that still need packing. Will someone please tell me what I don't know?"

"That could take a while," Stanford says.

"Give me a minute?" Val asks, looking at Commander Lee. The woman nods. "Thank you."

Val takes Hamish by the arm and leads him out of earshot of the others. She puts her hands on his cheeks and pulls his face to hers, their lips parting. The kiss is long and passionate.

"Okay, that was nice, but what is going on, Val?" Hamish asks.

"We aren't coming back," Val states bluntly. "We have no idea what may be down there and the odds just aren't in our favor."

"What? No, you're coming back," Hamish says. "You have to. You're DTA. DTA comes back."

"We're just Mates now," Val says. "DTA, DTB, doesn't matter. We're all that is left of the Teams. Even if we survive and somehow make it back up here, you will probably have the doors closed by then. You'll have to or the Z herd will get inside."

"Then we open the doors back up," Hamish snaps. "It's not that hard to figure out."

"Doesn't work that way," Val says. "Once the doors close, they stay closed for a long time."

"What?" Hamish cries. "Commander Lee never said anything about the doors staying closed!"

"What do you mean?" Val asks.

"Everyone thinks this will be for a couple of months," Hamish says. "That we're going inside to wait out the herd. We've been told that the Teams are going to a hidden base that has weapons that will wipe out the Zs, once and for all. Once the area is clear, we get to come back outside. Sure, we'll have a lot of rebuilding to do when we emerge, but that's just some sweat and labor."

"Are you joking?" Val asks. "My god. No wonder everyone is packing up and moving without freaking out. I can't believe Aunt Maura lied to the whole Stronghold."

Val looks back at the group of Mates and the stoic Commander Lee standing next to them all. She shakes her head and looks back at her love.

"Don't tell her you know the truth," Val says. "You keep this to yourself until she makes the announcement. If word gets out then there will be panic. You know what happens when people panic."

"People get hurt," Hamish says. "I know. I'll stay quiet. But only because I'm a doctor and won't let folks freak out and hurt themselves or others."

"Thank you," Val says and kisses him again.

They stay that way for a while until someone clears a throat from directly behind them.

"Time to go," Commander Lee says.

"Yes, sir," Val says. She pries herself from Hamish's grip, then rushes back to her comrades.

"She told you," Commander Lee states.

"Let's not talk about it," Hamish says. "Ever."

"Fair enough," Commander Lee nods.

They walk closer and watch the Teams load up into the helicopter.

Sister climbs into the front and starts flipping switches. She looks over and gives Commander Lee a thumbs up, then takes a deep breath. She flips one last switch and the engines sputter, sputter, fire up, cough hard, sputter, and die.

"Maybe they aren't going anywhere," Hamish says, his voice sounding very relieved.

There is shouting and swearing from the helicopter as Sister slams her fists against the instrument panel over and over.

"Dammit, she's going to hurt herself," Hamish says.

The side cargo door slides open and Val, Diaz, Cole, and Stanford all jump out.

"What are you doing, Mates?" Commander Lee shouts. "This mission is not over."

"I have an idea," Val says. "I think I know what will help the fuel system."

The four Mates take off running toward the center of town.

Sister just glares out the side window at Commander Lee.

EIGHT

COME DIE WITH ME! COME
DIE, COME DIE AWAY!

The helicopter soars over the massive Z herd, the sound of its rotors barely blocking out the combined groans and moans from the ocean of undead below.

The Mates stare out the windows at the impossible size of the herd, their eyes wide and shocked despite their experiences in the wasteland.

Seated in the cargo area, all looking a little green in the gills, are Cole, Diaz, and Alastair from DTA. Stanford, Shep, Carlotta, Lang, and Tommy Bombs from DTB1 are across from them with Billy and Santiago from DTB2 and Henshaw from DTB4 wedged between.

Off to himself, looking a lot sicker than the others, his eyes closed and arm strapped to his side, sits Scotty Kurowski from DTB4. Henshaw keeps glancing at him, then back at Cole.

After a few minutes, she finally speaks up.

"As his TL, I'm not cool with this!" she shouts over the rotor noise. "He should be back with the others and tended to!"

"It was his choice!" Cole yells. "He wanted to go out like a Mate, not like some patient waiting to be put out of his misery! Hamish cleared him for twenty-four hours!"

"He can't fight!" Henshaw argues. "He's only good for bait or as a decoy!"

"Both of which we may need!" Stanford shouts, joining in. "None of us are getting out of this alive anyway!"

"Maybe!" Henshaw says. "*Maybe* not getting out alive!"

"Keep dreaming, TL!" Stanford laughs. "Just keep dreaming!"

Up front in the pilot's seat, Sister grips the steering stick and throttle, her body looking relaxed and comfortable for the first time since joining the Teams. In the co-pilot's seat sits Val, looking the complete opposite of relaxed and comfortable as her hands grip her seat, her knuckles nearly pure white.

"Nice of your dad to give up his hooch!" Sister says. Val doesn't respond. Sister grabs a headset sitting on the dash and tosses it at her. "Put those on!"

Val puts on the headset and gives Sister a questioning look.

"I said it was nice of your dad to give up his hooch," Sister repeats, her voice clear in Val's headset. "Very one-for-all of him."

"Yeah, he gave it up like a toddler gives up a cookie snatched right from his hands," Val says. "The hard part was getting the rest from Bullet without getting shot. I think Kevin would have been jealous to see the stash of guns Bullet had hidden close to his still. He had almost as much as the armory."

"So now the Stronghold has more guns and we have the right mixture of fuel," Sister says. "It all works out."

"Yeah, sure, it all works out," Val says.

"He'll be fine," Sister says. "Your Hamish. He'll be fine. If we don't make it back then he'll grieve like everyone else, be a Gloomy Gus for a few months, heal, and move on."

"Gee, great, I feel so much better now," Val says.

Sister laughs and shakes her head.

"What?" Val snaps. "You think this is funny?"

"I think you're all spoiled children who have no idea how good you've had it over these years," Sister says. "I've lost more family than you can ever know. Lovers, friends, sisters. All of them are dead. I've been alone for a very long time. You've at least gotten to be with people, to be loved, to be held, to be a human being for longer than a half hour."

"Longer than a half hour?" Val asks. "What does that mean?"

Sister flips a couple of switches and the helicopter levels out. She lets go of the controls and makes an okay sign with one hand. Then slips an index finger through the hole back and forth, back and forth.

"Oh, alright, alright, I get it. You can stop now," Val says.

Sister grabs the controls again and flips the switch back. The two women are silent for a couple minutes.

"Who the hell have you been having sex with?" Val blurts out. "It's the wasteland."

"A girl gets it when she can get it," Sister says. "A woman takes it when she wants it. I may be old, but I still got it where it counts. Bumping uglies isn't just for the young, Little Baptiste."

"Okay, enough, I really don't want to hear more," Val says, holding up a hand. "Seriously. Don't tell me more."

"Wasn't going to," Sister says. "I need to concentrate on flying anyway. All the fires below are creating thermal things. Thermal things suck."

"Thermal things?" Val asks.

The helicopter shudders and jerks to the left and Val nearly shrieks. There are a few shouts from the back, but Sister gets the helicopter straightened out and everyone calms down.

"Thermal things," Sister says. "Hot air that pushes up. I'm trying to fly between the fires, but there're too many."

Val looks out her window and agrees with Sister. Basically all of Denver is ablaze. Thick, black smoke rises like ethereal flowers blooming high into the sky. Sister does her best to dodge around the columns of smoke, but the wind is picking up and the gaps between the fires disappear with each gust.

Val tries not to panic when their visibility turns to zero for a couple of seconds, then returns as they push through the smoke. Sister has a wide grin on her face each time they come out on the other side. The grin slips when they shoot through a fourth column.

"What is it?" Val asks. "What's wrong?"

"Nothing," Sister says.

"Bullshit," Val says. "What did you see?"

"Nothing," Sister repeats.

Val looks out her window and down at the burning city. All she sees is sector after sector lost to quickly spreading flames. She cranes her neck to get a view of what they just passed and is about turn her head back when she sees it. The water tower.

"Fitzpatrick!" Val shouts. "She's still alive!"

"Yes, she is," Sister replies, coldly.

"We have to go back for her!" Val yells. "We can't leave her there!"

"We don't have time," Sister responds.

"Then we make time, dammit!" Val shouts. She yanks off the headphones, unbuckles, and scrambles into the cargo hold. "Cole! Fitzpatrick is alive down there! She was waving to us as we flew by!"

"What?" Cole shouts.

"I said that Fitzpatrick is alive!" Val says.

"I know what you said, I just don't believe it," Cole yells. "Is Sister turning around for her?"

"No!" Val shouts.

"Fuck," Cole grumbles. He unbuckles and pushes past Val. "Hey!"

"Hey, yourself!" Sister responds. "We're not going back!"

"Yes, we are!" Cole says. "We could use the extra Mate. This mission could come down to us having one more shooter with us! Don't tell me you don't know that!"

Sister turns her head and glares at Cole. He starts to get a little anxious that she's not looking out the windshield and at where she's flying, but the anxiety dissolves as she nods to him.

"Fine," she says. "We go back. She gets one chance to climb

aboard. If she can't cut it, then she won't be any good to us anyway. Deal?"

"Deal," Cole says.

"Cole!" Val shouts as she shoves past him and back to her seat. "We have to give her more than one chance! She doesn't know how to climb into this thing!"

"And we don't have time to teach her!" Cole says. "No arguments, Val! One shot and then we go! The mission is all that matters, or there is no point in all of our friends and family getting locked up for a couple centuries just for their descendants to emerge into a wasteland still full of Zs!"

"Exactly," Sister shouts. "Now buckle up, buttercup! Shit gonna get bumpy!"

Sister yanks on the stick and the helicopter banks to the right as she turns it around. Cole has to struggle not to fall over. Everyone has to struggle not to throw up.

———

On an intellectual level, Fitzpatrick knows what she's looking at. It's a helicopter. She also knows all of the faces that stare out at her from the cargo hold windows. She doesn't know the face of the pilot, though, and that worries her slightly.

On an emotional level, she is shitting bricks as the helicopter hovers closer and closer to the water tower. It gets almost level with her, sending the thousands of Zs below into a frenzied rage from the noise. The helicopter stops and waits, more than twenty yards from the railing she is gripping tightly with both hands.

"I can't make it!" Fitzpatrick yells, but her words are lost to the roar of the rotors. "Get closer!"

Whoever the pilot is, she shakes her head at Fitzpatrick, then points up. Fitzpatrick frowns, then turns and looks at the water tower itself. She realizes what the woman means and sprints to the small ladder that is bolted to the side of the tower, curving up over the top of the bulbous reservoir.

Fitzpatrick fights off the dizziness and fatigue that threatens to cut her climb short. She forces her hands to move one over the other. Every time she lets go of a rung and reaches for another, she isn't sure she'll be able to close her hand over the cold metal. But she pushes on, digging for those last reserves of energy every Mate keeps deep down inside.

The helicopter hovering above isn't helping. The rotor wash is like a huge weight pressing down on Fitzpatrick, threatening to tear her free and toss her out into the air. She glances up and has to immediately look back down as the air rushing at her nearly dries her eyes from their sockets. She blinks a few times, the dizziness as strong as ever, and keeps going.

When she reaches the top, Fitzpatrick scoots across the reservoir on her hands and knees, takes a deep breath, and looks up at the helicopter. The cargo door is open and several Mates are leaning out, motioning for her to get up and hurry. Their mouths are moving, but Fitzpatrick can't hear a thing over the roar of the turbine engines.

Slowly, Fitzpatrick stands up and moves inch by inch across the slick metal surface of the water tower reservoir. The condensation of the cold morning dew makes every step unbelievably treacherous. She can only shuffle along, afraid that if she picks up a foot she'll lose her balance to the dizziness and go tumbling over the side and into the waiting claws and hands of the Zs below.

She chuckles to herself, thinking that if she's lucky, she'll snap her neck before the things can start eating her.

The helicopter hovers before her, the closest skid wavering back and forth, only a few feet from the surface of the water tower. Fitzpatrick shuffles, shuffles, then reaches the skid. She holds her arms out and is instantly grabbed by several hands and pulled up to the open door of the cargo hold.

Her boots find purchase on the helicopter's skid and the machine starts to bank away from the water tower. She beams a grateful smile at the faces of Cole, Stanford, and Diaz. But the smile is quickly lost as the helicopter shudders and the engines begin to whine. Her boots slip and she panics, her nails clawing into the flesh on Cole's and Stanford's arms as Diaz tries to wrap his bulky arms around her back.

The helicopter shudders again and jolts to the right, dipping fast toward the ground. Fitzpatrick looks down and sees the herd rushing up to meet her before the helicopter's engines stabilize and the whine turns back to a steady thrum.

But even though she knows absolutely nothing about helicopters, Fitzpatrick can sense that something isn't right with the vehicle she desperately clings to. The helicopter shudders again and starts to slowly spin to the right. Fitzpatrick can see a wisp of black smoke coming from the tail section where a small hole suddenly appears.

A bullet hole.

She starts to yell at Cole, to warn him of what is happening, but she doesn't get the chance. A sharp pain hits her side and she screams. She tries to suck in a breath, but her lungs won't fill with air. Then she feels the warmth trickling down her skin and she glances down to see bright red blood pouring out of her stained uniform.

There's another sharp pain and her whole body goes limp. The pain goes away, and all Fitzpatrick can think about is why she can't feel her legs. Why she can't feel anything anymore. She struggles to control her neck and is barely able to angle her head up to look at the panicked Mates trying to pull her dead weight into the cargo hold.

They are all shouting at her, but Fitzpatrick has no idea what they're saying. If they're trying to tell her to hang on, then they are out of luck. She has no idea if she is hanging on or not. All feeling is gone from her neck down. She has a strange sensation of weightlessness, like she is floating in midair, but she knows that isn't true.

The Mates keep shouting, the helicopter keeps spinning, and then everything gets smaller and smaller.

"I'm falling," Fitzpatrick thinks to herself as the helicopter is lost from sight and all she can see is the world tumbling about her.

She laughs as the last thing she sees are the wide-open and hungry jaws of a thousand Zs. At least she knows she won't feel anything when she's being eaten.

———

"Find the fucker!" Sister yells at Val. "The shots came from our right!"

Val flips open the window on her side and shoves the barrel of her M-4 through. She hunts the area through her scope but sees nothing. No person, no shooter.

"Find the tallest building!" Sister yells.

"I know how to hunt for a sniper!" Val says. "So shut the fuck up!"

She searches, searches, searches, while the helicopter's engines whine louder and louder. Then she sees him. A rag-covered man on top of a burning building about half a mile away. He has a high-powered hunting rifle to his shoulder and his cheek resting against the stock.

It's a long shot, but Val doesn't even think of the distance as she centers her scope and squeezes the trigger. The man's cheek is no longer resting against the stock as half his head evaporates. A bloody mist lifting high into the morning air. She sees the flash of the rifle's muzzle and pulls her carbine away, instinctively ducking.

The helicopter shudders and Sister lets out another long stream of curses, many of which Val has never heard as the woman struggles to maintain control.

"You get him?" Sister shouts. "Fucking tell me you got him!"

"I got him," Val says. She turns around and sees the looks on everyone's faces.

"I can hold it steady for another minute so they can get her inside," Sister says. "But no longer. We're going to be lucky to make it to Cheyenne at all."

"Don't bother," Val says. "Just go."

"What? Why?" Sister asks, looking over at Val.

"She didn't make it inside," Val replies. She points out the windshield. "Better hurry. The engines don't sound good."

"One is close to shutting down," Sister says. "The other is fine. It's why I picked a twin turbine chopper to be housed at the Stronghold. I knew if we needed it then we'd need every advantage possible."

Val glances sideways at the woman, again perplexed at how all of a sudden the crazy old lady sounds as clear and confident as any normal person, not like the wasteland nut she tries to pretend to be.

"What?" Sister asks, looking over at Val. She gets the helicopter back on course and frowns. "Something to say, Little Baptiste?"

"Stop calling me that," Val says.

"No," Sister says. "I used to call someone I knew very well that name…"

Val has no idea how to reply to that statement, so she doesn't. She just stares out the windshield and watches as they once again maneuver through the columns of black smoke.

———

The rest of the ride is nothing but silence from the Mates and from Sister. The damaged engine, on the other hand, is far from silent. It shrieks with a piercing noise that threatens to burst eardrums. Sister finally makes the decision to shut it down and switch all power through the remaining engine. Despite the rotor noise still being considerable, there is an almost audible gasp of relief from everyone inside.

"We tried," Sister says finally as she banks the helicopter west, taking it around the sharp curve of a mountain. "We tried."

"Yeah," Val says. "I just hope she didn't suffer."

"We all suffer," Sister says. "It's why we keep going. The ones who don't suffer are the ones who quit."

"I just mean I hope she didn't feel—"

"I know what you meant," Sister says. "But there's no way to know, so push it from your head. Move on. Time to get ready for the mission."

"How can you be so callous about this shit?" Val asks. "How can you be so cold?"

Sister shrugs. "I have to be. People used to die all the time pre-Z. No different now. Our time here isn't permanent. Not even for me."

"What the fuck does that mean? Not even for you?" Val snaps. "Why would it be different for you?"

"Because I'm different," Sister responds, giving Val a brief look of amusement. "Duh."

"I swear, before I die, I'm getting answers out of your ass," Val says.

"Answers come from my mouth, not my ass," Sister says. "Shit comes from my ass."

"Sounds the same to me," Val says. "How much longer until we're there?"

"We're here right now," Sister says, pointing at the mountainside in front of them. "See that clear space on that hill? That's where I'll put us down. We'll have a mile to hike to get to the entrance."

"A mile? Can't we get closer?" Val asks.

"Sure, if we want to alert everyone we're coming," Sister says. "Better to draw them away from the facility then sneak our way in."

"What? Who would we be alerting?" Val asks. "Who is still at this facility?"

"No one that I know of," Sister says as she carefully lands the helicopter.

Cole leans forward from the cargo hold and grabs Sister by the shoulder. He quickly lets go at the look she gives him.

"Why aren't we closer?" Cole asks.

"I was just asking her the same thing," Val says.

"I left the front door open," Sister says.

"You what?" Cole and Val ask at the same time.

The engine completely powers down and Sister takes her headset off, setting it on the dash. She turns and looks directly at Cole and says slowly, "I left the front door open. It was a huge pain in the ass to activate. I didn't want to have to take the time to do it all over again. So I left it open."

"That means there could be Zs inside," Cole says. "Or Code Monkeys."

"The Code Monkeys know how to get inside on their own," Sister says. "I haven't figured out how, but the little shits do. As for Zs?" She shrugs. "That's life, Mate Wright. Zs be everywhere, yo."

"You are insane," Cole stutters before he pushes away and starts shouting orders to the others.

"Come on," Sister says, opening her door. "I'm going to show you why leaving the door open doesn't matter."

"Great," Val replies as she opens her own door and jumps out of the helicopter onto shaky legs.

———

Hidden on a short rocky overhang, the Mates stare down at the chain-link compound that surrounds the wide opening in the side of Cheyenne Mountain to the former NORAD facility beyond. Within the chain-link compound are at least a hundred Zs, all milling about, shuffling from one part of the fence to another, the rusted chain link holding together enough to spring them away.

"There," Sister says. "That's why."

"I don't get it," Stanford says.

"Those came from inside, didn't they?" Cole asks.

"Yep," Sister responds. "And there could be plenty more still in there wandering the concrete corridors. Leaving the doors open means that at least some came outside for a look around."

She points to a half-collapsed gate where several Zs are snagged and stuck, their arms waving about, legs pumping but not taking them anywhere.

"If we can get that unblocked and make a little noise, then we'll have nothing but clear skies for miles," Sister says.

"What?" Diaz asks.

"We can draw them off so we can get in easier," Val says.

"Exactly," Sister agrees. "Couldn't have said it better myself. Like, really. I obviously couldn't."

The Mates stare at her for a split second, then shake it off and turn around to huddle up.

"Getting them out of there shouldn't be a problem," Cole says. "There are enough to break through that gate if they all press on it at once."

"But the noise is the problem," Stanford says. "To get them to come to the gate, we'll have to make enough noise to get their attention. That means other Zs in the area will hear and we could end up with part of the herd heading this way."

"That would be bad," Alastair says.

Scotty moans quietly and everyone glances at him, but no one's eyes linger too long.

"So, we need a noise to draw the ones in the compound to the gate, the ones at the gate through the gate, and any others that might hear us to go in a different direction than here," Henshaw says. "That's not going to be easy. The noise will need to be mobile."

"If it was night, we could use flares," Shep says.

"But it's not night," Tommy Bombs says. "What about demolitions?"

"Set off one of the phosphorous bombs?" Cole asks. "Too short. It would make a big bang, but we'll risk the Zs getting distracted before they leave or get far enough away. Not to mention that the person setting it off won't get away in time."

"I'll do it," Scotty says so low it sounds like another moan.

"We have guns," Val says. "One of us can fire a shot, draw them to the gate until they break through, then run like hell while still firing."

"Then we're down a man," Stanford says. "And that person is fucked."

"I said I'll do it," Scotty grunts. His face is covered in sweat and he is shaking hard. He clutches his arm to his chest and stares at the others with red-rimmed eyes and a distant, defeated look. His whites are bloodshot and his skin has a greenish tint to it. "I'll do it."

"I don't know," Cole says. "You don't look so—"

"I said I'll do it," Scotty snaps. "I don't have twenty-four hours. I have maybe twenty-four minutes before I go down hard and then come back up hungry. This is why you brought me, for something like this."

He starts stripping off his gear, but Cole holds out a hand.

"Scotty, man, let's talk this out," Cole says. "We may need you for something else."

"Anything else can be worked out inside the facility," Scotty says. "That's where you all need to be. I can draw them off and keep them away long enough for you to get in there and shut the doors. Once I know you're good, then I'll take care of myself."

He has stripped himself down to just his t-shirt and pants. Every bit of equipment is lying on the ground. Except for his 9mm. He looks at it and nods his head.

"I can move fast enough to stay ahead of them," Scotty says. "When you are inside, fire one single shot. I'll fire two right away so your shot doesn't turn them around. I'll make sure I leave a round for me. It's the only way, Cole. You know that."

"Yeah, I know," Cole admits. "It just sucks balls."

"Big hairy balls," Sister says. "And stinky. Hairy, stinky balls."

Scotty gives her a grin and shakes his head. "I will miss finding out what happens next."

"We complete the mission," Val says. "That's what happens next."

"Promise?" Scotty asks.

Everyone gives him a nod while Val stands and says, "Yes. We promise."

She hugs him tight and she can feel the fever burning under his clothes. He's like a wood stove fully loaded.

"Time to go," Scotty says, gently pushing Val away. "You're smelling good. Not in a sexy way, but in a make-my-stomach-rumble way."

"Then get the fuck gone," Stanford says. He stands and salutes. "You'll be remembered as a hero, Mate Scotty Kurowski."

They all stand and salute, each saying his name with respect and reverence.

"Jesus, I should sacrifice myself more often," Scotty says. He looks at the 9mm and then smiles. "Give me a few minutes to get in place. Don't waste any time. As soon as you see a break, go for it."

"Will do," Cole says.

Scotty clambers down from the overhang and starts walking toward the gate. Once the Zs notice him, he begins to wave his hands over his head. The moans and groans from the Zs make him hesitate briefly, but he overcomes quickly and keeps moving until he is only a few feet from the collapsed gate.

The Zs begin to push at the chain link, their bodies almost melding with the metal. They shove and reach and growl and hiss, but the gate doesn't move much.

Scotty tucks his pistol into the back of his pants and grabs onto the edge of the gate closest to him. A Z takes a swipe but misses by a good foot. Scotty doesn't even flinch at the attempted attack. He digs his heels into the dirt and pulls, pulls, pulls. The gate comes free from its last hinge and Scotty falls hard onto his ass, his pistol popping free and skidding a few feet away.

The Zs come for him, walking over the fallen chain link gate, their claws and mouths open, ready, hungry. Scotty scrambles to his feet and reaches back, but his pistol isn't there. He spins about and sees it. But not before a loud growl gets his attention.

From the back of the pack of Zs, what used to be a woman in a tattered and moldy uniform comes running. She shoves the other Zs out of the way to get to Scotty first. The man panics and runs as fast as his sick body will let him, straight for the 9mm.

The running Z is almost to him, only a few feet away, when a shot cracks and she falls to the ground, becoming a useless pile of bones and rags. Scotty turns and looks up, sees Stanford giving him a thumbs up, then grabs his 9mm and fires a round into the air.

He walks backward for a few yards and fires another round in the air. The Zs in the compound start to move in his direction, many using the natural path of the fence line to direct them to the open gate. Once free and on the open road, they shamble as quickly as their rotted legs will carry them, the promise of a fresh meal only a few yards away.

The Mates watch Scotty until he is around a bend and lost from sight. They can't help but flinch when he fires the first round where they can't see him. It takes about twenty minutes, but soon all of the Zs have filtered out of the compound and are on the road moving toward the sound of the now far-off gunfire.

"That's ten rounds," Henshaw says. "We better hurry so he has three left."

The Mates rush down from the overhang, using their blades and sharpened collapsible batons to put down the few stragglers that just couldn't get it together enough to follow the crowd.

"Always the rebels left behind," Stanford says as he jams his knife through the temple of a tall, bone-thin man dressed in the remnants of an MP's uniform.

"You mean the slackers," Cole says, dispatching a couple of Zs that look like they may have been cooks, their whites long since stained to a deep brown by their bodily fluids. "Only you would call them rebels."

"Only you would call them slackers," Stanford says.

"And only me would kill them without having to whip my dick out and show it to everyone," Val says as she stabs three Zs in a row, kicking their bodies aside as she follows Sister up the winding access road to the main doors of the facility. "Come on, boys. Grown-up time."

"You know, we're both TLs, Val," Stanford says. "You should talk to us with more respect. I expect a sir out of you from now on."

"Teams don't exist anymore, Ford," Val says. "We're all just doomed Mates now."

"Awesome," Alastair says as he stabs a Z, then shoves it against another one to give him time to yank his baton free. He stabs the second one and flicks the gore from the tip. "The doomed part really helps the situation."

"Telling it like it is," Val laughs.

"Preach it, sister," Sister says, her hands in the air. "Hallelujah."

They arrive at the doors to the facility and everyone stops except for Sister. After a couple seconds, she realizes no one is following and she spins about.

"Hello? We have to go inside, ya know," she says.

"You said doors," Cole says. "These are some big doors."

They stare at the opening, which is at least one hundred and fifty feet high and just as wide. The doors stand open, pushed against the massive walls outside the facility, each at least ten feet thick with recessed round bars in their middles. Corresponding holes are set between the bars, showing everyone that when the Cheyenne Mountain facility is locked down, it stays locked down.

"How did you get these open?" Cole asks.

"I had the code," Sister says.

There are few moans that echo to them from inside and Sister taps her foot impatiently.

"Are we doing this? Yes or no?" she asks.

"Yes," Cole says and marches toward her, his M-4 up.

He fires a shot into the air. Everyone waits a minute, then they hear Scotty fire two shots, one after the other. Then a third shot only a second later.

"Shit," Cole says. "He must have gotten trapped. We better hurry our asses inside."

"Good plan, genius," Sister says. "Y'all coming?"

Cole rushes up to her and inside the facility. The rest follow behind him and they are quickly swallowed whole by the mountainside.

———

Diaz drops a Z with a shot from his carbine then turns and drops a second one.

"I thought the place was going to be cleared out!" Diaz shouts as he fires a third time. "This is not cleared out!"

"How much farther to go?" Shep yells as he drops his third Z. He steps back from a fourth that almost grabs him and kicks the thing in the knee, shattering its leg and sending it falling to the ground. One stomp and it is silenced. "We've been walking for at least a mile now."

Lucky for the Mates, the huge concrete tunnel they are in has lights strung along the walls and ceiling. Only every third or fourth bulb works, but it's enough to see and fight by.

"About four more miles," Sister says as she snaps a Z's neck and throws it into two more coming for her.

She leaps into the air and breaks one's skull open. When she comes down, she goes into a roll and comes up with her shoulder buried in the third's belly. She lifts it off the ground and rams it into the wall, crushing it into a useless pile of undead flesh and splintered bones. It hisses at her, but that's about the only part of it that still works.

A stomp from her boot heel and the thing stops moving.

"Did you say four miles?" Cole asks, having shot five Zs and elbowed another hard enough its brains shot out its ear. It helped that half its skull was already hanging against its neck, barely connected by a couple threads of flesh. "Four?"

"Yep," Sister says, wiping her boot heel against the concrete ground. "They weren't fucking around when they wanted to secure a place. Five miles in and then another set of doors just like the ones at the main entrance."

"Are those open too?" Val asks.

"Sure are, little lady," Sister says in a bad cowpoke voice. "Wide open so the cattle can roam free."

"You are so fucked up," Stanford says. "Let's keep moving. Four miles is not a fun stretch."

"At least you don't have to deal with the trip wires and other booby traps the Code Monkeys set up," Sisters says. "You're welcome."

"We're making a lot of noise," Henshaw says. "When can we close the outer doors?"

"Not from inside the control room," Sister says. "Control lines to the exterior doors rotted out a long time ago."

"Where the hell is this place getting its power from?" Alastair asks, wiping gore from his vest. "No way it can be running off of old fuel."

"Geothermal generator," Sister says. She's met with a few blank stares. "The Earth's energy. They used to drill deep, deep holes down into the earth and use the natural heat to generate electricity via a bunch of pipes and machines and shit that goes vroom."

"She sounded intelligent for a second until the shit that goes vroom part," Stanford says.

"We'll see how intelligent you sound talking through a mouth without teeth," Sister sighs. "You can really be a rude jerk, Stanford Lee. Fucking knock it off."

"Damn!" Diaz laughs and is joined by almost everyone. "She put you down, dude!"

They keep walking for a couple miles, all thankful they only run into a stray Z here and there.

It's only a few more minutes before Tommy Bombs holds up a hand. "Hey? You hear that?"

Everyone stops and listens.

"Zs?" Shep asks, his voice low so it doesn't echo in the tunnel. "Probably just more stragglers."

"No, no, it's not footsteps or anything like that," Tommy Bombs says. "It sounds like machinery."

They listen, but except for a couple of moans far, far behind them, they hear nothing.

"Never mind," Tommy Bombs says, pointing at his ears. "Years of working with explosives means my ears are shit."

"I haven't found that to be true," Stanford says. "Stay alert, TB. You hear anything else, let us know ASAP."

"Will do, TL," Tommy Bombs replies, obviously happy that Stanford gave him a compliment.

"Not too many times," Alastair says as he and Diaz pick up the crate with the phosphorous bombs. "This thing gets heavier every time we fucking stop."

"That was nice of you," Val whispers as she sidles up to her cousin.

"I know how to work with my people, Val," Stanford says. "I'm not the rude jerk everyone always thinks I am."

"No, that's really Cole," Val snickers. "Sister got it wrong."

"I can hear you," Cole calls back from his position next to Sister.

They get another half mile before Tommy Bombs holds his hand up once more. "You guys can't hear that?"

This time they do, and everyone turns in circles, all trying to pinpoint the direction of the noise. Alastair and Diaz swear under their breath as they set the crate down yet again.

"It's coming from ahead," Cole says. "Maybe some Zs banging around in the facility?"

"Zs in the facility," Sister mutters, then her eyes go wide. "No! It's not Zs! Shit!"

She takes off running and is gone from sight as she sprints around a bend in the tunnel.

"God dammit!" Cole yells as he takes off after the woman.

Everyone else moves as fast as they can, hurrying to keep up with Cole and Sister. They jog for a half mile and then come face to face with the interior facility doors. Which are shut tight. Several red lights spin above the doors, bathing the tunnel in a revolving, bloody glow.

"No! No, no, no!" Sister yells as she pounds her fists against the closed doors. "Those shit fuckers! Those lousy, son of a bitch, shit fuckers! Why did they close the doors? There was no need to close the doors!"

"Who are the shit fuckers we're mad at?" Stanford asks.

"Code Monkeys," Sister says. "They're already here and heard us coming. But they wouldn't need to close the doors. Code Monkeys fight. They kill. They'd love it for us to walk inside into an ambush."

"Maybe it isn't Code Monkeys," Cole suggests. "Maybe someone else got in there."

"Do you need a code to close the doors?" Val asks.

"No," Sister says. "In an emergency, anyone can close them. Just slam a hand on a button and shut they go."

"Okay, so if Code Monkeys wouldn't close it, then who did?" Henshaw asks.

"Cannies," Sister snarls, her shoulders slumping. "Fucking cannies, of course."

"Or crazies," Shep says. "Could be ordinary wasteland crazies that stumbled upon this place and found the doors wide open."

"Nope," Sister says. "It's cannies. I know it is. They found a road and followed it because cannies do that. They follow roads, because roads mean people and people mean food."

"Yeah, we know how the whole canny thing works," Stanford says. "But how can you be sure it's cannies?"

"Because I can smell them now," Sister says. She raises her nose and takes a long sniff. "Yeah. It's cannies. Motherfucking cannies."

"Hey, guys," Alastair calls from behind them all.

"Just set the crate down, Al," Cole says without turning around. "We're going to be here a while."

"Yeah, we left the crate back there," Diaz says. "We brought something else."

"What?" Cole asks and everyone turns around.

Alastair and Diaz are on their knees, completely stripped of all weapons and equipment. Standing behind them, with blades to their necks, is a row of eyeless people.

"See," Sister says. "Those're the damn Code Monkeys."

From the line of Code Monkeys, Skye steps forward. She lifts a long blade and points it directly at Sister.

"Nice coat," Sister glares.

"Put your weapons down," Skye orders.

"Yeah, probably not going to happen," Cole says, his M-4 trained on her.

All of the Mates have their carbines up and pointed at the Code Monkeys.

"There are six of you and eleven of us," Cole says. "We have guns, you don't."

"We don't need guns," Skye says. "We have proven that before."

"They really don't need guns," Sister says.

"I know. I've seen what they can do," Cole says. "I watched them kill my friends and neighbors. Time for that debt to be repaid."

"Hold on," Sister says. "If they wanted to fight then they would have killed Alastair and Diaz. They didn't." She looks at Skye. "What do you want?"

"Answers," Skye says.

"That's all? Because I want like three days to soak in a hot tub and drink wine and eat chocolate," Sister says. "I miss wine and chocolate."

"What the hell is she talking about?" Val asks Stanford.

"No clue," Stanford replies.

"Okay, enough daydreams," Sister says. "You want answers, Skye? Then that means you have questions. Lay them on me."

"You gave us the rest of the codes. Why?" Skye asks.

"Huh? What do you mean?" Sister replies, but she sounds less than sincere. "You took my coat, Skye. I had them sewn into the sleeve. I didn't exactly give them to you."

"You wanted us to find them. Why?" Skye asks.

Sister starts to protest, then shrugs. "Oh, fuck it. Yeah, I gave them to you. You were supposed to use them to prep the launch sequences so all I had to do was come here with the second genetic match and press the damn button."

"You are not part of the way," Skye says. "Why do you consort with a Team, yet still want to bring about the end to everything?"

"Who said I want to bring about the end of everything?" Sister responds. "I just want to nuke the country, that's all. Is that so wrong?"

"When you say it that way, it is," Stanford whispers.

"Shut up," Val mutters.

"Valencia Baptiste," Skye says. "Your mother was a strong fighter. She could have been one of us if she was born into the right family."

"I don't think so," Val says.

"Let my guys go," Cole says. "No need to hurt them. You let them go and there's no need for us to hurt you."

"In this shit, we're on the same side," Sister says. "So everybody chill the fuck out."

"I don't know about that," Skye says. "You still have some convincing to do."

"Listen, Skye, sugar," Sister says. "There are fucking cannies inside the facility doing who the fuck knows what to all the equipment. The longer they're in there, the longer they screw things up.

I say we call a truce and kick their asses, then we can sit down and figure out where we stand with each other."

Skye says nothing. None of the Code Monkeys lower their blades, especially the blades being held to Alastair and Diaz's throats.

"Skye? Hello?" Sister says.

"Perhaps," Skye says finally. "But you must follow us."

"Where to?" Cole asks.

"To the other entrance," Skye replies. "Our entrance."

"We can do that," Sister says. "Uh, where is your entrance? Because I have been having a shit fuck of a time trying to find it."

"Back the other way," Skye says. "Outside."

"Through the herd?" Sister asks.

"Through the herd," Skye replies, smiling like a psychotic toddler who just killed her nanny for a candy bar.

"Yeah," Sister sighs. "I was afraid of that."

NINE
DOWN THE RABID HOLE

"It's in the middle of that?" Cole asks, pointing from the hillside down at the herd of hundreds of thousands of Zs that fill Peterson Air Force Base. "How the fuck are we supposed to get through that shit to get to your secret entrance?"

"Damn, they took this place down fast," Diaz says. "What the hell?"

"There's a connecting tunnel!" Sister nearly shouts as she slaps her forehead. "Duh. That's how you have been getting into the Cheyenne facility without me being able to figure it out."

Skye tilts her head and smiles.

"We prefer the dark," Skye says. "You should have guessed. *Sister.*"

Sister glares hard in Skye's direction, even though the eyeless woman cannot see her.

"How did so many get inside the fence line?" Val asks. "You had this place pretty secure."

"It is impossible to stop nature," Skye says. "The will of the Earth is not something one can stop with a fence."

"I don't think the Earth has anything to do with this crap," Stanford says. "Hell might. But not the Earth."

"Cole, we can't stand here forever," Henshaw warns.

"She's right," Lang says. "We have company."

Everyone except the Code Monkeys turn around to see a long line of Zs marching their way. They have split off from the main herd, which is less than a quarter mile from the hill they stand on and twists around the landscape to fill the AFB. Through sheer determination, and some uncanny guidance from the Code Monkeys, the Mates were able to find a narrow avenue of semi-safe passage and make it this far.

That semi-safe passage is gone.

"We're surrounded, TL," Tommy Bombs says to Stanford, a pair of binoculars to his eyes. He lowers them and shakes his head. "We can't get back to Cheyenne if we want to."

"Then you people better be on the fucking level," Cole says, pointing at Skye. He looks at his finger, at her eyeless sockets, back at his finger, and lowers it. "If this is a trap, then we plan on taking as many of you down as possible."

"If it was a trap, TL Wright, then you would be dead," Skye sighs. "You are one tedious man. And pointing is rude."

Cole frowns, then shakes his head. "Whatever. How do we get through that to your hatch?"

"You were watching us," Skye says and grins. "That means you have promise. We did not detect your observation. Perhaps you won't die as quickly as I thought."

Cole starts to raise his weapon, but Sister places a hand on his arm and shakes her head.

"She's shit fucking with you," Sister says. "Messing with your head to see how you hold up. Code Monkeys are head-messers. It's what they do."

"Let's cut the psychological warfare bullshit, okay?" Stanford snaps. "I've dealt with that shit my whole life. How do we get through that herd and to your fucking hatch so we can find your secret tunnel, sneak back into the Cheyenne facility, and kill some cannies?"

"Then press a button and blow up the world," Val says. "Don't forget that part, Ford."

"Yeah, that part too," Stanford says. "Whee."

"Just this country," Sister says. "Not the world."

"Not the world," Skye echoes.

"What the fuck does that mean?" Stanford asks.

"Never mind," Sister says. "Skye? Hit us with your plan."

"It's not a difficult plan," Skye says. "We walk through them."

"Really?" Cole asks and laughs.

"Guys," Henshaw warns. "We don't have time to talk."

Lang, Shep, Carlotta, Diaz, and Santiago all turn and take a knee, their carbines trained on the line of Zs encroaching on their position.

"TL, we need to go," Diaz says.

"They will accept you when you accept them," Skye says. "We know the way. We are born into the way. You cannot learn it in time, but you can take what you know and use it."

"What the hell does that mean?" Alastair asks.

"Be the zombie," Sister says. "*Be the zombie.*"

———

The stink of the smeared guts and gore that covers Val's uniform almost makes her vomit. With every step she takes, her shifting body pumps more of the stench up to her face, wafting the putrid odor right into her nostrils. She takes a deep breath and holds it.

But even taking that breath exposes her.

A hundred heads turn her direction as she and the rest of the Mates slowly shamble their way through the thousands upon thousands of Zs that fill the Peterson AFB grounds.

A firm hand presses against Val's back, keeping her moving when her instinct is to freeze at the attention the Zs are giving her. A hard shove makes her stumble but she recovers quickly, turning the stumble into a stutter step then back into a shamble. She turns her head, imitating the Zs that have focused on her, and moans. When she turns back, the Zs have shifted their attention from her and over to the huge bonfire that crackles on the hill above the base.

The light, the sound, the movement of the flames brings the Zs to it like undead moths finding a porch light for the first time in decades. Slowly, as only a mass the size of the herd can move, the Zs change directions from going further into the base to pushing toward the side fence line and the lure of the blaze.

While the herd alters its course, the Mates and Code Monkeys stick to the illusion of a rambling movement through the undead, cutting diagonally toward a small metal hut. They cannot take a straight route without drawing attention, so the Code Monkeys lead the mates on a zigzag course that cuts around long-forgotten and rusting jet engines and broken machinery. They loop and double back, go one way, then turn abruptly another way as the herd continues to shift.

Finally, after what seems like a hundred years, the group reaches the edge of the herd, a thin spot where only a few dozen Zs mill about, cut off from the herd and trapped by the piles of debris they stumbled into.

"We move quickly," Skye says.

Her voice draws hisses and groans from the Zs, but those noises are silenced almost as fast as they are produced. The Code Monkeys move from Z to Z, piercing skulls and stabbing brains with a speed and rhythm that would make any Mate jealous, especially since they do it all without eyes.

When the area is mostly clear of the undead, one of the Code Monkeys pushes on a specific pile of debris and opens the hatch that leads down through the broken tarmac and into the dark underneath the former AFB.

"Now," Skye orders. "We have only minutes to get below."

Cole looks at Stanford. Stanford looks at Val. Val looks at Sister. Sister shrugs and points at the hatch.

"I've already been down there," she says. "Your turn."

"In," Cole orders the Mates as he drops to one knee and takes a defensive position, his M-4 pointed back toward the way they came.

"Do not fire your weapon," Skye says. "It will bring the fast ones."

"Yeah, yeah, just go down your hole," Cole says. "Diaz, Alastair, Santiago, Chase. You stay up here with me while the rest go down. Once we have the all clear, we'll follow."

"You are being foolish," Skye says. "Get below now or you risk being overtaken. A part of the herd has already begun to move our way again."

"How does she know that?" Diaz asks, kneeling next to Cole.

"How do they know anything?" Cole replies.

"Go," Sister orders to the Mates who aren't guarding the position. "Then the Code Monkeys." She looks at Skye. "Have you thought of changing that name? I do not think it means what you think it means."

"We are the chosen," Skye almost snarls. "Our name is a mark of honor and—"

"Right, yeah, sorry, my bad," Sister says. "I shouldn't have brought it up. Mates? Get your asses down the hole."

"I'll go first," Val says and slings her carbine. She hooks a leg over the lip of the hatch and moves quickly down the ladder and into the dark. "I'm down."

There's a clang from above her and Shep follows right behind. Val moves out of the way and makes room for him, then Carlotta, Tommy Bombs, Henshaw, Lang, and finally Stanford.

"Damn," Stanford says. "Dark as hell down here. NVGs, Mates."

Hands move to belts and night vision goggles are unclasped, then pulled down over faces and eyes.

The tunnel they all stand in lights up in greens and grays, broken only by black shadows and the streaky tracers the goggles produce when a head turns too quickly. Which all of their heads do as the Mates realize they are not alone.

"Excuse us," Skye says as she and her Code Monkeys climb down the ladder. "Make room."

"How?" Stanford snaps, his hand on his M-4, ready to bring it up. "We're a little crowded down here."

"I was speaking to my people," Skye says. "Make room and stand down. We are using the Mates to our advantage, brothers and sisters."

"Someone call my name?" Sister asks as she follows everyone down the ladder. She looks around and nods. "Is this a party? How nice. Will there be cake? I miss cake. I miss wine and chocolate and cake. Chocolate cake! Oh, man, chocolate cake was the best!"

"You know we had cake back at the Stronghold, right?" Val says.

"That's not cake," Sister says. "Not real cake. That's cake-like. Just not the same."

"Make room for the Mates," Skye orders. "We are taking them through the sacred passage and into the cathedral."

There are several gasps and more than a few angry grunts at the news.

"They are here to bring about the end with us, brothers and sisters," Skye says. "We welcome the help, since they bring the blood of the chosen to unlock the gates to eternity."

"DNA and all that shit," Sister says. She looks up at the hatch above and is about to call out for the others, but stops when she hears the gunfire erupt. The Mates rush the ladder, but she blocks their way. "No. They can handle it and follow. We need to keep going."

"You don't give orders," Stanford says.

"Not an order," Sister replies. "We have a mission. *You* have a mission. Cole and the others are fighting up top so we can complete the mission. It's what Mates do."

Stanford starts to argue again, but Val grabs him and yanks him away from Sister.

"Come on," Val says. "We have to go or those cannies can do damage that we can't repair."

"She's right," Skye says. "Your comrades are well trained. I will leave two guides here to bring them to us after they have secured the area."

"What if they can't secure the area?" Stanford snaps.

"Do I need to answer that question?" Skye replies. "Come. We must go to the sacred passage."

Sister snickers and all heads turn to her, eyeless and those with NVGs.

"Sorry," Sister says. "Sacred passage just sounds dirty. Doesn't it sound dirty?"

———

Cole whips his M-4 to the right, fires a burst of six rounds, then whips it back to the left and fires another six, dropping only eight Zs, a fraction of the number coming at them.

"TL!" Diaz shouts. "We're gonna be toast in like six seconds!"

"Alastair! Santiago!" Cole yells. "In the hatch now!"

"Come on, Cole!" Alastair shouts. "I'm not leaving you up here!"

"Go!" Cole orders.

Santiago pulls at Alastair's shoulder and turns to the hatch. His way is blocked by three Zs, mouths open, rotten teeth ready for flesh.

"Shit!" Santiago yells and opens fire with his M-4, taking one of the Zs out at the legs. It collapses against a second Z and the two tumble to the ground.

That leaves one Z. It throws itself at Santiago with a speed the Mate isn't prepared for. He fires his carbine until it is empty, ripping open the Z's belly, spilling rotten intestines and organs down onto his boots.

The Z goes for Santiago's throat, undeterred by its guts dangling from its abdomen. Santiago gets an arm up to block the thing and its teeth clamp down hard, chewing and sawing side to side in order to rip through the protective sleeve of Santiago's uniform.

Alastair moves fast and places the barrel of his carbine against the Z's temple, pulls the trigger, and yanks the thing from Santiago's arm.

"Thanks," Santiago gasps. "That was close."

"Get in," Alastair says and points at the hatch.

Just before a Z leaps onto his back and rips into his neck.

Alastair screams and bats at the undead monster, trying to pry it loose, but the Z won't let go, its jaw locked tight. Santiago sends two rounds into the Z's forehead and the monster goes slack.

Collapsing hard under the dead weight of the silenced Z, Alastair's head slams into the broken tarmac. He tries to push up onto his hands and knees, but blood flows so fast from his neck wound that he can't gather the strength. Santiago rushes over and pushes the dead Z off, then takes a couple of steps back.

"Al?" Cole yells, his back to them. "What's going on?"

Cole can't turn around and look without risking being overrun by the Zs that swarm towards them and the hatch.

"Al! Talk to me!" Cole yells.

"I'm good, TL," Alastair responds, his voice a ragged croak. "Just helping Santiago get in the hatch."

"Good! Move ass!" Cole shouts.

"TL! Your right!" Billy yells as he swings his M-4 in the direction of four Zs rushing at them. The things move too fast, and Billy can only drop one before the others leap and dive through the air. "DOWN!"

Cole and Diaz drop to the ground as Billy opens fire on the leaping Zs. One skull explodes open, but two make it through and tackle him about the waist and chest. Billy's carbine swings out from the impacts, still firing, and the rounds catch Santiago in his side, obliterating his ribs and shredding his lungs.

The man staggers a couple of steps then falls, his life leaving his body in the blink of an eye.

Cole pushes to his feet and grabs Diaz. He yanks the big man back toward the hatch, his eyes locked onto the screaming form of Billy as he's eaten alive by the two Zs. His M-4 clicks empty and he throws it aside. Cole pulls his 9mm and puts a bullet between Billy's eyes, then shoves Diaz toward the hatch.

"Get the fuck in there now!" Cole yells. "Al! Come on!"

Cole looks over and sees Alastair on the ground, blood everywhere.

"Not happening, TL," Alastair whispers. He manages to pull two grenades from his vest and put the pins in his mouth. He winks at Cole and Diaz, then pulls the pins and lets the grenades drop to the ground as his last breath slowly eases from between his lips.

Cole and Diaz literally dive at the hatch.

They tumble fast, but their landing is softened as several bodies move into position to catch their fall. The grunts of the men and women Cole and Diaz have landed on are lost in the noise of the grenades going off above. Dirt, debris, chunks of pavement, and plenty of body parts, rotten and fresh, rain down through the hatch.

Cole rolls to his side and stares up at the hole, then scrambles to his feet as a Z crawls to the edge and falls right at him. Before he can hunt for his 9, a Code Monkey stabs the Z through the back of the skull, then clambers up the ladder to close the hatch.

"It is gone," the Code Monkey announces. "The hatch is destroyed."

"We take them to the scared passage," a woman next to Diaz says. She shoves the man, and he groans as he struggles to stand up. "We have seconds. Get up and follow us."

"Come on," Cole says, helping Diaz to his feet. "We can't stay here."

Two Zs try to force their way into the hatch, but the Code Monkey at the top of the ladder slices their heads off with his blade. Black, bloody sludge drips from the necks in globs that add to the gunk Cole and Diaz are covered in.

"Great," Cole says. "Now I smell even more like them."

"Fuck me, my head," Diaz says.

"Ignore the pain," the woman Code Monkey snaps. "Follow or be left behind."

She disappears ahead of them into the pitch-black passageway. Cole and Diaz scramble to get their NVGs on and limp their way after her. They are only a few yards into the darkness when the Code Money on the ladder screams. A scream cut off midway by a harsh gurgle and a choking noise. Cole and Diaz do not stop to look back. They know that sound and what it means.

It means they are out of time.

———

"What the fuck was that?" Lang asks. "Did you hear that? Sounded like frags going off up top."

"It was," Skye says. She cocks her head, as do the other Code Monkeys. "Our space has been breached. The unclean abominations are now below. I hear the scream of a brother dying."

The far-off cry, then strangled end, barely reaches the Mates' ears.

"No time for waiting," Skye says. "Your friends are lost."

Sister looks at Skye and starts to say something, then closes her mouth and nods. "Open sesame."

Two Code Monkeys move to the wall in front of them and push old crates and piles of trash out of the way to reveal a large, steel door. They each grab a metal ring set into the door and pull, bracing their legs against the wall. It takes a few seconds, then the door begins to budge, slowly at first, then faster as the hinges loosen and the rust falls away. With the heavy steel door open, the two Code Monkeys gesture for Val and the others to step through.

"Rust?" Sister asks. "You haven't been this way in a long time."

"We have no need for it," Skye says. "We can navigate the herd easily without harm. This is our sacred passage and is only to be used when the end is finally upon us."

Sister gives Skye a strained smile that she knows the blind woman cannot see. Skye smiles back.

"You've been using the front doors this whole time?" Sister asks. "How? I haven't seen you go in or out."

Skye gestures to the door.

"If you please," Skye says. "Our time down here is over."

"You first," Stanford says, picking up quickly on Sister's suspicion. "We'd hate for it to be a trap."

Skye sighs and shakes her eyeless head, then moves through the doorway and into the corridor beyond. Two of the Code Monkeys follow her while the rest wait for the Mates to move.

"You have something you want to say?" Stanford asks Sister.

"I don't know," Sister says. She leans forward and sniffs the air coming from the doorway and corridor. "This way hasn't been used for a really long time. If ever."

"It is the way to the cathedral," one of the Code Monkeys says. "The sacred passage leads to the facility where your blood will unlock the end for all."

"Creepy fuckers," Shep says.

"Sister?" Val asks. "What's wrong?"

"Everything," Sister says.

"We are in this together," Skye says, stepping back out of the corridor. "We do not deceive you. All danger is shared danger from now on."

"Yeah," Sister says. "Okay." She takes a step forward. "Follow me, Mates."

She moves past Skye and into the corridor. Val looks at Stanford and he shrugs.

"Your guess is as good as mine at this point," Stanford says.

"Come on," Val replies and follows after Sister.

The rest of the Mates fall in line with the last Code Monkeys behind them.

Once everyone is inside, the door is pulled closed. After a few seconds, a bright flash appears next to the handles and a white-hot flames works its way around the door completely, welding it shut.

Only a few seconds after that, the woman Code Monkey, Cole, and Diaz come running into the room and head right for the door. They grab the handles and pull, but it is no good.

"Fuck," Cole mutters. He pounds on the door, then stops immediately at the huge booming sound it makes.

"What now?" Diaz asks, cringing as the echoes of Cole's pounding slowly fades out.

"We look for another way," Cole says. "There can't be only one secret entrance from this base to Cheyenne Mountain." He turns to the Code Monkey. "You'd know, right? There has to be another way."

"This is the sacred passage to the cathedral," the woman says.

"That's not a fucking answer," Cole snarls. "Is there or isn't there another way in?"

"The sacred passage is the way when the time is at hand," the woman replies. "Only with sacrifice will we be worthy to enter the cathedral."

"Sacrifice? What does that mean?" Diaz asks. "TL? That sound good to you?"

"No," Cole says. He reaches for the woman, but she swats his hand away and easily steps out of his reach.

"The door to the sacred passage is now sealed," the woman says. "The sacrifices have entered the gauntlet and will be tested until their time of truth is revealed."

"It's a fucking trap," Cole snarls. "I knew it. I fucking knew it."

"This scared passage thing," Diaz says. "Uh, it's special? Only to be used when the end is close and all that shit?"

The woman turns her focus on Diaz and nods. The man shivers at the sight of her empty sockets and the way she appears to be more of a phantom than a person in his NVGs.

"So you people have been going in and out of the facility a different way, haven't you?" Diaz asks.

Cole stops grumbling and whips his head toward the woman.

"Shit. You're right, Diaz," he says, then aims his 9mm at the woman. "You're going to take us to the other entrance."

"I am going to do no such thing," the woman responds.

Cole places his finger on the trigger and pulls back the hammer with his thumb.

"Then looks like you're going to be a sacrifice out here instead of in your fucking sacred passage," Cole says.

"Then that is my fate," the woman says. Before Cole can even blink, she steps forward, grabs the pistol, places it to her forehead, and pushes Cole's finger down on the trigger. The muzzle flash is muted by the woman's blood and brains spraying everywhere. Cole jumps back as the Code Monkey's body falls to the ground.

"Dammit!" Cole yells.

"TL, we can't stay here," Diaz says. "That gunshot just told every Z down here where dinner's at."

"I know, I know," Cole says. "But how the hell are we going to find another secret entrance? Secret is secret for a fucking reason."

"Rats," Diaz says.

"What?" Cole asks.

"Rats," Diaz repeats. "They always find a way."

"So fucking what?" Cole responds.

The sound of groans and a mass of shuffling feet echoes down the corridor behind them.

"Diaz, just say what you need to fucking say," Cole snaps.

"We look for rats," Diaz says. "If these people have been going back and forth through a different tunnel, then the rats will be too. My dad was a rat catcher as a teenager before he joined the Teams. He always said if I got stuck somewhere to follow the rats."

"Why the fuck would rats lead us to the Cheyenne facility and not just outside?" Cole asks.

"Because the Zs have that way blocked," Diaz says. "The rats will be high-tailing it out of this bunker and headed for a safer place."

"I'm not sure you know what you're talking about, but it's not like I have a fucking choice," Cole says. The groans and shuffling feet are considerably closer. "Gonna have to trust you and your dad's special rat knowledge. Lead on."

"Search the ground," Diaz says.

"For what?" Cole asks.

"Rats," Diaz says. "Aren't you listening to me?"

"Rats. Right," Cole says. "Look for the rats."

They move off away from the sealed door with Diaz in the lead.

"Never thought a mission would be decided by if we do or do not find rats," Cole says.

"Are you really surprised?" Diaz chuckles, then lowers his voice to a whisper as several moans behind them answer his laughter. "We're DTA. Of course we have to follow rats."

"Yeah," Cole snorts. "Of course we do."

————

"How far are we going?" Shep asks. "If the tunnel from the front doors to the interior doors at the main entrance is five miles, then how long is this tunnel?"

"Has to be at least ten miles or more," Val says.

"We will travel eight miles precisely before we reach the entrance to the cathedral," Skye says.

"Eight miles?" Sister asks. "That doesn't seem right. When you say the cathedral, you mean the nuclear control room, right?"

"I mean the cathedral," Sky says. "It is what it is called. It is what it was named. That is where we're going."

"This no-answer bullshit is starting to wig me out," Stanford says. "They've already shown us the way. I say we ditch the nutjobs and double time it to the facility on our own."

The Code Monkeys stop moving and all turn to Stanford.

"Good one, Ford," Val says. "You couldn't have kept that thought in your head?"

"Yeah. Sorry," Stanford says and holds out a hand. "I was just talking out loud. By ditching you guys I didn't mean kill you. Just leave you behind so we can finish our mission."

"Your mission is our mission," Skye says. "And you will need us to complete it. The sacred passage is not for the sighted."

"What the hell does that mean?" Stanford asks. "Because I'm really, really sighted. I even have NVGs on, which makes me super sighted."

"The Code Monkeys will take on the trials for you, is what I mean," Skye says. "We will make sure you arrive at the cathedral to finish your mission."

"And stop the cannies," Sister says.

"If that is what must be done," Skye says.

Sister shakes her head and motions down the long, pitch-black tunnel.

"Not much choice now, huh?" Sister sighs.

"There has never been a choice," Skye says. "It has all been predestined."

"Then let's predestine our asses along," Stanford says.

Skye smiles, and her teeth shine a bright gray in Stanford's NVGs. The man shivers at the sight. He is not the only one.

———

Three miles in and the Mates are violently informed as to what Skye meant by the Code Monkeys taking on the trials for them.

A woman, small and agile, leads the group. She stops and holds up her hands. The rest stop instantly, nearly causing the Mates to walk right into the backs of the blind men and women.

"It begins," Skye says. "Anita? This is your trial."

The woman in the lead nods her head and takes a step forward, a heavy pipe in her hand.

Before the Mates can even react, there is a click and a swoosh.

The woman, Anita, dives into a forward roll, bringing the pipe in front of her face as she comes up to a knee. A loud clang is heard and Anita is knocked back a couple of feet onto her ass.

"Anita?" Skye asks. "Have you completed the trial?"

"Not yet, Skye," Anita replies. "One more obstacle to go."

Anita picks herself up into a crouch. She doesn't move, just waits there, her entire body shaking with tension.

"What the hell is going on?" Henshaw asks.

"Shhhh!" Skye snaps.

Anita springs ahead, raising the pipe up to her shoulder as she twists her body to the side, using the wall of the tunnel to push off from with her feet. She flips into the air, her back arching as the pipe is knocked from her grip. She does a backward handspring and lands on her feet, her chest heaving from the exertion.

She places a hand to her right shoulder and it comes away black with blood. She sniffs it and nods, then stands straight up.

"I have been marked, but I am not injured badly," Anita says. "The first trial is complete. We may proceed."

"You have done well, Anita," Skye says. "You will be worthy to enter the cathedral."

"Thank you, Skye," Anita says and nods.

"Yeah, we're going to need some explaining," Stanford says, his M-4 up and pointed at Skye's head. "Like now."

The rest of the Mates move in close to Stanford, their weapons up as well.

Sister pats him on the shoulder, then moves away from the group of Mates.

"Hold on," she says as she walks forward. She approaches Anita and holds out a hand. "Can I take a look?"

"Yes," Anita says. "Please do. My wound is a badge of honor."

Sister leans close so her NVGs pick up the details of Anita's shoulder wound. She studies it for a few seconds, then nods and moves away, her attention focused on the walls of the tunnel.

"Sister?" Val asks. "What do you see?"

"Trials," Sister replies, her fingers tracing a long groove in the wall. She turns to Skye and holds up her fingers which are black with old grease. "Trials."

"Yes. Trials," Skye says. "The sacred passage is only a way for true warriors to go."

"This isn't a normal tunnel, is it?" Sister says.

"This is the sacred passage to the cathedral," Skye says. "It is the only way for us to complete our mission, which is your mission."

"I swear to god I'll start shooting if someone doesn't tell us what the fuck is going on!" Stanford shouts.

"Don't shoot," Sister says. "We need them. They are taking the trials for us."

"Good for fucking them!" Stanford snaps. "We're Mates, so we know all about trials. We have them back at the Stronghold. It's how you get onto the Teams."

"Yeah, those aren't like these," Sister says. "Those are tests in a gym."

"Then what are these?" Val asks.

"Booby traps," Sister says. "Security measures put here a long time ago by someone who is pretty sick in the head."

"Who?" Val asks.

"That's a long story," Sister says. "And not one I really plan on telling. Ever. There's no need. Just know that the bastard got his in the end."

The Code Monkeys all hiss and some even spit at Sister. Skye holds up a hand and they back off.

"Thank you for revealing who you are, Sister," Skye says. "This is good news to us. We will finally have what the old world called closure. Today is truly the end of it all. The end of everything."

"Yep. End of everything," Sister says. "How many more trials are there?"

"More than enough for all of us to be tested," Skye says.

"Great," Sister says. "Just shit fucking great."

———

Diaz shoves a stack of moldy boxes out of the way and is not surprised they move as one unit, rolling to the side on a hidden platform that swings out into the corridor.

"Rats," Diaz says, pointing down at the litter of rodent droppings that sit next to a seam in the wall.

"I'll be dipped in Z guts," Cole says.

"You already are, TL," Diaz laughs as he moves his hand up the seam. It takes him a few passes, but he finds what he is looking for. With a loud click, the wall pops out about two inches. "There we go."

Diaz and Cole grab the wall with their gloves and pull it all the way out. It becomes a door that nearly blocks the entire corridor they have been following for close to an hour.

The smell hits them fast and they both put a hand up to their noses.

"What the fuck is that?" Cole says.

The two men raise their weapons and take a few careful steps into the passage revealed by the hidden door. They only get a few feet before the passage takes a sharp turn to the right.

"Holy shit," Diaz says. "They've been hacked to pieces."

Cole takes a cautious step toward the pile and studies the miscellaneous body parts.

"These aren't Zs," he says. "The tissues are rotting, but not necrotic like the undead. These parts belong to people. People who were alive when they were chopped up."

"TL? You noticing what I'm noticing?" Diaz asks. "There's something missing here."

Cole looks at the pile again and then nods.

"No heads," he says.

"Yeah, no heads," Diaz says. "Where the hell are the heads?"

"I'm guessing we need to follow the trail of blood," Cole says, nodding at the wide, dark smear that leads down the passage and away from the grotesque pile.

The two Mates walk for a while before there is another turn in the passageway. Cole stops by the corner then ducks his head around quickly. He pulls back just as quickly and closes his eyes.

"Found them," he says.

Cole moves around the corner with Diaz right behind him. In a row that stretches from wall to wall sit close to two dozen heads, their necks stuck to the concrete floor by the pools of blood that have leaked and congealed from them.

"Watch yourself," Diaz says as Cole moves toward the heads. "Could be rigged."

"Could be," Cole says. "But I don't think they would bother. No one was supposed to come this way."

He gets close to the heads and kneels down. Very slowly, he reaches out and grabs one by the top of the skull. Despite his assumption, Cole lets out a deep breath when nothing happens after he picks the head up. He turns it this way, then that.

"Code Monkeys?" Diaz asks.

"They have eyes," Cole says.

"Oh, right."

Cole grabs the head by the chin and pulls down, opening the jaw. He stares at what's inside the mouth then sets the head down, stands, and looks right at Diaz.

"Cannies," Cole says.

"What?" Diaz says.

"Cannies," Cole says. "Their teeth are sharpened. These fuckers are canny heads."

"Cannies? Why the hell would there be hacked-up cannies in a secret passage leading from the AFB to the Cheyenne facility?" Diaz asks. "How'd they even get by the Code Monkeys to get down here?"

"I have a hunch," Cole says. "Come on."

The two men step over the rows of heads and keep going down the passageway. There is a distinct trail of blood that leads around each turn, smeared across the floor from the bodies being dragged along the concrete. Then the trail starts to thin out and the blood becomes more random, like splatters instead of a wide path.

"Yeah. This isn't good," Cole says, pointing at the splatters on the floor and then corresponding ones that cover the walls. "Look at the trajectory."

"I am," Diaz says. He takes off his pack and rummages through it. He pulls out a hand crank flashlight and yanks his NVGs from his face. "Going bright."

Cole pulls off his NVGs as Diaz cranks the flashlight to life and points the beam at the blood on the walls. The spray fans out in one direction.

"They were running," Diaz says.

"Yeah, they were," Cole agrees.

"They were trying to escape," Diaz says.

Cole only nods.

"There aren't any cannies in the facility anymore, are there, TL?" Diaz asks, pocketing the flashlight and putting his goggles back on.

"I don't think so," Cole says.

"That means the Code Monkeys set this all up," Diaz says.

"Looks like it," Cole nods and puts his NVGs back on as well.

"So what now?" Diaz asks.

"We're the rats," Cole says. "We find a way."

"A way to what?" Diaz asks.

"A way to find our friends before whatever the Code Monkeys have planned happens."

"They're gonna kill them, aren't they?" Diaz asks. He drops his pack and straps his M-4 tight to his back.

"Not if we get there first," Cole says, doing the same with his pack and holstering his 9mm.

The two men nod, then sprint as fast as they can down the passageway.

TEN
HOUSES OF THE HOLY SHIT

"Zora," Skye says quietly. "It is your turn to be tested."

A tall woman with long, black hair that hangs down to the middle of her back nods at Skye and moves away from the group. She takes a few steps and then stops, her head cocked and listening.

Instead of moving forward, she steps sideways and places her back to the wall. She takes a deep breath, then begins to cartwheel herself down the tunnel, her back never leaving the surface of the wall. There is a tiny whoosh of air and Zora grunts but keeps moving.

When she is close to thirty yards away, she stops cartwheeling, landing on her feet without even a stumble.

"Nora? Can you continue?" Skye asks.

"I can," Nora replies.

She sticks her hand in her pants pocket and pulls out a handful of small objects. To the Mates wearing NVGs, the objects shine in their enhanced vision. To the Code Monkeys, they do nothing but change the density of the air around Zora's hand.

The woman throws the objects out, back toward the group. They fly through the air but quickly drop to the ground. More whooshes fill the air, and the Mates take a couple steps back as they watch small projectiles shoot from one side of the tunnel to the other.

"Is that all of them, Zora?" Skye asks, a tone in her voice that makes it plain that is not all of them.

"No," Zora responds.

Another deep breath, and she runs a couple of feet before putting her hands out in front of her. She throws herself forward and flips onto her hands, then back to her legs, onto her hands, back to her legs, her body tumbling end over end down the tunnel back toward the group.

Six whooshes. One cry.

The final whoosh drops Zora and the woman lies on the ground, her hand to her leg. Blood seeps out around a small shaft. The skin on her face is tight with pain as she tilts her head up to face Skye.

"That is all," Zora gasps. "The way is clear."

"You are sure?" Skye asks.

"I am sure," Zora says. "This was my trial. I have cleared it as I was trained."

"Good," Skye says. "Is the dart poisoned as foretold?"

"It is," Zora says, her voice shaky and weak. "I can feel it flowing inside me. It hurts like nothing I have ever felt. It is glorious."

"Are you shitting me?" Stanford whispers. Val nudges him with her elbow and he shakes his head. "We have entered levels of cuckoo I never thought existed. And you know how warped my brain is."

"You do not understand," Skye says as she kneels next to Zora. "Your kind can never understand."

"Glad that I don't," Stanford says.

Skye ignores him and focuses on Zora.

"Would you like relief? Or will you endure the trial to the end?" Skye asks.

"I will endure," Zora gasps.

Her body starts to shake and her eyes roll up into her head.

Foam leaks from the corners of her mouth, followed by a trickle of blood. The trickle becomes a stream and is joined by blood pouring from her nose, her ears, and even from her empty eye sockets. The woman's limbs twist and contort, followed by her back as it bends, bends, bends, and finally snaps.

Zora lets out one last cry, a choked gurgle, then goes still.

"Her bravery will be logged," Skye says. "She will be forever remembered in the cathedral."

"Fucking A," Tommy Bombs whispers.

"Yeah," Shep agrees.

"We keep moving," Skye says. "More trials await us."

Val looks over at Sister before they get moving again, but the woman keeps her goggles focused on the way ahead, giving no indication to Val what she is thinking.

———

Blades that slice at the legs from the floor.

Spikes that rain down from the ceiling.

Flames that nearly blind the Mates before they can yank their NVGs off in time to see a man cooked alive.

Acid that sprays out from cracks in the concrete.

And finally a large pit with no way across.

The trials are brutal and deadly, killing two more Code Monkeys before everyone stops at the edge of the large pit.

"The final trial," Skye says. "My trial."

Sister crouches by the edge of the pit. She runs a hand across the surface, reaching down inside to feel the wall that lines it. She pulls back quickly, then laughs.

"There's a bridge, isn't there?" Sister asks. "I felt a groove a foot down. Does it extend across or is there half on the other side that meets in the middle?"

"It extends across," Skye says. "But only halfway. And from the other side."

"Only halfway?" Lang asks. "So we have to jump the rest of the way?"

"If I complete the trial, yes," Skye says.

"If you don't complete it?" Henshaw asks.

"Then I and my brothers and sisters will be stuck here with you forever," Skye says.

"We could just go back," Shep suggests. "Figure out another way in."

"This is the only way in to the cathedral," Skye says. "And there is no going back."

"No going back," the other Code Monkeys say. Three men and two women are what remain of Skye's party. They nod their heads at Skye, then face the pit. "Only forward to the cathedral."

"Then get on with it," Stanford snaps. "Go forward and fetch us this mighty half bridge."

"When we reach the cathedral, you will be tested yourself, Stanford Lee," Skye says. "You will wish you had not mocked the trials."

"I wish a lot of things," Stanford says. "They rarely come true anyway."

Skye faces him for a few seconds, then nods. "I believe that."

She turns quickly and flings herself into the pit. Everyone except for the Code Monkeys gasp.

The Mates stare at the vast darkness that even their NVGs can't penetrate.

"I'm guessing that, since the blindies aren't worried, we shouldn't be either," Stanford says. "So… we wait?"

The minutes tick off before a slow rumbling is felt from the ground. There are a series of clicks and thuds, then a loud, harsh grating sound as the half bridge begins to extend from the opposite side of the pit. It moves out until it is exactly halfway across, then stops and shudders before several loud clangs freeze it in place.

"It is secure," one of the Code Monkeys says. "We may proceed."

"That is a long way to jump," Val says. "It's going to be tricky."

"DTA afraid of a little tricky?" Stanford asks.

"Yes, Ford, DTA is afraid of a little tricky," Val replies. "You got me."

One by one the Code Monkeys step back from the edge of the pit, then take a running start before leaping out over the empty space. They each land with a couple of feet to spare then turn and regard the Mates with their eyeless sockets.

"You all must pass this trial," another of the Code Monkeys says. "This is not one we can do for you."

"I thought this was Skye's trial?" Stanford yells.

"You all must pass the trial," the Code Monkey says again. "This is not one we can—"

"Yeah, yeah, I get it," Stanford says.

"Our packs are going to weigh us down," Henshaw says. "We should toss them over first."

She takes off her pack and gets close to the edge. She swings the pack out, back and forth, building up momentum until she finally lets go and it flies out in a long arc, landing heavily next to the Code Monkeys.

"Come on," Henshaw says. "Everyone now."

The Mates follow suit and fling their packs across the space. The Code Monkeys merely step aside when the packs land, giving them zero attention.

"Your time is now," a third Code Monkey announces. "Jump or be left behind forever."

"That's not an option," Stanford says.

He cinches his M-4 tight to his back, takes a couple deep breaths, then sprints and leaps. His arms pinwheel in the air as he braces his legs for the landing. The bridge rushes up at him and he slams into it, his legs going out from under him right away. He rolls a few feet, then is stopped just as he is about to go off the side of the bridge.

A Code Monkey has him by the ankle and pulls him back to safety.

"Thanks," he says as he's helped to his feet.

"You are needed," the Code Monkey says.

Everyone else follows, making it across with only minor difficulties. Leaving only Sister on the far side.

"Where is Skye?" Sister asks.

"She is preparing the cathedral," a Code Monkey replies.

"Uh, no, pretty sure she fell down a big hole," Stanford says.

"She did not," the Code Monkey responds. "She jumped to exactly where she needed to be. Now she is inside the cathedral, readying it for our arrival."

"That's what I thought," Sister says.

She runs at the pit, her legs springing at the last second. When she lands, she comes up out of a roll and then slams a fist into the gut of one of the Code Monkeys, doubling the man over. Her knee comes up and cracks him in the face, sending him stumbling backward until his feet slip and he is sent falling from the bridge.

"Run!" Sister yells as she spins about and cracks another Code Monkey in the face with a strong roundhouse kick. "Go!"

The Mates barely register what is happening, but none of them hesitate. They grab whatever packs are at hand and take off, running as fast as they can away from the bridge.

The Code Monkeys step toward Sister, who is blocking their way off the bridge. She holds up her hand and they stop.

"Y'all are amazing," Sister says. "You know I have something in my hand, don't you?"

"You are holding a grenade," one of the men says. "But you have not pulled the pin free yet."

"Let me fix that," Sister says and pulls the pin from the grenade. "I'd say something witty, but I'm just too fucking tired. So I'll whistle for a minute to give my friends time to get away."

"They cannot get away," the man says. "They are going exactly where they need to go."

"Yeah, I know, I know," Sister says.

Then she starts whistling.

One of the Code Monkeys makes a move and Sister waves the grenade at her. She stops immediately, her head cocked and listening.

"They have reached the cathedral doors," the woman says. "You should be there to witness their sacrifice."

"And there we have it," Sister says. "I knew one of you would slip up. You didn't keep it ambiguous enough that time. Nope. That time you specifically said that my friends are going to be sacrificed. I had a feeling that was where this might be going. If there's one thing I know, it's how crazy people think."

She taps her head with her grenade hand and a couple of the Code Monkeys flinch. Sister grins, then sighs. She tosses the grenade at the bridge and takes off running as fast as she can.

———

The Mates hear the explosion a split second before they reach the double doors set into the end of the tunnel. The walls around the doors are rough and look like rock, not concrete. The doors themselves look old and like they haven't been opened in forever, if at all.

Turning back to the tunnel, the Mates unstrap their carbines, each take a knee, and aim into the darkness. There are no more explosions, but there are the sounds of footsteps.

"Confirm your targets," Stanford says, his finger resting on his trigger. "We still have a friendly back there."

"What the hell set her off?" Henshaw asks. "We were good until the pit, then she lost it."

"She didn't lose it," Val says. "She knew exactly what she was doing. I think we've been tricked."

"No," a voice says from behind them. "You have been led."

Everyone spins around on their knees and sees Skye standing in the doorway, both doors wide open.

"You must oil those hinges every fucking day," Stanford says.

"The cathedral is a holy space for us," Skye says. "It is about to become more holy."

"Good for you," Stanford says. "Val?"

"I think we've dealt with her enough," Val says.

"Have you?" Skye asks. "But have you dealt with all of us enough?"

The doorway fills with Code Monkeys. Close to two dozen of them stand behind Skye, various weapons held in their hands. Various sharp weapons.

"You will be able to kill one or two of us, but not all of us," Skye says. "Put down the weapons and I will let you enter the cathedral alive."

"But will we get to leave alive?" Stanford asks.

"You were never going to leave the facility alive," Skye says. "You knew that. Why does it matter now?"

"The assumption was we wouldn't leave alive," Stanford says. "Doesn't mean it's written in stone."

"It is all written in stone," Skye says. She points up at the rock above the doorway. "See."

The Mates look up and see the faint outlines of words etched into the rock.

"Shall I read it for you?" Skye asks. "It says, "Welcome to the cathedral. Let all who pass through these doors taste immortality. Let only the worthy grasp it."

"Okay, that is one lame message," Stanford says. "Let only the worthy grasp it? Sounds like what I'd say to some of my ex-lovers."

The Code Monkeys hiss and spit over and over until Skye holds up a hand.

"Put down the weapons," Skye says.

"Fucking shoot them!" Sister shouts from behind the Mates as she comes running down the tunnel. "Just shoot them!"

"All I needed to hear," Stanford says and opens fire.

The Code Monkeys scatter, diving inside the open doorway,

lost from sight as the Mates get to their feet and press the attack, their carbines barking fire the whole way.

"Reloading!" Lang yells as she ejects a spent magazine and pops in a fresh one. She racks the slide, then screams as she looks down at the blade embedded in her chest. "Fuck!"

She falls to the ground, blood bubbling from her mouth and nose.

"Mate down!" Stanford yells.

"Reloading!" Shep shouts. He ejects his magazine but doesn't even get his fresh one in before he is falling to the ground as well, his throat a wide-open gash that spews blood everywhere.

"Fuck!" Val yells as she enters the cathedral and spins to the right, spraying that direction with bullets while Stanford stands at her back and sprays the other direction.

Henshaw, Tommy Bombs, and Carlotta follow right behind, their carbines spitting lead as fast as they can pull the trigger.

Val sees a blur on her left and turns, but not before a fist hits her in the temple. The world spins and her NVGs go flying from her face, plunging her into pitch blackness. Another blow to her head and she drops her M-4. A third blow knocks her to her knees. A fourth knocks her completely out.

———

The screams bring Val back around. Her eyes shoot open and she is surprised she can see. The room is filled with soft, flickering light. It's not much, but it's enough for her to see what is happening clearly. She instantly wishes she couldn't.

"Oh, fuck," she whispers.

"Just stay quiet and still," Sister says from close by.

Val risks turning her head and sees Sister pushed up against a wall, a dozen Code Monkeys all guarding her with sharp-looking blades. A couple of them even have M-4s, which makes Val wonder how the hell they can fire them without sight. Not that they have much trouble doing anything without sight.

Right next to Val, and looking unconscious, is Stanford, with Carlotta and Tommy Bombs next to him. Both of them are wide awake, and their eyes stare in horror at what is happening to Henshaw.

The woman is completely naked and being held by her ankles above a large tank. Her skin hangs off her in long strips, stretching down into blood that is slowly filling the bottom of the tank.

"A vein," Skye says, slicing at Henshaw's thigh. Blood pours from the cut and joins the rest in the tank.

"A vein," the Code Monkeys say together.

"Let the cathedral accept this sacrifice so that it may gather what it needs to finish its work," Skye says.

"Let the cathedral accept this sacri—"

"Oh, shut the fuck up!" Stanford shouts, obviously awake. "Just fucking kill us if you're going to kill us!"

Hisses and spit are flung his way.

"Yes, I get it, you guys don't like me," Stanford says. "Welcome to the club."

"Stanford, be quiet," Sister says.

"Fuck that," Stanford replies. "Come on you crazy, no-eyed assholes! Kill us! Get it over with!"

"Very well," Skye says and slashes Henshaw's throat wide open. She saws at the woman's neck until the head comes free. Holding it by the hair, Skye raises it up. "The first sacrifice is complete! He shall be pleased with us!"

"He's dead!" Sister yells. "I killed him years ago!"

"NO!" Skye roars. "He lives forever!"

"I gutted the motherfucker and watched him die," Sister says. "It took him three days to bleed out. When it was done, I gave his body to a canny group I stumbled across. Only fitting the asshole became canny shit."

The Code Monkeys begin to scream and screech at her, moving forward, their sharp blades coming dangerously close to her body.

"Do not harm her!" Skye shouts. "She is one of the keys!"

"Yeah! She's one of the keys!" Stanford shouts. "So back off!"

"You are not," Skye says, pointing her blade at Stanford. "Save the Baptiste woman and kill the rest. The cathedral will still favor us with their sacrifice, even if we do not collect their blood."

"Whoa! Stop!" Stanford yells as the Code Monkeys descend on him, Carlotta, and Tommy Bombs. "Just kidding! JUST KIDDING!"

There's a loud whistle and everyone stops moving. All heads turn to the opposite side of the room, which now that Val can see clearly enough, looks like some weird laboratory and not like a cathedral at all. Not any cathedral she has ever seen.

"Hey there," Cole says, his 9mm leading his way into the room. "Back away from my friends."

He doesn't even give them a chance to comply before he opens fire. Two Code Monkeys lose their heads as slugs rip into them, while a third doubles over from three shots to her belly.

"Back away faster!" Diaz shouts as he follows Cole into the room.

He swings his carbine to the right and takes down four Code Monkeys before they can get halfway across the room. He swings back toward the others, and his eyes go wide as he watches in horror as Carlotta's throat is slit and blood geysers out, coating Tommy Bombs.

"No!" Diaz yells and empties his magazine into the man who had slit Carlotta's throat.

He ejects the spent magazine, but before he can pop in a new one, two Code Monkeys are leaping at him. He uses his carbine as a bat and swats one to the ground, the man's neck angled in a way that nature did not intend.

The second Code Monkey hits him hard and stabs a long blade through his left shoulder. Diaz screams and rolls with the attack, putting the Code Monkey between him and the ground. He drops fast, using all of his weight to crush the woman who stabbed him. She grunts and coughs as the air is knocked from her lungs. Diaz pushes up, yanks the blade free from his shoulder, and jams it into the woman's left eye socket. She twitches once, then goes still.

Cole drops three more Code Monkeys before the rest try to escape out the double doors and back into the tunnel.

"I have them!" Sister yells and is gone from sight as she takes off after the Code Monkeys.

Cole sweeps the room, sees no other threats, and runs to the blood-covered Mates.

"Report!" he orders as he slides to his knees, pulls a knife, and starts cutting at the restraints holding Val's wrists together.

"I'm fine," she says, rubbing her wrists once they are free. "How the hell did you get here?"

"We found the other entrance," Cole says.

"And a lot of heads," Diaz says, walking over to them, his hand pressing a rag to his shoulder.

"Heads?" Stanford asks as Cole cuts him free.

"Cannies," Diaz says. He winces and blinks a couple of times. "Shit, this hurts."

"I'll dress it," Sister says as she comes back into the room, her clothes considerably more bloody.

"Any of that yours?" Cole asks, looking over at her.

"None," she says. She looks around. "Where's Skye?"

"She wasn't with the ones who tried to escape?" Cole asks, getting Tommy Bombs free.

"If she was, then I wouldn't have fucking asked where she was!" Sister roars.

"Okay, okay, calm down," Cole says. "She was standing in the middle of the room when I came in. I don't know where she is now."

"Shit," Sister curses. "Come on, we have to find her."

"Why?" Cole asks, helping Tommy Bombs to his feet. "Our mission is to use your genetics to unlock the controls so Commander Lee can launch some nukes. That is the priority, not chasing after one last blind crazy."

Sister starts to argue, then nods. "Yes. You're right. Follow me."

Everyone does. They do not hesitate, do not ask where she is going, they just get up and follow, grabbing weapons on their way through the doors opposite the tunnel entrance.

———

Three corridors later, and several turns that nearly make the Mates dizzy, they arrive at a steel door with multiple warnings stenciled across it, all faded from time.

The Mates stop and Sister pops a panel open to the right of the doors.

"Give me a minute," she says.

While Sister works, Stanford takes Val by the arm and looks her over.

"You okay?" he asks.

"I'm fine," Val says. "But I'm worried about Tommy Bombs."

They both glance at the man covered in blood. His usual jitteri-ness has doubled and he stands there, literally shaking in his boots as he stares off into space.

"Seeing Carlotta die like that messed him up," Val says.

"It didn't mess me up," Tommy Bombs says. "So stop talking about me like I'm not standing right here. Just a lot to fucking take in, okay?"

"Okay, sorry," Val says.

"Got it," Sister announces, and the steel door slides open to reveal a fairly ordinary-looking room with a bank of control panels bolted above several metal desks. "The genetic authorization panel is the middle one. Let's get this done, and then we need to hurry and find a communications station. The one in here doesn't work. I've tried."

"A communication's station?" Cole asks. "Why?"

"So we can warn the Stronghold," Sister says. "Did you think those were all of the Code Monkeys?"

"What are you talking about?" Cole asks.

"The ones we killed back in the lab," Sister says. "The ones I chased down. That's not enough. There are more. Plenty more, and I know where they are headed."

"Oh, Jesus," Stanford says. "Skye said that everyone must die. She means the Stronghold too, doesn't she? Does she know all of the Mates are down here?"

"She might," Sister says, rushing over to the authorization console. "Doesn't matter. There are Code Monkeys heading to the new Stronghold now. If only a few get in there, it'll be slaughter."

"I'll go look for a comm system," Cole says. "You punch in the codes."

"Do you know how to work a comm system?" Sister asks. "Have you ever worked a comm system?"

"I can figure it out," Cole says.

"No, you can't," Sister says. "Just trying to dial in the right channel can take a rookie an hour. This isn't like lighting a signal pyre."

"And Skye is still out there," Val says.

"Exactly," Sister responds. "Help clean Diaz's shoulder and pack it with gauze. There's a first aid kit hanging on the wall over there,"

Cole doesn't argue, just walks to the first aid kit, muttering curses under his breath.

"You," Sister says and points at Val. "Come here and get ready to have your finger pricked. The system needs DNA confirmation before we enter the final codes simultaneously and send control up to the new Stronghold. The real Stronghold."

ELEVEN
A STRONGHOLD STATE
OF MIND

Hamish stands by the massive doors to the new Stronghold, his doctor's eyes surveying the residents as they straggle inside once their names and numbers have been called.

He knows almost everyone by their health history. There goes the bleeding ulcer. The sprained knee is busy arguing with the infected toenail by the far wall. Tinnitus is flirting with severe hemorrhoids. Stomach cancer is telling jokes to carpal tunnel and rosacea.

Hamish looks about the huge entryway behind him, a massive room nearly a hundred feet tall and just as wide and deep, and sees years and years of care. Generations of families he's gotten to know even in his short few years as head physician at the Stronghold hospital.

But one case he doesn't see is severe cirrhosis of the liver.

"Hey, Sheriff?" Hamish asks, catching the attention of Sheriff Marsh as the man walks by with an armload of blankets and sheets. "Have you seen Collin? Collin Baptiste?"

"No. Why? What has he done now?" Marsh asks. "Did he try to steal your compounds again? I told him the next time he pilfered from the pharmacy I was going to throw him in a deep dark hole for a year."

"No, he hasn't stolen anything," Hamish replies. "At least, not that I know of. It's just with Val gone, I said I'd watch out for him and make sure he got into the new Stronghold safely."

"Kinda failed at that job, didn't you?" Marsh laughs. "Hold on. Let me set these down and I'll help you look."

"Oh, you don't need to do that," Hamish says. "You're busy. I can probably find him on my own."

"I've known Collin my whole life, Doc," Marsh says. "That man can hide if he wants to. Lucky for you, I know all of his regular haunts. We'll try at his house first."

"You think he'd hide there?" Hamish asks. "That's pretty obvious."

"Collin is a drunk and a junkie," Marsh says. "But more than all of that, he's a lazy son of a bitch. If he can get high without leaving his house, then he'll do it."

"Okay, thank you," Hamish says. "I really appreciate it. If I lost him and Val found out, I don't know what I'd do."

Marsh looks at Hamish for a second, a kindness in his eyes.

"It's good you have hope she'll come back," Marsh says. "Hope gets us through a lot."

"She's coming back," Hamish says. "I know it."

———

The porch step squeaks as Collin places his left foot on it. He lifts his foot, then sets it down again, making the squeak at will. Up and down, up and down. Squeak, squeak.

He takes a swig from the Mason jar, its clear contents sloshing about but not quite spilling. Collin doesn't even wince as the highly flammable liquid slides down his throat. It would take molten lava to affect the seasoned esophagus of such a veteran drinker. Years of pounding homemade alcohol has conditioned

Collin's entire system for the flaming hammer blows the hooch delivers from lips to gut.

Squeak, squeak. Sip, sip. Burp. Laugh. Fart.

"Excuse me," Collin says to no one. He takes a deep breath and gags. "Oh, man, damn. That is dead. Whatever is up my ass is dead. Dead, dead… dead…"

Collin squints into the darkness of the late autumn night. Barely any stars out and the moon stuck behind a bank of thick, gray clouds, makes visibility nearly impossible, but Collin is not just a veteran drinker. He's a veteran survivor. He saw something. He knows it.

"Well," Collin mutters. "Let's go have a look."

Without letting go of the jar of hooch, Collin picks up a 12-gauge pump-action shotgun and grips it in one hand. Not the most steady hand, but steady enough for a shell of buckshot to do some damage.

He walks down off the porch and stares into the deep, dark shadows across the street. The Gunndersons had left with all of their belongings a couple hours ago, so he knows what he saw wasn't Larry double-checking that the windows were boarded tight. Which was totally something Larry Gunnderson would do. The guy obsesses about following Stronghold council orders.

Collin, on the other hand, couldn't give two wet, runny shits about anything the council has to say. Hence the one last jar of hooch before being tossed inside some fortress with all the rule followers, normals, and morons. One last jar of hooch before he finds out what the harsh reality of a full detox feels like. That was what the shotgun was for.

Collin hasn't quite decided if living inside the new Stronghold is his cup of tea. He might just skip the door closing ceremony and gnaw on the barrel of the shotgun. Gnaw and gnaw until the thing accidentally goes off. Another reason for the jar of hooch. Liquid courage is a coward's best friend.

He crosses the street, shotgun in a relaxed aim at the shadows.

"Larry?" he calls out, even though he knows it's not Larry.

Collin can't think of what else to call out. "Hey, Gunnderson? That you?"

It is not Larry Gunnderson.

Flashbacks of bloody violence in the streets of the Stronghold rush through Collin's mind as the eyeless person sprints toward him, blades in both hands.

The blast from the shotgun is extremely loud and surprises Collin enough that he almost drops his hooch. Almost. He stares down at his weapon but doesn't see smoke coming from the barrel. In fact, he doesn't remember any kick either.

The Code Monkey writhes on the ground, his rib cage exposed to the night air, blood spilling into the Gunnderson's front yard, staining the brown dirt and stray pine needles.

"You're welcome," Marsh says from the next yard over. "I wouldn't want you to put your booze down or anything."

"Thanks for that," Collin says, lifting the jar in Marsh's direction. He takes a quick sip and nods at the dying man at his feet. "Looks like we got ourselves a Monkey problem again."

"Looks like it," Marsh says.

"What happened? What was that gunshot?" Hamish asks, jogging up behind Marsh, extremely winded and looking like he's going to throw up. "You took off running so fast I couldn't keep up."

"This is what my daughter chooses to love," Collin says and smirks before taking another sip. "She's man enough for both of them, I guess."

"Come on, Collin," Marsh says. "We need to get back to the new Stronghold and warn everyone. There could be more."

"Probably are," Collin agrees. "What do you think, Doctor Turdlington?"

"Terlington," Hamish corrects. "And go fuck yourself, Collin."

"Gonna have to say I approve of your daughter's choice, Collin," Marsh says. "He knows where to stand with you."

Collin lifts the shotgun, and Marsh's eyes go wide just before he grabs Hamish by the arm and dives to the ground. This time it is Collin's shotgun that breaks the silence of the night. A woman screams and grabs at her face, the machete in her hand falling into the dirt only a foot from Hamish. Blood pours through her fingers as she collapses to her knees.

Collin steadies himself from the recoil of the blast and then smiles at the bleeding woman. He walks over to her and puts the shotgun to her head. She shrieks and starts to bat it away, but Collin pulls the trigger a split second faster than her hands can move.

The woman's brains spray out the back of her head and create a fanlike mosaic of gray matter, blood, and bone upon the ground. Collin drinks deeply from his jar and cocks his head.

"Looks like a volcano," he says, pointing with the shotgun at the bloody mess. "Hey! Hamish! What do you think it looks like?"

Marsh picks himself up then helps the doctor to his feet.

"Leave him alone, Collin," Marsh says. "That's two just here. That means not only are there more, there are probably a lot more. We need to go now."

"Nah, you guys go on," Collin says. "I'm going for a walk. Gonna listen to the Zs pound on the wall for a bit. It's soothing."

"The only walk you are going on is with me to the Stronghold," Marsh says. "And by walk, I mean a fast run. Put the hooch down and puke now if you need to."

"Puke?" Collin laughs. "And waste perfectly good alcohol? Fuck you, Ward."

"You blew her head off," Hamish says, staring at the corpse. "She was wounded and you shot her again."

"Good observation skills, Doc," Collin says. "You might have a future in the sciences. You should look into that."

"But she was harmless," Hamish says.

"That's bullshit," Marsh responds. "None of these bastards are harmless. Not ever."

Collin looks up into the sky suddenly.

"What?" Hamish asks, spinning around quickly, fear on his face. "What do you see?"

"I was looking for flying pigs," Collin says. "Because Sheriff Ward Marsh just agreed with me."

"We run," Marsh says. "Now."

Collin is about to argue again, but two things happen.

There is the sound of several screams of pain in the direction of the new Stronghold.

And the sound of metal and wood cracking and crashing to the ground in the direction of the main gate.

"Sounds like we're about to have a party," Collin says and lifts his jar. "L'chaim!"

———

"The system has been activated and we now have control over the full nuclear arsenal on this continent," Kevin Ross says as he sits at a dusty console in a dusty room. "We can launch on your orders, Commander Lee."

Commander Maura Lee takes a deep breath, then stands from the dusty chair set in the middle of the dusty room. She stares at the winking and blinking monitors that fill one wall of the room, all showing various angles of large missiles housed in silos across hundreds of miles to the north. The Silo Teams had done their job getting the cameras working, the Code Monkeys had done theirs getting the missiles prepped. Now she must do hers.

She says a silent prayer over the lives that were lost making everything happen. Lives she willingly sacrificed in order to have the weapons needed to hopefully eradicate the Z menace that has finally overtaken the land.

"Commander?" Kevin asks. "Shall I initiate the launch for you?"

"Yes, Kevin. It is time to—" Commander Lee begins, then stops as noise from outside the room reaches her ears. While not soundproof, the room is fortified enough that whatever is happening must be extremely loud to penetrate the walls. "What is that?"

She looks at two guards that stand on either side of the door and points at one.

"Go see what is happening out there," Commander Lee orders. "I'm sure it's someone arguing about food or where they've been assigned to sleep. People do not seem to grasp what is at stake anymore."

"I don't think people know what is at stake at all," Kevin responds. "Since no one has actually explained it to them."

"Not having this argument again, Kevin," Commander Lee snaps.

The guard opens the door and steps into the hallway. He makes it a foot before he stops dead in his tracks. Literally dead in his tracks as a machete pierces his chest and out his back. The guard stands for a second, then collapses into a heap, his rifle clattering to the ground and sliding across the concrete right to Commander Lee's feet.

The experienced soldier doesn't hesitate or wait for the other guard to react; she picks up the rifle, puts it to her shoulder, and steps out into the hallway. Even before she sees the attacker, she knows what she will find. Two shots and the Code Monkey's head explodes.

Commander Lee steps back into the room and slams the door shut. She punches in a code, and there is the sound of several heavy bars sliding into place within the walls. She hands the rifle to the stunned guard and moves next to Kevin's spot at the launch console.

"All targets are confirmed?" she asks. There are several muffled gunshots and more than a few barely audible screams from outside the room. Kevin turns and looks toward the door, but Commander Lee smacks him upside the head. "Kevin! Are all targets confirmed?"

"Yes, Commander," Kevin replies, rubbing at his head. "One hundred and sixty-five missiles all locked onto the largest urban centers. Or former urban centers. Two hundred and fifteen missiles locked onto the various rural and open space locations the woman gave us. The launch should wipe out nearly ninety percent of the Zs out there."

"Ninety percent," Commander Lee says. "Will that be enough?"

"It will be enough to give humanity a fighting chance," Kevin says. "We've all seen the numbers, Commander. If we can double the population inside here, then we will be able to stage an offensive once we emerge. If we emerge."

"No ifs, Kevin," Commander Lee says. "We will emerge. I just pray there are others like us who will emerge as well. God only knows what will happen when the time comes to open those doors and we are all that is left."

"That's the risk we're taking launching at all of the major urban centers, Commander," Kevin says. "The death of possible survivor pockets the woman hasn't found."

Commander Lee smirks. "I do not believe there are such things out there."

There's a high squelch and crackle and Commander Lee jumps. The guard by the door twists around and brings up his rifle, but Commander Lee holds up a hand and glares at him.

"Keep it in check, Mr. Jorgens," she snaps. "It is the comm system."

"Yes, sir," Jorgens nods. "My apologies."

"Hello?" a voice calls out from the static. "This is Cheyenne Mountain calling the Stronghold, over. Please come in, over."

Commander Lee moves to the comm system and picks up the handset.

"This is the Stronghold. Commander Lee speaking. Identify yourself," she replies, then looks at Kevin and frowns. "Over?"

"Sister here, loud and clear, talking at ya from deep inside the mountain," the voice responds. There is some muttering and some scuffling.

"It's Val, Aunt Maura," Val calls. "I have the comm now." There's a shout in the background. "No, I am using it. You're just going to say weird things like always."

"Val, what the hell is going on?" Commander Lee asks.

"Just Sister messing with the comm," Val says. "Listen, we think there may be Code Monkeys heading your way."

"We are aware of that," Commander Lee says. "And they are already here."

"How many?" Val asks. "We killed a lot, but not enough. You could have close to a dozen inside the walls."

"I have killed one, so make that under a dozen," Commander Lee says. "I have the launch room secured and we are initiating the launch now. Will you be able to return before we close the outside doors?"

Val's voice is muffled, then grows strong again. "I doubt it." More muffled talking. "Really? You can do that? Bullshit."

"Val? What is she saying?" Commander Lee asks.

"She thinks we can get back to the Stronghold with the fuel we have left in the helicopter," Val says. "We may not make it all the way to the front doors, but we'll get close."

"Val, you know we can't wait for you," Commander Lee says. "With the Code Monkeys attacking, we need to shut the doors now."

"We know," Val says. "We're leaving the Cheyenne Mountain facility in just a couple minutes." She pauses. "Uh, Sister is going to get the helicopter for us."

"Get the helicopter? What does that mean?" Commander Lee asks.

"We're not quite sure," Val says. "Something about flying it through the tunnel to the interior doors."

"Commander?" Kevin interrupts.

"Hold on," Commander Lee says to him.

"But, sir, you need to tell her that one of the missiles is aimed at Denver," Kevin says. "They need to either get here now or…"

Commander Lee sighs.

"I heard that," Val says. "You didn't let go of the button."

"I'm sorry, Val," Commander Lee says.

There is the sound of a huge explosion, and the walls shake as dust falls from the ceiling, adding to the many layers that dominate the room.

"What the hell was that?" Commander Lee shouts.

There's another explosion and the lights flicker.

"Val, I have to go," Commander Lee says. "Do what you need to do. You might want to stay where you are. I am sorry to say that, but if you can't get here in time then you will be stranded outside with the herd of Zs and a nuclear winter."

There's no response.

"Val?" Commander Lee shouts, clicking the handset button again and again.

"Let me see," Kevin says, taking the handset from Commander Lee.

He clicks it himself, getting a harsh look of disapproval from his boss, then begins turning dials and knobs on the comm system console.

"The equipment is working," Kevin says. "It went dead on their end."

There's another explosion and emergency claxons ring out.

"What is going on?" Commander Lee shouts. She goes and gets the dead guard's rifle, then points at the door. "Jorgens? Open the door."

"Commander, that will leave this room vulnerable," Kevin protests.

"Lock it down after we leave," Commander Lee says. "If I am not back in five minutes, then launch. Do not wait a second longer. You launch those missiles and finish this."

Kevin blanches with fear, but he nods. "Yes, sir."

"Jorgens?" Commander Lee says.

The guard keys in the code and the door clangs open. Wisps of smoke and the smell of burning metal quickly fill the room. Commander Lee and Jorgens rush out into the corridor and are lost from sight. The second they are gone, Kevin hurries over and locks the room down once more.

Then he turns and looks at the launch console, his blood turning ice cold.

———

Diaz drops to the ground, his hands around his throat, his trachea only a pinhole after the blow from Skye's boot. He gasps for air, struggling to keep his eyes open as his airway closes. He looks up in time to see a second boot come at his face, and there is nothing he can do to stop it. Lucky for Diaz, it is stopped by someone else.

"I don't think so, you blind twat," Stanford shouts as he kidney punches the Code Monkey and wraps a forearm around her throat from behind.

The woman grunts and sends an elbow back at Stanford, but he dodges to the side and avoids the blow. Which sends him right into Skye's other elbow. The wind is knocked out of him as his diaphragm spasms and seizes.

Skye pries Stanford's arm away from her neck and twists it hard, flipping the man head over heels onto his back. He tries to grunt from the impact, but his diaphragm still won't obey, and all that comes out is a choked cough.

A shot rings out and Skye spins to the side, dodging the bullet before it can tear into her back. She leaps into the air, plants a foot on the communications console, and then jumps back in the direction of the gunshot, her left leg whipping out and kicking the pistol from Cole's hand. She lands three blows to his face, her fists moving at a speed that can barely be seen, and the TL rocks back on his heels before landing hard on his ass. Her right leg catches him across the chin and his eyes role up into his head as he takes a break from the conscious world.

A loud alarm echoes through the facility, the entire place bathed in red flashing lights.

"Emer-emer-emergency purge in t-t-t-ten minutes," a scratchy and stuttering computerized voice announces. "Emergency-cy-cy pur-pur-purge in ten minutessssss."

The voice degrades into a static hiss turned up to the highest volume possible. Skye clamps her hands over her ears and cries out as the noise penetrates straight into her brain.

"Good to know something hurts you," Val says as she rushes forward and tackles Skye about the waist.

The two women go flying through the air as Val's impact lifts them both up off their feet. They hit the ground sideways and Val's head smacks into the concrete, dazing her briefly. One of Skye's hands comes loose from its position over her ear, and she screams as the static stabs into her brain like a burning hot poker.

Val rolls a few feet away, shaking the fuzziness from her head, and shoves up onto her knees. She sways a bit as she catches her balance, then struggles to get up on her feet.

"I've trained my whole life to be a Mate," Val says as she shuffles over to Skye, her legs wobbly and crooked. She stops and takes a deep breath before moving again. Her hand goes to her head and comes away coated in blood. "Fuck. What was I saying?"

She reaches Skye and kicks the woman in the gut as hard as she can. Skye grunts but doesn't scream. The Code Monkey's entire being is focused on keeping her hands clamped to her head.

"Right, right," Val mumbles. "I trained my whole life to be a Mate. I've been fighting since I could walk. Before that even. I remember watching my mother train, her body drenched in sweat, her skin bright red from the exertion. The Teams have been my life before I was even born."

She kicks Skye again and then again.

"You know what? I'm fucking sick of it," she says. "I am not shitting you sideways, as my cousin would say. I am sick of fighting. It's why I fell in love with Hamish. I knew one day I could quit and still contribute. Maybe join him in the hospital and help save people instead of killing them."

She kicks once more, but her foot is blocked by Skye's foot. The impact sends Val off-balance and she stumbles back a couple of feet. Skye flips herself upright and comes at her fast. Val barely gets an arm up in time to block the kick aimed for her head. The blow knocks her into the communications console, and she cries out as her ribs meet metal.

Without her hands leaving her ears, Skye goes on the attack. She kicks out at Val's knee, then thigh, then side. Val is able to roll along the console and dodge most of the kicks, but not all of them. She goes down on one knee as a boot nails her calf, sending shooting pains all the way up her leg.

A second boot catches her right between the eyes and Val's head slams back against the console. More dizziness and the feeling of fresh blood on the back of her scalp are added to her world.

Skye comes in with a knee to Val's chin and the Mate rocks back, then comes forward onto all fours. The boot that comes for her face whiffs by as Val tucks and rolls, sending herself right into Skye's legs. The Code Monkey shouts as they both end up in a tangle on the floor once again.

"All of you must die!" Skye yells, then screams as one of her hands comes loose because Val's jaws are clamped down tight on her bicep.

Skye screams and screams as she leaves her other ear unprotected and starts punching Val in the side of the face to get her to let go. Instead of letting go, Val doubles down and bites harder, then starts shaking her head from side to side until she actually rips through the hide of the coat and right into bare flesh.

Blood spurts from between Val's lips as she yanks her head back, a huge chunk of Skye's arm coming away with her mouth. Skye's screams turn into full body roars, and Val has a split second to spit out the deer hide and arm flesh before she's grabbed around the throat and lifted up off the ground.

"You are not chosen!" Skye screams. "You are not worthy of glory! Your place will be to rot here for eternity! Your corpse will come back, and you will wander the halls of this facility for the rest of time!"

"Eternity means the same as the rest of time," Tommy Bombs says from behind Skye.

"What?" Skye shouts as she drops Val and spins about.

The blade, Val's long blade that had fallen from her belt, stabs all the way through Skye's belly but doesn't go out the back. Tommy Bombs halts the motion and then angles the blade upward. He gives it one last push and blood explodes from Skye's mouth. The woman reaches for Tommy Bomb's face, her fingers smearing blood from his forehead down his cheeks and to his neck.

"Did you get a good look?" Tommy Bombs asks before he pulls the blade free. Blood gushes from the wound and all over his boots. He looks down and frowns. "Fuck. That's nasty."

Skye lands on her knees, her hands clutched to her belly. Her body is still as a statue.

"Uh… are you dead?" he asks. "Oh, fuck it."

With one hard swing, he takes her head off and then her body collapses onto the concrete. Tommy Bombs kicks the severed head away from him as it rolls toward his feet.

"Everyone forgets about Tommy Bombs until they need something blown up," Tommy Bombs says to himself. "It's nice to step out of the box."

"Are you talking to yourself?" Stanford asks as he gets to his feet. He stays bent over, his hands on his thighs, and takes a couple of slow, easy breaths. "Oh, fuck me. That hurts."

"My everything hurts," Val says, still on the ground. "Help a Mate up, will ya?"

Tommy Bombs walks to her and offers her his hand. She takes it and he pulls her up, then offers her the blade.

"You hang onto that," she says. "My hands are shaking too much to hold anything."

"I know the feeling," Tommy Bombs says. The static starts to get worse and he winces. "How do we shut that off?"

"I don't think we do," Val says. "It sounded like some sort of self-destruct. Might be a good idea to leave."

"Self-destruct?" Tommy Bombs asks. "Why would that Skye bitch set a self-destruct? She was talking about killing you and letting you walk around as a Z forever."

"She didn't set it," Sister says as she comes running into the room. "I did." She skids to a stop and her eyebrows rise nearly to her hairline. "I left you five alone for only ten minutes and look what happened." She frowns. "Ah, man, my coat."

"I killed her," Tommy Bombs says quickly. "Just want that on the record. Killed her with a blade, not with explosives."

"Good for you," Sister replies. "We'll get you a medal or some other shit."

"How?" Stanford asks. "We're stuck here forever."

"Nope," Sister says, hooking a thumb over her shoulder. "I brought our ride to the front door."

"I don't understand," Val says. "How?"

"I told you I'm really, really good at flying helicopters," Sister says and grins. Then the grin falters a bit. "There is one problem."

"What's that?" Val asks.

"Uh, I better show you," Sister says. "We need to get the shit fuck out of here, and it's gonna take a while to help get Cole and Diaz to the chopper." She laughs. "Get to the chopper!" She laughs harder. "I am funny."

Everyone awake looks at her more like she's insane. Sister shrugs and moves to get Diaz up.

"Tommy Bombs, help me out," she says. "Val, you and Stanford get Cole."

"I'm good," Cole mutters from the floor. Then he rolls to the side and vomits. "No, I'm not."

There's a static burst and the red lights stop flashing and stay solid red.

"Five minutes to boom time," Sister says. "This is going to be cutting it shit fucking close."

———

"I don't want excuses!" Commander Lee yells. "I want those doors closed and sealed!"

A woman stands with her hands on her hips and shakes her head.

"That isn't happening!" she yells back. "The crazies blew up the closing mechanisms! These doors are open permanently!"

"No, that is not acceptable," Commander Lee growls. "If we don't get those doors closed then this whole place, our one shot at survival, will be flooded with radiation within a week!"

The woman takes a step back, her face full of confusion.

"What?" she asks, the fight leaving her quickly. "What did you say?"

"What did she say?" someone close by asks as well.

"Did she say radiation?"

"What radiation?"

"In a week? How long are we going to have to stay in here?"

"The council has been lying! We've been put in here to die!"

The crowd that fills the huge entranceway to the new Stronghold starts to panic. Voices are raised, fingers are pointed, and Commander Lee suddenly finds herself in the middle of an angry mob.

She points her rifle in the air and fires.

"Everyone will shut up and calm down!" she yells. "We do not have time for rumors and accusations! What matters is getting these doors closed! I want everyone from the engineering department and from the construction department on this ASAP! I do not want to hear excuses! I do not want to hear complaints! We will work together and we will close those doors so all of us are safe!"

She gets only accusatory looks in response. No one moves a muscle.

Commander Lee levels the rifle at the crowd and turns in a tight circle.

"The Code Monkeys have been killed, but we are not out of danger," she says. "In only a minute, a button will be pressed launching hundreds of missiles, each with multiple nuclear warheads, at specific targets across this country. I am sorry I have kept that from you, but we have lost the war against the Zs, and we need to cleanse the land of their presence so future generations may live out in the world in peace."

There are some mutters and mumbles, but still no one moves.

"This hasn't been an easy choice to make," Commander Lee says. "But it is one that has been coming for some time."

"You've known this would happen?"

"What about the Teams? Can't they keep us safe?"

"How do we know you don't have some other secret plan when we close the doors?"

"Yeah! How do we know that?"

"Hey!"

"Listen to me," Commander Lee pleads. "We have all been trained from our first day that—"

"HEY!"

There's a shotgun blast, and the crowd turns toward the entrance.

"Why do you have to do that?" Marsh asks, yanking the shotgun from Collin's grasp. "You just freak people out."

"It softens the blow from the real bad news," Collin says and looks at all the faces turned his way. "Zs. They're inside. The gate and front wall have collapsed. They'll be up here in only a few minutes."

He looks over his shoulder at the smoking ruins of the machinery that opens and closes the doors.

"These things going to close or what?" he asks.

Commander Lee growls long and loud.

"Hey, sis," Collin says and winks. "You look stressed out."

"Jesus," Marsh mutters, then looks at the crowd. "I do not know what is going on in here, but we need to barricade this entrance, then get everyone armed now! NOW!"

The crowd scrambles into action, everyone well-drilled on

what to do if the walls collapse and the undead world outside comes for a visit.

———

Val wants to scream, but she doesn't as she holds her head out the window of the helicopter. Instead of looking forward, she is looking back, making sure the top rotors don't hit the sides of the tunnel or the ceiling. The need to scream is because there is about two feet clearance on her side and up top as the helicopter races backward out of the tunnel.

Her headset almost comes off her head, but she clamps a hand down to keep it in place.

"Adjust to your right!" Val shouts. "Your right! YOUR RIGHT!"

"Sorry!" Sister shouts back from the pilot's seat. "I thought my right was your right!"

"It's not! Your right is your right! My right is your left!" Val yells. "I thought you said you were really, really good at flying this thing!"

"Are you shit fucking kidding me?" Sister yells. "You have no idea how good I am if you have to ask that question! I'm fucking flying a helicopter backward in a fucking tunnel! I'm a shit fucking GOD!"

"Wouldn't that be a goddess?" Stanford interrupts.

"Don't be a sexist ass!" Sister replies.

"I'm not," Stanford says. "You're a woman, so you would be a goddess, not a god."

"So a woman can't be a god?" Sister asks.

"What? No, I'm not saying that," Stanford replies. "No, wait, maybe I am. It's just—"

"You're a sexist dick knuckle!" Sister shouts. "Why'd I even give you a headset?"

"A sexist what knuckle?" Stanford asks. "And I have a headset to help you see on your side!"

"That was dumb of me," Sister says. "You're just distracting—"

"PAY ATTENTION TO FLYING THIS THING!" Val screams. "You're going to hit the ceiling!"

The helicopter shudders and Sister flinches.

"Sorry," she says.

Val briefly looks down at the ground and the hundreds of Zs that were chopped to bits when Sister flew the helicopter inside the tunnel. Those intact enough try to reach up and grab the helicopter; many just stare with undead eyes as a meal flies by. Other than screaming, Val wants nothing more than to blow the whole tunnel up and bury the fucking things.

"How am I looking?" Sister asks.

"We're almost to the entrance!" Val replies. "You need to turn to your left, my right! Do you understand?"

"Got it!" Sister says then adjusts the stick.

"More!" Val yells. "MORE!"

Sister adjusts again.

"Less!" Val yells. "LESS!"

Sister adjusts again, and then the helicopter is flying out into open air. As soon as it is clear enough, she swings it around and takes it up into the night sky. She flies up and around, her eyes locked onto the dark curve of the mountain.

"They used to have red lights that blinked on every tall structure or obstacle in the whole country," Sister says. "That way helicopters wouldn't fly right into a tower or building."

"Or mountain?" Stanford asks.

"Or mountain," Sister says. "How are we looking out there?"

"I can't see anything," Val says, pulling her head back inside the cockpit. "It's too cloudy out."

"We're clear," Stanford says. "I snagged a pair of NVGs. Oh, shit!"

Half the mountainside explodes into flame. Burning hunks of rock fly everywhere and Sister pulls up, sending the helicopter climbing above the exploding mountainside.

"Uh, could I have those NVGs?" Sister asks. "Might help keep us from crashing."

"No problem," Stanford says. "I was looking right at the tunnel when it blew. I can't see a fucking thing now."

Sister reaches back for the goggles and Val gasps.

"Both hands on the stick!" she snaps as she grabs the goggles from Stanford and hands them to Sister. "Jesus."

"Val doesn't like flying," Sister states.

"Not anymore," Val says. "As soon as we land this thing, I'm done. No more helicopters."

"As soon as we land this thing, I'm done too," Sister says. "Can't top that move back there. Best to quit on a high note."

"You are so fucked up," Val says.

"True dat, homey," Sister replies.

"None of that makes any sense," Stanford says.

"Never does," Sister says.

TWELVE
IT AIN'T OVER UNTIL THE UNDEAD LADY SCREAMS

The barricade isn't anywhere near high enough, deep enough, strong enough to stop the herd that slowly comes toward the new stronghold. Everyone who stands behind it, firearms in hand, knows that fact. They are very aware of it, and more than a few people turn and throw up from nervousness.

Commander Lee walks back and forth behind the residents, unhappy that once again she must instruct her people on how to hold the line. It was supposed to be easy. Just get everyone inside, close the doors, push a button, and the world outside goes away. But she had deluded herself.

Nothing is ever easy when the undead are the ones that truly rule.

"You take them out at the legs!" she shouts. "Drop the first wave and let them muck it up for the others behind them! I want to see piles! I want to see a wall of downed Zs! Then when the others climb over, you put bullets between their eyes! The dead ones will weigh down the still-alive ones! We turn them into the barricade we need! We turn the Zs against themselves!"

There's no cheer or cry for victory. Not that she expects there to be. People are too scared. They've faced a Z herd before, but nothing even close to the scale of what is coming at them now.

She looks over her shoulder as residents flee further into the new Stronghold. Once all the firearms were handed out, she'd instructed the remainder of the residents to move themselves, and all supplies, as deep into the Stronghold as possible. The secondary doors will hold against the Zs, but not for long. It is the main entrance doors she needs working.

"Kevin!" she shouts as soon as she sees the man push through the fleeing crowd. "What are you doing here? Did you push the button?"

"No," Kevin says. "I was able to figure out the intercom system and heard everything that was going on in here. We can't launch the nukes until we have the doors closed."

"I gave you an order, Mr. Ross," Commander Lee says.

"I ignored that order when new information presented itself," Kevin says, standing his ground. "If I'd pushed the button, Denver would have been a nuclear crater fifteen minutes ago."

"The radiation wouldn't get to us right away," Commander Lee says. "We've checked the winds."

"No, but the EMP would fry all of the circuits in this place without those doors closed," Kevin says. "They're shielded to withstand the pulse. If I'd pushed the button then we'd be back in the Dark Ages. Forever."

"Shit," Commander Lee says, then clasps Kevin on the shoulder. "Good call. Keep making those calls in case I miss anything."

"We're all going to miss something," Kevin says. "Look around. This is a different world now. We're in the real Stronghold."

"Here they come!" Marsh yells from the barricade.

"On my mark, open fire!" Commander Lee orders as she hustles away from Kevin and joins the line at the barricade. "Ready! Aim! Fire!"

———

Sister and the Mates go silent as Denver comes into view. Despite the night's darkness, there is plenty of light coming from the many conflagrations that burn through the city. Everyone in the helicopter becomes very aware of the state of the world below them.

"What the hell is up with all the fires?" Val asks. "Look at them all. There's even more than before. No way they could have spread that fast."

"Crazies," Sister says. "I've seen it before. When the Zs overrun a city, the crazies go even more crazy and just start lighting shit on fire. Sacramento, Montgomery, Indianapolis. They've all been burned to the ground because of crazies."

"I don't see signs of them. All I see are Zs," Stanford says. "Holy shit. This herd is insane. Are we looking at millions?"

"Not for long," Sister says. "Hey, Tommy Bombs!"

"What?" Tommy Bombs replies after Stanford shoves a headset into his hands and he puts it on. "You need me?"

"You notice what I got in the cargo hold with you?" Sister asks, a smile in her voice.

"What? Where?" Tommy Bombs asks. He's quiet for two seconds then he starts laughing. "Oh, shit! You put the bombs back into the helicopter?"

"I did," Sister says. "I think Tommy Bombs has earned some fun. What do you all think?"

"He saved our asses," Stanford says.

"He sure fucking did," Cole agrees.

"Tommy Bombs, light up the night, Mate!" Sister yells. "Woo hoo!"

"Why are we going lower?" Val asks. "Sister?"

"Make it easier for Tommy Bombs," Sister says, "and because we only have one turbine and limited fuel. I'm keeping our altitude low until we are forced to climb."

The burning city below grows larger and larger until Val can actually make out shapes of old office furniture and debris inside rooms as they pass by the taller buildings.

"First one out!" Tommy Bombs shouts as he tosses one of the phosphorous bombs out the cargo hold door.

The explosive device plummets hundreds of yards until it lands in the mass of Zs that steadily move through the cracked and broken streets. Thirty seconds later, the bomb goes off and the world behind the helicopter becomes a flash so bright it's as if the sun has come out for a split second.

"Holy shit," Tommy Bombs whispers, blinking a few times. "That was awesome!"

"Good thing I closed my eyes," Sister says. "Or I'd be blind as a Code Monkey with these NVGs on."

"Do not close your eyes when flying!" Val shouts. "Don't do that again!"

"Hey," Stanford says. "Did anyone see that?"

"See what?" Cole asks.

There's a flash from one of the buildings they pass, and a split second later Cole hits the deck of the cargo hold, his hand to his cheek.

"Someone's shooting!" Cole yells.

"That's what I saw," Stanford says. "Fucking crazy snipers."

"You got him?" Val asks.

A bullet pings against the helicopter and everyone ducks their head instinctively. Stanford starts rummaging through the miscellaneous gear in the cargo hold.

"Ford!" Val shouts as another bullet pings against the helicopter. "There's more than one!"

"I got this," Stanford says as he finds a night vision scope and slides it onto a rifle strapped above his seat. He chambers a round and puts the rifle to his shoulder, then begins sighting through the scope. "Come on, assholes. Gimme one more shot."

"We don't want him to shoot again!" Val shouts. "Ford!"

There's a muzzle flash from the building they start to fly by and Stanford squeezes the trigger.

"You get him?" Val asks.

"I got him," Stanford says, still watching the buildings as they fly over the Z-clogged streets of Denver. He squeezes the trigger a second time, a third time, and a fourth. "Got those assholes too."

"Tommy Bombs!" Sister calls out. "Get back to fucking shit up!"

Tommy Bombs looks at Cole and Stanford and they nod.

"Might as well," Cole says. "Take out as many Zs as we can."

"And crazies," Stanford says. "I fucking hate crazies."

Tommy Bombs grins and grabs up another phosphorous bomb.

––––––

As soon as weapons click empty, the shooters move from their positions and let a new line of Stronghold residents take their place, fresh magazines loaded into the carbines and rifles of the replacements.

"We're going to run out of ammunition soon," Marsh says to Commander Lee as he reloads his rifle, slapping in a fresh magazine as he tosses the empty one onto a pile where folks are busy grabbing those up and pushing cartridges in as fast as they can. "We aren't making a dent. This isn't like last time. I can't even see an end to this herd."

There's a loud clanging noise and all heads turn toward the giant doors. One of them starts to move then shudders, stops, and retreats back into its recessed housing.

Lee stares at the doors, then shakes her head.

"The Code Monkeys had no reason to attack us this time," Commander Lee says. "We'd given them what they needed to activate the missiles."

"Maybe they wanted control themselves," Marsh suggests.

"No," Commander Lee replies. "If that was true, they wouldn't have needed to disable the doors. They could have just pressed the button and gone away."

"You lost your mind, Maura?" Collin cackles. "You want to find logic with those eyeless bastards? Guess what? You can't find logic with crazy people. They're a fucking cult that cuts their own eyes out and then trains like super ninjas. You'll go just as crazy trying to figure out what's in those heads. Don't matter now, anyway. We got Zs to deal with."

There's a scream by the barricade and several people begin to run in the opposite direction, heading for the far doors and the hope of safety. Another scream and Marsh, Collin, and Commander Lee see a Z leap at a woman, its teeth sinking into her throat, ripping at the flesh over and over, barely chewing before gulping down the bloody meat.

"Fast one!" Marsh says. "Put it down!"

"Watch out for our people!" Commander Lee shouts as several rifles turn and open fire.

The woman's body dances and shudders as round after round rips into her and the attacking Z. Finally, one cracks open the monster's head and its putrid brains plop onto the floor, where a man stomps on them over and over again.

"I think it's dead," Marsh says. "Get back to the line, Freddie."

A man kneels by the dead woman, cradling her in his arms as he rocks back and forth, tears streaming down his face.

"Someone help Paul," Marsh orders. "Get him and Connie to the back." He looks at Commander Lee. "She didn't take a shot to the head."

"I'll take care of it," Commander Lee says. "You keep people firing and holding tight."

Marsh nods and pulls on Collin's elbow. "Come on. We're up."

Rifles and carbines start to click empty, and Marsh switches places with a woman who looks like she's asleep on her feet. Collin sees her as well and nods to the others who stand behind the barricade, their fingers squeezing triggers in rapid succession, every one of them looking as if they are locked in a bad dream.

"Waiting to die," Collin says. "We better do something soon, or folks'll just sit their asses down and give up. Everyone knows this is a losing battle."

"It's not a losing battle until the battle is lost," Marsh says. "Don't be a quitter, Collin."

"Fuck, man," Collin grins. "I'd have to have the motivation to start something before I quit it."

———

"Are we going to make it?" Val asks, watching Sister closely. "You keep looking at that gauge. Is that the fuel gauge?"

"We'll make it," Sister says shortly.

"You sure?" Cole asks, leaning forward. "You didn't think this would be a two-way trip before."

"Only one turbine," Sister says. "We need less fuel."

"We're also going a lot slower because of that," Stanford says. "There're still crazies out there taking pot shots at us. I'm taking down as many as I can, but seems like the whole apocalypse rifle club is out there tonight. Faster would be better."

"Not crashing into an ocean of Zs would be best," Val says.

"You know, if we live through this, I'm never letting you forget this," Stanford says. "The great Valencia Baptiste is afraid of flying in a helicopter."

"People are not meant to fly!" Val snaps. "If they were, they'd have wings and—"

"Fire in the hole!" Tommy Bombs yells, and everyone counts to twenty-nine, then closes their eyes.

Even with closed lids, the flash is intense.

"We're heading up," Sister says. "Last stretch, Mates, then you're home."

"*We're* home," Val says.

Sister gives her a weak smile, which is more than creepy since her eyes are covered with NVGs. Val shakes off the creep factor and leans toward Sister.

"We're home," Val says again. "You can't stay out in the waste-land. Not once the nukes go off."

"Why haven't they?" Cole asks. "This place should have been a crater by now."

"Whoa, what?" Stanford asks. "Denver's getting nuked? That's a little close for comfort."

"Look down, Ford," Cole says. "You think Tommy Bombs can take care of all of them? He's having fun and making dents here and there, but there is no way we have even a fraction of the explosives needed to kill this herd."

"Can we watch the nuke go off?" Tommy Bombs asks.

"You need help, Mate," Stanford says.

"Come on, TL," Tommy Bombs grins as he readies another phosphorous bomb. "I've always wanted to watch a nuke go boom."

"We may get to," Sister says. "If the Stronghold is already locked down. If that's the case then not only will we get to watch it blow, we'll get to taste that sweet, sweet fallout. Nothing like the taste of fallout on a cold autumn night."

"Yeah, that doesn't sound so fun anymore," Tommy Bombs says.

"Ah, come on," Sister says. "Fallout ain't so bad. Trust me."

"Gonna have to take your word on that," Stanford says.

"The Stronghold may not be locked down yet," Val says, a small bit of hope in her voice. "That's probably why Denver hasn't been nuked."

"If that's the case, then why isn't it locked down?" Cole asks. "What went wrong?"

———

"Another fast one!" Marsh yells as a Z shoves through the herd and rushes right for him.

The thing's head explodes, and Marsh turns to see Collin racking the slide on his rifle.

"Saw that one coming a ways back," Collin says. "Look out there. See how some of the Zs start to stumble and move to the side? That means a fast one is heading our way through the herd. Like a snake parting grass."

"You all hear that?" Marsh asks the few people on either side of him and Collin. "You see the Zs part and you take aim! We can't have more of those fast ones get in here!"

Several bangs and a harsh grating noise makes everyone jump. The doors on either side of the entrance start to move.

"Get back!" Kevin yells. "Get inside!"

People don't wait to be told twice. They scramble away from the barricade and get inside the Stronghold entrance, making sure they are well past the deep tracks the doors run on. Parts of the barricade stick out and block the tracks, but the heavy doors make short work of the debris and shove it out of the way.

Then they stop and smoke begins to billow from the right-side door.

"Dammit!" Kevin yells. "I need all hands on this motor! We might be able to manually crank these shut!"

"Ain't gonna matter," Collin says, pointing his rifle at the twenty-foot opening still left between the doors. "We gave up the advantage. The Zs are breaching the barricade."

The barricade just outside the doors begins to wobble and crash, pieces and chunks tumbling to the ground as the Zs leading the Z herd collide with it. A fast Z scrambles over, followed by another and another, their dead eyes locking onto the first living target they see.

"I still need help!" Kevin yells as he waves a wrench over his head. "Come on!"

Most of the residents flee running and screaming toward the back of the massive entranceway while others only stand there and stare in horror at the Zs coming at them. And the ones heading for Kevin as he keeps trying to get people to help him manually close the doors.

"Shit," Collin says, seeing two fast Zs turn their attention on the man.

He drops to a knee, takes aim, and blows one Z's head off.

He's about to fire again when the second Z's head is obliterated as well.

"You don't get all the fun," Marsh says. "Come on. Looks like we're on mechanic duty too."

Marsh starts firing at the Zs cresting the barricade outside the doors as he rushes over to help Kevin. Collin hesitates, looks at the people trying to flee to safety, looks over at Kevin as the man frantically starts barking orders at the few helpers who join him, then looks at the Zs that are tumbling over each other to get at the meat inside the Stronghold.

"Dammit," he mutters and opens fire too, following behind Marsh. Collin shakes his head over and over as he takes Zs out. "This is stupid. I should just bail and get lost in this place. I'm good at getting lost."

A fast Z zeroes in on him, but Collin kneecaps it, sending it rolling right at him. He jumps to the side and then aims his rifle at the thing's head, avoiding the thrashing arms and hands trying to snag his ankles and pull him down.

The Z's face becomes nothing but a bloody mist. Collin looks up in time to see two more fast ones heading his direction. Before they can reach him, they are dropped hard by gunfire behind him.

"We got this!" Commander Lee shouts, having rallied a group of residents to pick their guns back up and provide cover for those working to close the doors. "Get your ass over there and help!"

Collin nods at her and slings his rifle as he sprints toward Kevin, Marsh, and the others who have their arms stuck inside the wall of the Stronghold, grease smeared all the way up their elbows. When he reaches them, he's amazed to see the size of the gears that work the doors. He finds a spot, shoves his arms in as well, and grabs onto a gear.

"That one goes clockwise!" Kevin yells at Collin and the couple of other people who have grabbed the same gear. "Be careful of your fingers! They get caught in the teeth and we can't stop to back the gear up! You stop being careful, you will lose your fingers!"

"Kinda like dealing with Zs," Collin says. "Gonna lose a body part if you ain't paying attention."

"The place is lost," Val says as the helicopter flies above the hundreds of thousands of Zs that tromp over the fallen walls of the old Stronghold. She points toward the northeast. "We need to see if the Zs have reached the new Stronghold. The Gym should be that way."

"The Stronghold entrance isn't at the Gym," Sister says. "It's this way."

She banks the helicopter to the left and skirts Baseline Dr, which is the border of the old Stronghold. The herd below them has decimated everything. Not a single one of the wall panels that had guarded so many people for so many decades is left standing. There are nothing but Zs now.

"Flagstaff Rd," Stanford says. "Where those big old houses are. We used to sneak out of the Stronghold and go explore them when we were kids."

"Then I'd have to go find your asses when your parents freaked out because I was older and already training," Cole responds. "You two were huge pains in my ass."

"Still are if we're doing our jobs right," Stanford says.

They come up over a small ridge, and then everyone in the helicopter gasps at the sight below. Where there should be only a hillside is the huge opening to the new Stronghold. Bright light filtering out from the gap in the two massive doors shows the Mates the fallen barricade and the thousands of Zs bottlenecked and trying to get inside.

"What do we do?" Val asks. "We can't land in that."

"I'll make some room," Sister says. "Tommy Bombs? Let's clear this backlog a bit, alright? Do that voodoo you do so well!"

No one says a word.

"Just drop the shit fucking bombs," she says.

"Got it," Tommy Bombs replies and begins tossing the last of the bombs out the window as they zoom toward the Stronghold entrance.

In seconds the bombs go off, cutting a huge swath of land clear of Zs. Those that aren't completely blown apart shuffle around, setting others on fire as the bright hot phosphorous burns their putrid bodies.

"I got one left, but we're too close," Tommy Bombs announces.

"Hang on to that one," Sister says. "I can clear some space myself." She looks over her shoulder and back at Stanford, Cole, and Tommy Bombs. She glances down at the passed-out figure of Diaz. "Anyone checked his pulse lately?"

"He's sleeping," Cole says. "He lost a lot of blood. We got to get him inside or he loses the whole arm."

"Make sure he stays alive," Sister says. "I don't want to do this awesome thing I'm about to do and then get my face eaten because no one is watching whether Diaz kicks it and turns into a Z."

"Awesome thing?" Stanford asks.

He gets his answer as Sister dips the nose of the helicopter forward and brings it lower and lower toward the herd of Zs still converging on the Stronghold entrance. Everyone starts shouting, especially Val, as Sister doesn't pull up, just keeps the helicopter angled once she's at the perfect height.

The height of Z heads.

The windshield of the helicopter is splattered with gore as the edges of the rotors tear into the undead. Stanford and Tommy Bombs scramble to get the cargo hold doors closed before they are covered in too much Z gunk. Val screams and shouts at Sister as she grabs onto her seat.

Sister just laughs and laughs.

"You go splat!" Sister exclaims. "And you go splat! Splat for you and splat for you! Oh, did I miss you? Here ya go! Splat! Splat, splat, splat!"

Val almost throws up as Sister turns the helicopter in a tight circle, widening the swath of destruction. In just a few moments, almost every Z within a hundred yards of the Stronghold entrance is chopped to bits by the helicopter's rotor blades, leaving a semi-open area for Sister to set down.

But, before she can, alarms start bleeping in the cockpit and the helicopter shudders, then drops hard. Sister manages to get the skids close to level as the helicopter plummets the thirty feet to the shredded bodies of the Z herd that covers every square inch of land below.

Val lets out one last shriek as the helicopter hits the ground. It rocks to the side, one skid higher than the other due to a random piling of Z corpses, but it doesn't go over.

"And that's how you do that," Sister says. "If anyone wants to stay they can, but I'm getting the shit fuck out of here and inside where it's safe."

She opens her door and climbs out, trying not to slip on the slick, gore-covered remains that are everywhere.

"Gonna need a new pair of boots after this," Sister says as she leaves the helicopter behind and starts working her way to the collapsed barricade and the Stronghold doors beyond.

"Uh, is she leaving us?" Stanford asks.

"What?" Val asks and opens her eyes. "Son of a bitch. Grab gear and let's go."

They all look down at the passed-out form of Diaz, who is not a small man by any stretch of the imagination.

"Rock, paper, scissors?" Stanford asks. The far-off sound of the rest of the Z herd reaches them and he shakes his head. "Fuck it." He slaps Diaz across the face. The man starts to stir. "Diaz! Come on! Get your ass up so we can help you inside!"

———

"Hey there. Howdy. How you folks doing? Oh, crap, that looks bad. That a bite? Hope not or I'll have to put you down," Sister says as she walks into the Stronghold. "Just shit fucking with you. I don't even know you. I'll let your family put a knife in your skull. Hey! Commander Lee! We made it back! What's up with the doors?"

Mouths hang open and eyes seem to swim in peoples' heads as they stare at Sister. The woman gives them nods and smiles, waves at some kids, holds her thumbs up to the people filling magazines with cartridges, then walks over to Kevin and his crew as they continue to struggle to get the doors closed.

"Having a problem there?" Sister asks.

"Motor is shot," Kevin says.

"That's why you didn't fire the nukes," Sister states. "I get it now. You tried the backup motor system? It's not as strong as this one, but it'll get the doors closed. You'll want to pull all the debris free from the tracks first. Can't have debris blocking things."

Kevin frowns, his brows coming together until they are one. "Backup motor system?"

"Backup motor system," Sister says. "You didn't think these doors would rely on one system only, did you?"

"I, uh, only knew about the one system," Kevin says.

"Let me show you the other one," Sister responds, then points at a group of men and women staring at her. "You folks, go clear the tracks. Come on! Move ass, people!"

The people move ass and start pulling out miscellaneous debris from the door tracks. They stop only to let Val and Stanford by as they help Diaz walk into the Stronghold with Cole and Tommy Bombs right behind.

Hamish sprints up to Val, looks at her until she nods, and then starts checking Diaz.

"Someone, grab a stretcher!" Hamish shouts. "I want this man off his feet and in the infirmary now!"

"Do you know where the infirmary is?" Val asks him.

"Not a clue," Hamish says then shouts, "Someone show me the infirmary!"

Kevin yells at a couple of men who had been helping him. They rush over and take Diaz from Val and Stanford and lead him through the confused clumps of people who stand around the Stronghold entrance area.

"They'll show you," Kevin says, then points back at Sister. "You show me the backup motor. Now!"

Sister's eyes go cold. Very cold.

"Please?" Kevin says.

Sister shoves by and looks in the open wall with the massive gears and smoking motor. She reaches in all the way to her shoulder, then pulls a lever. A hatch pops open to her right and she stands back.

"Press the button," Sister says.

Kevin moves up next to her, pulls the hatch open, and stares at the single red, plunger-like button that is mounted on a recessed square in the wall. He looks at Sister and she nods. His hand presses the button and the doors protest as metal begins to shriek and grind.

"Are you sure about this?" Kevin shouts over the noise.

"Nope," Sister says. "Never seen it done. Just knew it could be."

Slowly, like they are pushing through molasses, the doors begin to move. Inch by inch they get closer and closer. Tommy Bombs runs up, tweaks the phosphorous bomb in his hand, and throws it through the gap in the doors just before they slam shut with a noise so loud that quite a few people cringe and stagger.

The doors are so thick the noise of the bomb going off can't even be heard inside.

"Uh, is that phosphorous going to eat through the doors?" Stanford asks, looking at Tommy Bombs.

"Oh, shit," Tommy Bombs says. "I thought I was just going to clear out some more of the herd."

"Don't worry about it," Sister says. "These doors can handle anything. Maybe not a direct nuclear blast, but pretty fucking close."

She spins about and then nods at Commander Lee.

"Speaking of nuclear blasts, time to get the end over with," Sister says.

———

At one end of the room sits Stanford, Val, Hamish, Marsh, Cole, and Sister. The other end of the room sits Commander Lee and the Stronghold council.

"We have confirmed that all missiles have been launched," Commander Lee says. "We can't confirm if they have hit their targets, but I would say from that small quake we felt yesterday that Denver is gone."

"That's good," Cole says. "So why are we here? You made that same announcement this morning to the full assembly of residents. Is there something else we need to do now?"

"I think there is, since she called us in here, Cole," Stanford says. "My mother is not one to repeat herself for no reason. Unless it's to tell me I'm a total dipshit. She never gets tired of that one."

"I did call you in here for something else," Commander Lee says, standing and looking at the council before she looks back at those seated. "This is something that Sister here already knows, but you need to know as well."

"I told the Mates," Sister says.

"You what?" Commander Lee gasps. "You told them what?"

"That these doors ain't opening for a very, very long time," Sister says. "That's what you were going to say, right?"

A look passes between the two women, one that is not lost on anyone in the room.

"Yes," Commander Lee answers finally. "That is what I was going to say."

"So what does that mean?" Marsh asks. "I haven't been told shit. Someone want to clue me in?"

"The Stronghold doors will not be opening for at least a hundred years, maybe more," Commander Lee says. "We will need to rebuild society from within this structure. As you already know, the Stronghold is a massive complex of levels and sectors. It is almost as large inside as the old Stronghold was outside."

"But Z-free," Sister says. "That's nice."

"Yes, it is," Commander Lee says. "Which brings us to something else I want to say. We have all been raised to be aware of those who may be sick or dying. If someone dies and turns, then we have a Z problem again. Outside in the old Stronghold, we had the space to deal with the issue. In here, we are a contained unit, and if someone turns, it could spread fast if not controlled. I want all of you here to be part of the new advisory board we are putting together to come up with procedures and policies to prevent an outbreak occurring."

"First line of defense again," Cole says. "We're a new Team."

"Teams are over," Commander Lee says. "For now. You'll all have other duties as well, we all will, but for right now I want you to focus on this task. If we let one turned resident slip detection, then it could be all over well before those doors unlock."

Val holds her hand up. "Can the doors be opened at all? Is there a manual override?"

"No," Sister says. She doesn't elaborate.

"Okay then," Val nods.

"Meet when you can and work on this issue as soon as possible," Commander Lee says. "In the meantime, explore the Stronghold. I want every one of you to know this place inside and out." She looks at the council. "Anything any of you would like to add?"

No one replies, they all just look uncomfortable and exhausted.

"Very well," Commander Lee says. "Dismissed."

"Actually, I have something," Stanford says. "If the Teams are gone, then why are you still in charge? Shouldn't we elect someone new to lead us?"

The uncomfortable silence that fills the room almost strangles everyone inside. Until Sister claps her hands and stands up.

"I'm hungry," she announces. "Gonna go eat something and

turn in. Big day of exploring tomorrow. Not to mention the whole still healing while feeling like I'm still dying at the same time thing. It's a rich life I lead. Yes, it is."

She claps her hands again, turns on her heels, and leaves the room quickly.

There's a confused pause, then Val stands up and follows. Stanford is quickly on her heels, with Cole right behind. Hamish and Marsh look at each other, then at Commander Lee.

"Go," Commander Lee sighs. "Meeting is over."

———

Over the next few days, several ceremonies are held to honor those who fell fighting for the Stronghold. It is a long list of names considering the Teams were nearly wiped out. Val attends each ceremony, including the ones for the random residents who died fighting off the Zs at the barricade. Everyone counts.

By the end of the week, she hasn't had any time to explore the Stronghold, let alone feel like she's had a chance to settle in to her new quarters, which she gets to share with Hamish. Who is busy sitting on their bed, his head in his hands.

"You coming down for dinner?" Val asks as she steps out of the small bathroom of their quarters. "I have no idea what it is. The food service crew is opening a new crate of rations they found, so it should be interesting. One of the cooks told me they'll have some hydroponics up and fresh greens growing by the end of the month. That's nice, right?"

She waits, but Hamish doesn't answer.

"Hame?" she asks, gently taking one of his hands from his head. "Are you alright?"

"What if I die and turn in the night?" Hamish asks. "I'll attack you, and then what? You turn and we both just get stuck inside here?"

"Probably," Val replies.

"Someone comes along and hears us banging around, they

open the door, and then they get bitten," Hamish says. "Then it spreads. We need something to keep these doors from being opened from the outside."

"That shouldn't be a problem," Val says. "I'm sure Kevin and his crew can come up with something."

"Yeah, I'm sure they can," Hamish agrees. "But what we really need is some sort of way to stop people before they turn. Something that detects when folks die and fries that part of them that turns them into a Z."

"What part is that? The brain?" Val asks. "How would that work?"

"I don't know," Hamish says. "But it's going to drive me nuts until I figure it out."

"Well, figure it out later," Val says. "The last ceremony was today and I'm ready to finally relax. Ford and Benji are meeting us for dinner, so get your ass up and move."

"Are they back together?" Hamish asks.

"Once Ford told Benji that we'd be in here for the rest of our lives, they decided to work things out," Val says. "The rest of your life is a long time to hold a grudge toward an ex."

"Yeah," Hamish says, then cries out as Val flicks him across the nose. "Ow!"

"Get up," she says. "We are going to go eat and have fun with friends. You can think about your brain killer later. Or never. Let someone else figure it out. You have enough to do."

"Yeah, yeah, you're right," Hamish says and gets up. He kisses her, then nods toward their door. "Okay, let's go have fun."

"After that kiss, I think dinner can wait a minute," Val says, working at his belt.

"Okay, we need to discuss these mood swings," Hamish says. "Are we leaving or are we staying?"

"Really?" Val asks. "Just go with it, Hame."

———

The corridor is dark and cold, the walls slick with condensation as Commander Lee walks with a crank flashlight through the bottom level of the Stronghold. After a few turns, and several more wet-looking corridors, she comes to a plain door. She knocks lightly and waits.

The door opens, Sister looks her up and down, then steps aside so the Commander can enter. Commander Lee quickly moves inside and takes a seat in an old-looking swivel chair, one that could have been in any office in any city across the country. Former country. Former land. Now a land that's nothing but radioactive slag. Most of it, at least.

Sister grabs her own seat in an identical swivel chair and points at one of the many video monitors that fill the wall in front of them.

"I just talked with some guy in Paris," Sister says. "He was a dick. Didn't want to give me an update on their containment measures. Stupid prick kept saying I didn't have the authority. I rattled off some nuke codes and told him I could authorize his ass to be vaporized. He says that the EU is safe and still Z-free. Not a single case since this country closed its borders."

"You should really let me do all the communicating," Commander Lee says. "Or maybe someone with a slightly more diplomatic way."

"Right now, it's just you and me, Maura baby," Sister says.

"And the council," Commander Lee says. "They had to know as well. What I do not understand is why you stopped me from telling everyone else in that meeting? It would have gone a long way toward them understanding the real reason we had to nuke everything."

"Don't tell them," Sister says. "And make sure the council doesn't tell them either. If they do, I'll have to do something about it."

"Like what? Kill everyone who knows?" Commander Lee asks. "Why?"

"Because if anyone in here knows that the rest of the world

exists and never was infected, then there will be hell," Sister says. "Trust me. I've seen what the news can do to a person not prepared to hear it. It spells trouble for everyone. T-r-o-u-b-l-e. Trouble."

"Then what are we going to tell them?" Commander Lee asks. "We have to say something. I wanted the residents to know there was hope for the future. Maybe not for this generation, or even the next couple of generations, but at some point everything we work for in here will mean something because there actually is a world outside, and our descendants get to be a part of that."

"I know what to tell them," Sister says. "Leave it to me."

"They don't know you," Commander Lee says.

Sister smiles, but it is sad and full of years of suppressed grief. "They know me. They won't believe it, but they know me."

There's a bleep from one of the monitors and Commander Lee looks up. "That's the EU defense council."

"Then answer, and let's see how they plan on protecting the rest of the world from our fallout," Sister says.

———

Sister turns as her name is called. She smiles as she sees Hamish and Val walking towards her.

"I brought it like you asked," Val says, patting her blade on her hip. "Want to clue me in?"

"You'll see," Sister replies.

"Been a couple weeks since I've seen you," Hamish says. "I need to look at the progress with your wound and I also want to do a full work up regarding your cancer. The supplies and facilities in this place are incredible. If we're lucky, maybe I can find some sort of treatment to slow down the progress of the cancer."

"Don't worry about me," Sister says and lifts her shirt. "My wound is just a scar now."

"That can't be," Hamish says. "It's much too soon for it to heal that fast."

"I've been getting some sleep," Sister says. "Sleep helps."

"But it shouldn't help like that," Hamish says. He starts to say more, but Val puts a hand on his shoulder and he stops.

"Then at least let him treat the cancer," Val says.

"This crap?" Sister laughs, pointing at the splotches on her skin. "I've been dealing with this for decades now. I have a long while before it takes me down."

"Decades?" Hamish asks. "That's not possible either."

"I'm an impossible person," Sister says and shrugs. "Best get used to it. We're gonna be stuck in here together for a long, long time." She gestures toward the wide-open doors a few feet away where people are filtering through. "You two coming to the big announcement or what?"

"Yes, we're coming," Val says, yanking on Hamish. His mouth just opens and closes, opens and closes in a mix of confusion and frustration. Val places a finger under his chin and pushes it fully closed.

"Leave it alone," Val says. "We'll figure it all out later."

"That's my philosophy," Sister says. "If I had one."

The three follow the other residents through the doors and into the main entry area. The residents of the new Stronghold stand around chatting and greeting each other as the space quickly fills. But it doesn't fill completely up; it can fit everyone with plenty of space leftover. That goes for the rest of the facility. Not even close to a half of the quarters are filled, and there are more rooms, halls, and various training spaces throughout that it would take a person over a month of searching to find and see every one.

Commander Lee steps onto a ladder set in the middle of the entry area and holds her hands up for it to be quiet. Sister stands near the ladder and nods as Val and Hamish find a place close by. Only a few feet from them are Stanford and Benji, with Cole, Diaz, and Tommy Bombs standing right behind them.

"Hello," Commander Lee says. Voices are raised in acknowledgement. "Thank you for gathering here. I know we have had plenty of these things lately as we get oriented with our new home and also as we have paid tribute to the ones who fell getting us in here."

"Everyone counts," half the crowd says.

"We always remember," the other half responds.

"As much as I would like to tell you all the hard part is done, I think you'd know I'm full of it," Commander Lee says.

"No shit," Stanford mumbles, and few people give him harsh looks. He gives them right back.

"We will be in here for a long time," Commander Lee says. "But, unfortunately, as some of you have guessed, it will be a lot longer than you were originally told. There is a failsafe protocol in place that will keep those giant doors behind you closed for a very, very long time."

"Due to the radiation, right?" someone shouts.

"Due to that and other factors," Commander Lee says. "Some of these factors are within our control, some are not. As we start to live and flourish in this new home, many of you will come to learn the importance of these factors. Many of you won't, and I count you the lucky ones. Just know that, no matter what our fate is, we will always be the people of the Stronghold, and we live by a code of honor and integrity that will outlive us all."

"I'd like to say a few words," Sister says.

Commander Lee looks down at her, hesitates, then nods.

"Most of you know that we have someone amongst us who has lived out in the wasteland for many years," Commander Lee says. "Sister has been instrumental in gathering intel on other survivor areas, both friendly and not so friendly. I can say with one hundred percent certainty that, without her assistance, we would not be safe within this facility right now."

"True dat!" Stanford exclaims.

"What does that mean?" Benji asks.

"Not a clue," Stanford says. "Just something Sister says."

"Thank you, son, for your continued contributions to my

speech," Commander Lee says. More than a few people chuckle. "Sister? Your turn."

Sister and Commander Lee swap places. The battle-worn woman stares out at the many faces. She takes a deep breath, climbs to the top of the ladder, and sits down.

"I am a lot older than you might think," Sister says. "I am by far the oldest person in the Stronghold."

There are some grumbles of disagreement from the elderly residents and Sister smiles.

"No, it's true," Sister insists. "I've been around since the very beginning of all of this mess. I have loved and lost more people than I even remember. But of those people, there were four who meant more than anything to me. They were my family. Not by blood, but by the heart. They taught me that if you are to survive in life, you need your family with you. And when you have family with you, you can accomplish anything. I'm not shit fucking you here, people. With family you can accomplish anything."

Commander Lee clears her throat at the use of profanity and Sister rolls her eyes.

"For as long as I am alive, I plan to treat every one of you like my family," Sister continues. "I plan on passing down everything I have learned in my one hundred years plus on this stupid planet." More grumbles of protests and even a few gasps of disbelief. "Yeah, yeah, you don't believe me. I get that a lot. And I don't really care. What I do care about is that you are all prepared. That future generations are prepared. That when those doors open, the people of the Stronghold will have the training and strength to take on whatever insanity is still out there. I want you to be the seeds that will eventually sow the residents of the new world."

"How will you do that, old lady?" someone shouts. There's nervous laughter.

"You aren't part of the Teams," someone else yells. "Have the Teams teach us."

"They will," Sister says. "We have just enough Mates left to help me with this crazy crap. I'll pass on to them what I know, and they will pass that on to those willing to learn. The knowledge will spread faster than a Z herd."

No laughter on that one.

"But I can see the doubt out there," Sister says, scanning the faces of the crowd. "I'll prove to you all who I am, and I can guarantee that before I kick the bloody bucket there will no longer be a single bit of that doubt left in this Stronghold of my true identity."

She motions to Val to come forward.

"Can I see that?" Sister asks, holding out her hand.

Val doesn't hesitate and hands Sister her blade.

"Many of you know the legend of this blade," Sister says, holding the weapon above her head for all to see. "I'm going to tell you now that the legend is true. I was there when this blade was handed over to Granny G. I was there because I handed it to her myself."

Voices grow, there are shouts of protest and disbelief. Several people call for her to step down and quit the crap.

"HEY!" Sister bellows. "Don't be rude!"

The crowd quiets down. Mostly.

"I was born Carly Michelle Thornberg pre-Z," Sister says. "I have had a lot more names since then. But there is only one name I call my own."

She takes a deep breath and points the blade at the crowd. Every last mumble and mutter goes silent.

"My name is Elsbeth, but you know me as the Great El," she says. "And when I am done with you, there won't be a single person in this place who can't kick some serious ass."

She smiles wide and her face lights up enough to brighten the massive space.

"And I ain't shit fucking you on that promise. Not at all."

The place explodes into shouts of alarm, disbelief, and even some hope. Eyes stare at the woman and she stares back, that bright smile on her face.

They may be angry and confused, but they are now her family.

Every one of them. Sister looks for Val and finds her. She gives a small wave. Val waves back, shaking her head, then starts laughing. All of the Mates join in, and the laughter soon becomes infectious.

Sister looks about and knows that, no matter what, she will do everything she can to prepare these people, and their children, and children's children, for that time far off in the future when the doors open and the people of the Stronghold venture out into the unknown of the wasteland.

THANK YOU FOR READING THE STRONGHOLD

We hope you enjoyed it as much as we enjoyed bringing it to you. We just wanted to take a moment to encourage you to review the book. Follow this link: **The Stronghold** to be directed to the book's Amazon product page to leave your review.

Every review helps further the author's reach and, ultimately, helps them continue writing fantastic books for us all to enjoy.

———

Also in Series:
NO EASY DEAD
THE STRONGHOLD

———

Want to discuss our books with other readers and even the authors? Join our Discord server today and be a part of the Aethon community.

Facebook | Instagram | Twitter | Website

You can also join our non-spam mailing list by visiting www. subscribepage.com/AethonReadersGroup and never miss out on future releases. You'll also receive three full books completely Free as our thanks to you.

Looking for more great Science Fiction from Jake Bible?

The Bloody Conflict is long over. The lands are now controlled by despots, crooked cattle barons, energy hoarders, and anyone with enough might to keep the local folks under control. For Clay MacAulay, none of that matters. He roams the land in a war machine from a time gone by. He wants nothing to do with small desert towns or brutal dictators. He only has his sights set on a new life. Unfortunately for Clay, too many ruthless people want the war machine he pilots. The battle mech that shouldn't exist anymore. But they will have to pry Clay's cold, dead body out of that pilot's seat to get it.

Get A Fistful of Mechs Now!

Something else has been living beneath the Earth. Now, it's their time to rule... The Yellowstone supervolcano has begun to erupt, sending North America into chaos and the rest of the world into a panic. People are dangerous and desperate, knowing this will plunge the continent, and the world, into perpetual winter. Until they realize that the eruption is the least of their worries... Out of the massive chasm comes more than ash and lava. Giant monsters emerge, bent on destroying everything in sight. Federal Marshal Lu Morgan and a ragtag group of survivors and soldiers must fight hard to stay alive and beat back the invasion of massive creatures. It is a race against time, and a race for survival, as all involved struggle to find answers as to where the monsters came from and how to stop them.

Get Out of the Earth Now!

AUTHOR'S NOTE

It has been a blast playing in the world of *DTA*. Which is, if you haven't already noticed, the same world as my *Z-Burbia* series, just well after those events. If you haven't read that series, then go back and you'll learn a lot about how the Stronghold came about and also who the crazy woman known as Sister/Elsbeth/Great El is.

Oh, and for those keeping score, yes, this Stronghold is the Stronghold which shows up in *Dead Mech* and the *Apex Trilogy*. Want to know what the future is like for the residents of the Stronghold when they finally open those doors? Check out the *Apex Trilogy* and you'll see all!

Thanks, as always, for reading!

Cheers,
Jake

ABOUT THE AUTHOR

Jake Bible is a Bram Stoker Award nominated-novelist, award-winning novelist, short story writer, independent screenwriter, podcaster, audiobook narrator/producer, and inventor of the Drabble Novel.

He has entertained thousands and reached audiences of all ages with his uncanny ability to write a wide range of characters and genres. He's the author of 65+ novels, including the bestselling *Z-Burbia* series, the bestselling *Salvage Merc One*, the bestselling *Out of the Earth* series, the bestselling *ROAK* series, the *Apex Trilogy* (*DEAD MECH*, *The Americans*, *Metal and Ash*) and the *Mega* series, as well as the YA zombie novel, *Little Dead Man*, and the Bram Stoker Award-nominated Teen horror novel, *Intentional Haunting*.

Find Jake at jakebible.com or jakebible.substack.com

Printed in Great Britain
by Amazon